Angry Nurse

MW00596241

By Karl Bort & Thekla Madsen

Madsen Communications, Inc.
River Falls, WI

ANGRY NURSE

Madsen Communications, Inc.
River Falls, Wisconsin 54022
www.bort-madsen.com
Facebook: Bort-Madsen Books

ISBN 978-0-692-89725-6

Cover design by Chris Cheetham |
www.chrischeethamdesign.com

Formatting by Rob Bignell, Inventing Reality Editing
Service | http://inventingreality.4t.com/editingservices.html

Manufactured in the United States of America

First printing May 2017

Also by Karl Bort & Thekla Madsen

Bad JuJu in Cleveland

The First Book in the Detective Nicholas Silvano Crime Thriller Series

"There very well may be BAD JuJu in Cleveland, but Bort and Madsen have conspired to write a very, very GOOD novel, which will please hardcore police procedural fans and general readers alike."

-Dave Wood, Past Vice President,

National Book Critic Circle

Find It At:

www.bort-madsen.com

Facebook: Bort-Madsen Books

Dedicated to those who
Protect, Serve, Defend, and Care

This book is dedicated to those who protect, serve, defend, and provide care for all of us, especially our veterans and officers who may suffer from Post Traumatic Stress Disorder and individuals experiencing mental health issues. Those who protect, serve, defend, and care don't have eight-hour work days and their "offices" are the emergency rooms, hospitals, and streets both local and far away; wherever there are people in need.

If you, or someone you know is suffering from
PTSD or mental health issues, there is help.

PTSDHotline.com | 1-800-273-8255
National Alliance on Mental Illness (NAMI) |
www.nami.org | 1-800-950-6264

Acknowledgments

As with our first novel, *Bad JuJu in Cleveland*, selected locations, businesses, and characters may be real or have a factual basis and are portrayed fictionally in this novel. Any resemblance to actual persons, places, or situations (current or historical) is unintentional. Special thanks to those who allowed their real names to be used (you know who you are!), Lieutenant G. Williams of the Hudson, Wisconsin Police Department, Rob Bignell for his e-publishing expertise, our panel of reader/reviewers, our spouses, and Chris Cheetham for another great cover design.

Prologue

"Whoa!" Kat chased after a bunch of papers that blew off the coffee table.

"Sorry," Nick slid the door shut. "Here, let me help you with those." He got down on his hands and knees, picked up the papers and set them on the kitchen counter.

"Where did you get this?" he gestured to the crayon drawing at the top of the pile.

"One of my patients drew it in art therapy and gave it to me," Kat answered.

"Art therapy, huh?" he commented. The drawing depicted two figures lying on a bed. Red crayon slashes cut through the figures and over the entire page.

"Are they always this gruesome?"

"It can't be all hearts and flowers when you're dealing with damaged minds," she said.

Chapter 1

"*A*ssholes!"

Registered Nurse Joshua Ramsey's grey eyes narrowed and his lips pressed together tightly as he looked at the scene playing out in the patient Day Area. Three student doctors were gathered around a young girl, his patient, who sat hunched over a table, sobbing quietly. Her hands cupped her face; a shield to protect against the taunts coming from the would-be doctors performing their required psych rotation. Joshua had enough.

He got up from the counter that served as a desk, opened the door separating the Nurses Station from the patient Day Area, and made his way over to the group. He overheard the tallest of the three say, "Honey, why don't you tell Doctor Haldol here what is bothering you? My name is Doctor Ativan and this other gentleman is Doctor Valium. We're here to help you get better."

The trio surrounded the trembling girl, their arms folded in front of the short white physicians' coats to conceal their name tags. Joshua slipped between them, took the girl's hand, and helped her to stand. Ignoring the trio, he adjusted the girl's hospital gown over her rail-thin body and guided her down the hallway to Room 242.

The tiny room was sparsely furnished with one unmovable bed and a small brown dresser with four drawers. The only other creature comfort was a metallic mirror screwed into the wall above the dresser. A large plastic St. Luke's Hospital mug sat on top of the dresser. It was half-full of ginger ale and had a flexible plastic straw sticking out of the top. The lone window to the outside world faced the parking lot. Adjustable blinds captured between double panes of unbreakable glass ensured patients couldn't use the blind cords to hang themselves.

The sun was just beginning to rise over the steel mills of Cleveland's Flats area and reflected into the room off the gold top of the Key Tower bank building, the city's tallest structure. For Joshua, the sunrise signaled the end of his work day.

The Behavioral Health Unit within St. Luke's Hospital was a locked unit with eighteen identical rooms housing the most violent and sickest mental health patients in Northeast Ohio. Although Theresa's waif-like countenance inspired sympathy, a history of cutting herself and four documented unsuccessful suicide attempts fully qualified her for residency at the facility.

Joshua hit the red call light button for assistance and heard the muted "bing-bing" of the chime signifying that any available staff members should come to his location. Within a few seconds a mental health technician rushed into the room.

"What is it, Josh?"

"Henry, can you sit with Theresa while I get some medication?" Joshua asked the aide.

"Sure, Josh. You gonna give her a B-52?" Henry asked as he turned to hit the Cancel call light button. B-52 was nurse slang for the drug cocktail consisting of a mixture of Benadryl, Haldol, and Ativan.

"No, she's not out of control, just upset. Going to draw up a little Ativan, that's all she needs right now," Joshua said as he walked out of the room. He returned to the Nurses Station, swiped his hospital ID card through the electronic card reader, and waited until he heard the click that signified the door was unlocked. He moved to the freestanding Pyxis machine and tapped his "secret code" that allowed access to the medications and selected Theresa's name from the list of current patients. Her prescribed medications displayed on the screen. He selected Ativan and stepped to the side so the metal drawer would not hit his leg when it automatically opened. After counting the vials of Ativan dispensed by the machine, he pressed "9" to acknowledge the number of remaining vials, known as the count, and pushed the drawer shut. After drawing up the medication, he signed off the Pyxis. Next, he reached into the small red box of alcohol wipes sitting on top of the machine and grabbed several, placing them into the side pocket of his maroon scrub top, then returned to Theresa's room.

Unwrapping one of the alcohol wipes, he swabbed the girl's left shoulder then deftly injected the calming medication into her deltoid muscle. It was an action he had performed hundreds of times during his five years of nursing mental patients at St. Luke's hospital.

"It's okay, Theresa," Joshua spoke softly as Henry gently laid her onto the bed and adjusted the pillow under her head. "I won't let those men bother you again." Both men watched her expression slacken as the meds took hold. After Theresa's eyes closed, Joshua motioned Henry to follow him into the hallway.

"Those damned interns were at it again," he said, explaining that morning's scene in a hushed, angry voice.

"What are we going to do about this, Josh?" Henry asked. The mental health worker had worked at St. Luke's for seventeen years; most of it spent on the night shift. "Those wanna be doctors are the worst group I've ever seen come through this unit - and I've seen a lot of bad ones!"

St. Luke's, a one hundred year old teaching hospital, was located on the near west side of Cleveland, Ohio and surrounded by century old homes housing a mix of races and cultures. The area businesses were comprised of run-down liquor establishments, Arab-owned deli's and empty storefronts. The hospital was owned by Cuyahoga County taxpayers and serviced mostly poor and indigent patients. The hospital's quality of care, however, was excellent. St. Luke's had a Level One Trauma Center. A helicopter pad identified by a big red "X" painted in the center was just below the Behavioral Health Unit Center One floor. The sprawling dark brick hospital had five medical floors, a pediatric "crack baby" unit to care for infants born to addicted mothers, and a nationally acclaimed burn unit.

Just above Center One was another identical floor aptly named Center Two, giving the facility a total of thirty-six psych ward beds to serve the 1.2 million residents of Cuyahoga County. Most days, it wasn't enough.

"I don't know yet, Henry," replied Joshua. "It's almost 6 a.m. so let's wait and see which doctor is coming in to teach this morning."

Retaliation by doctors to the nursing staff and other employees was common at St. Luke's. The recent changes to "improve" insurance and healthcare administration did little to bring money into the hospital system and employee morale was the lowest Joshua had seen since coming to St. Luke's. Future doctors had little interest in studying their craft in a place they knew they would not stay at and the turnover of medical professionals was high.

Joshua and Henry stepped back into the room and conducted a quick search for any hidden plastic pieces of a fork or spoon that Theresa could use to cut herself; as the numerous scars on her arms and thighs revealed a history of self-abuse. Satisfied there was no hidden contraband, they left the room and Joshua went back to the Nurses Station.

He glanced at the Lexapro-logo clock affixed high on the wall over the Medical Secretary's desk. Most of the hospital's office supplies sported drug company product names, much like NASCAR driver jumpsuits sported automotive product patches, and came from the various drug company representatives hoping to influence doctors' choices of medication. It was fast approaching 7:30 a.m. - quitting time and the end of his twelve-hour shift. But he still hadn't finished his charting.

Logging into the last available computer in the Nurses Station, Joshua began checking and signing off on new orders placed into the system. Doctors frequently placed orders using computers from their home or car and with no medical secretary on the night shift to alert the nursing staff, it was up to the nurses to stay current. Just as he was almost done, the Nurses Station phone rang. Caller ID revealed it was Intake with a new admission. Joshua ignored the ringing phone. One of the other nurses in the room could pick it up.

"Joshua!" the Charge Nurse barked after the phone rang

a couple more times. "You have the next admit – pick it up!" She returned to reading her *People* magazine.

He picked up the phone. "Center One, Joshua speaking," he said, reaching into the file cabinet drawer next to his chair for an intake sheet.

"Hi, Joshua. This is Donna from Intake. We have a Direct Admit for you guys. You ready to write?"

A Direct Admit meant the patient had not been pink-slipped, so there was no medical information from an Emergency Room or Doctor's office available. Usually, when someone was admitted to St. Luke's they had a Pink Slip that listed the reason for admission and the patient's medical history. With a Direct Admit, none of that important information was available and left the nurse to guess at the patient's medical and emotional condition. It was done infrequently and usually meant the patient was some kind of celebrity. This designation also avoided revealing the patient's identity or condition to the ambulance and emergency room personnel, as well as the outside world.

"Go ahead, Donna. I'm ready," Joshua replied, glaring at the Charge Nurse flipping through the magazine.

"Patient's name is David Feighan. Presenting with schizophrenic paranoia and intermittent explosive disorder. He was brought into his doctor's office by his wife and attorney after they found him running naked on the property of his Edgewater Drive mansion. According to his wife, the husband has been acting strangely for the past couple of months. His admitting doctor wants to be called after the patient is processed. I'll fax over what I have but it's not much. All I can say is good luck."

Joshua looked over the sparsely completed intake form before answering. "Sure Donna. Just put the doctor's contact phone number on the fax for me, will you?" As he hung up the phone, Joshua tried to recall why the patient's name sounded familiar. Then, it came to him - David Feighan was the Cleveland millionaire philanthropist who had amassed a fortune buying out troubled businesses all over the world. Sort of like a local Donald Trump, he thought.

While Feighan's business ventures were legendary, equally impressive was the man's social life which was rife with multiple marriages to much younger women that ended in extremely messy divorces. Feighan threw his money and political weight around to get what he wanted and also had a history of drug abuse. "Fucker probably overdosed and now he's going to be my problem," Joshua muttered. Privately, he had less sympathy for the wealthy who could afford better healthcare than the average citizen. But rich or poor, mental illness was an equal opportunity affliction. He leaned back in his chair and glanced at the clock.

"Finish up the Admit and try to do it without too much overtime," the Charge Nurse told him. She dropped the magazine on the counter and got up to leave.

"Bitch," he whispered to her back as she walked toward the exit.

Chapter 2

Joshua heard the door buzzer then looked at the video monitor affixed to the Nursing Station's counter and saw a man and woman standing behind a wheelchair. He was halfway out of his chair when he felt a heavy hand on his shoulder.

"I got it, Josh," Henry said. "I'll stay and help you with the admission. Screw 'em if they don't like me getting overtime. Let them write me up. Good luck finding another aide to do what I do in this looney bin!"

"Thanks, Henry," Joshua said and went to the small room off the Day Area that was used to admit new patients. He watched as Henry struggled to hold open the double entrance doors with one elbow while maneuvering the wheelchair through them. The couple just watched without offering any help.

"What is wrong with you people?" the woman exclaimed loudly to Henry's back as he turned to make sure the two doors closed and locked behind him. "We have been at this all night. My husband needs help now!" she announced, stomping down the hallway, her high-heels echoing like rim shots off the bare walls.

Henry had to stop and pull out a corner of the blanket that had become entangled in the wheels. He ignored the woman's complaints and rolled his eyes at Joshua as he pushed the patient into the interview room.

"What room, Josh?" Henry asked after he locked the wheels of the chair.

"Room 252 is the only one left. Check and make sure it has been cleaned and then see if there is an extra breakfast ordered, okay?"

"You got it, sir," Henry said and turned and left the room. Joshua closed the door, sat at the desk, and adjusted the computer used for new admissions. He motioned for the man and woman to take a seat.

"Whuu...whuuu...am I?" the man stammered, his fingers clenching the sides of the wheelchair in a futile attempt to stand.

"You're in the hospital, dear," his wife said, her manicured hand pressing down on his shoulder as she leaned over to face him.

"Hosp...hospital?" he questioned, turning his head from side to side.

"Yes, the hospital," she snipped.

Do I detect sarcasm? Nurse Joshua Ramsey wondered. He thought he saw a grimace cross her perfectly lined and Chanel-painted lips. *Yes, definitely sarcasm.*

"You're at St. Luke's hospital," Joshua supplied.

The woman's companion, a trim man in a pinstriped suit demanded, "Who's in charge here?"

"I'm Joshua Ramsey, the Registered Nurse on this floor who will be admitting the patient this morning," he replied, glancing at the man in the wheelchair and then back to the pair. "Won't you please take a seat so we can begin?" Joshua waited as the pair reluctantly took seats.

"Please tell me your relationship to the patient," Joshua addressed the woman.

"The *patient* is my husband, David Feighan," she said, pausing to see if Joshua's expression changed with this information. Seeing nothing, she continued. "I am Johanna Feighan and this is Michael White, our attorney," she nodded to the man in the suit.

"David has been acting very strange over the past month and last night, when Michael, ah, Mr. White, brought me home after a charity event, David was at the front gate of our home - naked!" She cast a furtive glance at her husband, who was nodding his head from side to side. "He was barking and growling like some sort of animal," she shuddered.

"The First District Police were already there but they didn't have the code to open the gate," the lawyer said. "When I punched in the numbers, David charged the cops. They yelled that they were going to Taser him then David suddenly froze and they were able to get him in the ambulance."

He knows the gate code, Joshua thought. *Interesting.*

"They wanted us to follow them to Fairview Hospital for David to have a psych evaluation in the emergency room but we called his doctor, who told us to bring him directly here to St. Luke's."

Joshua took notes on his admission sheet, thinking the cops were probably only too happy to rid themselves of a doped-up millionaire with a bitch wife and pompous lawyer. But, Joshua wondered, why did the man's behavior suddenly change when he was threatened with being tazed? He glanced at his new patient. *Did the guy just smile?* He must have imagined it.

"Look here," said the wife. "This has to be kept quiet. We don't want any media attention. David's name is synonymous with charitable giving in this city and we don't want his name dragged through the dirt."

The lawyer nodded. "That's why we called David's personal physician, Toby Abernathy. He was supposed to have everything arranged with your hospital to bring David directly here until we can take appropriate action, but..."

Joshua held up his hand to stop the attorney in midsentence. "I'm sorry but you are going to have to clue me in on a couple of things. You're telling me that Toby Abernathy, the CEO of this hospital and also the patient's doctor, told you to bring him here without having him taken to an emergency room first to check out his medical condition? That's not protocol and I find that hard to believe!"

Michael White stood. "Nurse Ramsey is it?" he asked. "As the family attorney I will advise you that you are not qualified to question Dr. Abernathy's judgment regarding David. Keep your opinions to yourself, do what we tell you to do, and everything will be just fine."

Joshua's gut tightened with the man's dismissive comments. *Who the hell did he think he was?* Before his mouth could catch up with his thoughts, he held himself still and inhaled deeply...one, two, three, and four. And exhaled...one, two, three, four, five, six. He repeated the breathing exercise once more as he had been taught in anger management classes. *Better.*

"Mr. White, is it?" Joshua parroted. "My job is to determine the patient's current state of mind and to assess his health and welfare. To do this I need information. I would ask that you please refrain from answering my questions and allow Mrs. Feighan to answer, if you don't mind."

"Ramsey," White responded, his voice rising. "Let's get this straight right now." He removed his cell phone from the inside suit coat pocket and made a call.

Joshua stood. "Mr. White, per hospital policy, cell phones are not permitted on this floor to protect our patients' privacy. Please stop or I will be forced to summon Security."

White waved his free hand at the nurse as if swatting away a fly and turned away. "Toby, this is Michael White. Johanna and I are at St. Luke's with David. There's a nurse here giving us a difficult time. I need you to take care of this. Johanna is quite tired from this ordeal and I have to get her home to rest."

White turned and, with a visible smirk, held the phone out to Joshua. "Here, Ramsey. Your *boss* wants to talk to you."

Joshua took the phone from the attorney's hand. "This is Nurse Ramsey."

"Nurse, Mr. Feighan is my patient. Just do the admission with the information you currently have," Dr. Abernathy instructed. "This is a very sensitive situation. David Feighan has a charitable organization that does a lot of good for St. Luke's which is why I requested the police take him directly to our Behavioral Health unit. Johanna and Michael are the administrators of the charity and I want them happy, do you understand? Just admit my patient. I will be in this morning to give orders. Do not discuss this with anybody and do not perform any routine blood tests or treatments. I will be his doctor of record so he is not to be assigned to any of the psychiatric doctors on staff. Do I make myself clear?" the CEO asked pointedly.

"Yes, sir," answered Joshua. He placed the lawyer's phone on the desk, stood and opened the door. "Henry, will you take Mr. Feighan to his room? I'll be right in after I put his information into the computer."

Michael picked up his phone and said to Johanna, "I think we've made our point. Let's get you home to rest now."

Johanna stood and as she walked past him, Joshua heard her hiss, "I'm going to see to it that you get fired!"

Joshua watched them leave. Neither seemed interested in accompanying Feighan to his room to make sure he was comfortable. So much for being a loving wife, he thought. After they left the Unit, Joshua glanced at the video monitor that provided the staff a view of the hallway outside the doors.

"What the....?" he uttered. There, in grainy black and white, were the patient's wife and lawyer caught up in what appeared to be a very passionate embrace and exchanging a long kiss before walking away arm in arm. *So, that's how it was.* He shook his head. *I'll bet they have no idea they're being filmed.* The thought caused him to grin.

Joshua gave his Nursing Report to the oncoming day shift which summarized each patient's activity and state of mind during the night shift, finished his charting that was interrupted by Feighan's admission, and went to Room 252 to check on his new patient before clocking out.

David Feighan was sitting on the edge of the bed eating from a breakfast tray Henry had found for him. Without looking up he said, "Isn't she the bitch of all bitches, that one? And that tool who is my attorney, I can't wait to finish that prick off!"

Joshua stared in amazement at the man, who only moments ago, seemed catatonic.

David stood and placed the now empty tray onto the window sill before turning to face his nurse and said, "I got lucky with you, Josh," speaking like they were longtime friends. "I was worried I'd get some touchy feely nurse but I can see they pissed you off too."

"What's going on?" Joshua asked, bewildered. "What kind of game are you playing?"

"It's not a game, Josh. Those two were planning to *kill me* and I had to protect myself. It might seem extreme but I needed to be somewhere safe until I could sort this out. She can't get to me in here!"

Joshua was skeptical. David's paranoid behavior was typical of people on drugs. But yet, he couldn't explain how the man went from a mumbling mess in a wheelchair to the person now calmly talking to him.

Noting the nurse's confusion, David said, "I've got proof! I can prove they're trying to kill me, but I can't show it to you right now. Can I trust you to keep this between you and me?" David asked. "Just for a day. Then I'll explain everything."

"Okay," Joshua replied. "You've got till tomorrow." He knew a lot could happen between now and the next day. David Feighan could be discharged or another nurse could be assigned to him; then it wouldn't be his problem. What the hell, he thought. What was one more looney in the bin? Besides, this guy had enough clout to make trouble for him if he wanted.

"It will be extremely worth your while to help me. I guarantee it," the new patient said.

Joshua left the room. *What was he getting himself into?*

Chapter 3

I t's called *Behavioral Health* for a reason, Joshua thought as he retrieved his nursing bag from the Nurses Station. But this was the first time anyone has ever played "crazy" to get *into* a psychiatric ward. He really should report David Feighan, but to who? Toby Abernathy was the highest authority and he already knew the situation.

Doctor Katrina Westerly, a recent graduate of Case Western University's School of Psychiatry and one of the resident psychiatric doctors on staff, entered the room. She dropped her shiny red bag onto the counter and removed her white physician's coat and stethoscope from the bag.

"Morning, Josh. How was your shift?" She slipped on the short physician's coat, smoothing it with both hands, and then placed the stethoscope around her neck.

Joshua gazed at her admiringly before mustering his answer. "Fine, the usual stuff, Doctor," he said while thinking, *if you only knew.*

Kat, as she was called by her friends, was in her late 20's and stood almost six feet tall. With short blonde hair and athletic build, she could have been an Olympic beach volleyball player. Intelligent green eyes sparkled under the fluorescent lights. She had paid for her college education by working nights as a barmaid and attending classes during the day. Rumor had it she was living with a Cleveland Police Homicide Detective, Nick Silvano, a cop the newspapers loved to cover who had a reputation for being a bad-ass. That additional credential served as a deterrent to anyone who might harbor romantic thoughts toward the new doctor on the ward.

She pinned her name tag to her coat; it read, Doctor Katrina, in bold black letters over the blue St. Luke's Hospital staff logo. The hospital's Behavioral Health unit workers had requested and received permission to utilize only first names after the Unit's prior Charge Nurse received a midnight phone call placed to her home by a patient. The delusional man had threatened her life and called her a "devil bitch" for not believing the government had placed a computer chip in his head and also for her refusal to spend taxpayers' money to perform surgery to remove said imaginary chip.

While the official story was that the patient used an online search engine to locate her number, Joshua had heard that a disgruntled hospital worker had given the nurse's phone number to the patient after being fired for drinking and using drugs on duty.

After looking around to make sure they were alone, Joshua spoke. "Kat, I'm having a problem with your student doctors." He related the incident between the students and his patient, his voice betraying the anger he felt. "Those damn students think this is a big joke. Theresa is very sick!"

Kat listened to the nurse's account and thought carefully before responding. "Josh, I'm the newest doctor here. My situation is touchy. The veteran docs all squeezed out of instructing those jerks and I got stuck with mentoring them through their psych rotation. But I will deal with them. This will not happen again. Thank you for telling me," she said as she stood up, coffee cup in one hand and a patient Census sheet in the other.

"I just get really pissed when stuff like this happens," Joshua vented. "None of the other staff seems to care except me and Henry. Night shift robots, that's all they are! I gotta go and punch out before I get written up for abusing my overtime and get points placed into my employee jacket file," he said sarcastically. "Never mind that the overtime was due to Toby Abernathy's admit."

Doctor Katrina Westerly watched Joshua walk down the hall toward the exit and noticed the nurse seemed to be limping slightly. She remembered hearing he had been wounded in the Middle East. She thought about their conversation. While his concern over the student doctors was legitimate, his anger seemed amplified beyond what the situation warranted. She made a mental note: "Registered Nurse Joshua Ramsey seems to be exhibiting signs of nurse burn-out."

Chapter 4

J oshua left Center One forty-five minutes past his scheduled quitting time of 7:30 a.m. He'd probably have a note in his mailbox or an e-mail when he got into work tonight wanting to know why he had overtime. He was so sick of the administrative bullshit. It always seemed to matter more than the patients. And while he tried to just ignore the crap and do his job, all he seemed to get him was threats of discipline and write-ups.

He swiped his employee badge through the Kronos time clock outside the men's locker room and allowed his right index finger to be read by the machine to prove it was really him and not someone pretending to be him. An electronic chirp confirmed his identity. He entered the dimly lit locker room, removed his maroon hospital scrubs and tossed them into the wheeled laundry cart. It was still full with yesterday's dirty clothes. Joshua decided to load up his locker with the hospital-supplied scrubs before they were all gone.

"Who knows when those lazy laundry trolls will get around to doing their jobs," he muttered as he sorted through the pile looking for his size.

He grabbed some towels and soap from the supply closet. Might as well shower here and use their water, he thought. Removing the rest of his clothing, Joshua Ramsey stood naked in front of the full-length mirror at the entrance to the green-tiled shower room. He could hear the water running from an unattended shower someone before him had carelessly left on.

Joshua Ramsey was average height with a short cropped military buzz haircut rendering his brown hair almost invisible in the dimly lit room. The scars to his body, however, were very visible. His right side looked like a shark had taken a bite; the aftermath of a roadside bomb that had exploded in Afghanistan during the Battle of Ramadi, tossing the Humvee he and three other soldiers occupied high into the air before ejecting his shrapnel-riddled body onto the sandy roadside. One kidney and two ribs were gone. And he was one of the lucky ones. The only other survivor was Doc Stafford, now a physician's assistant at St. Luke's emergency room, whose quick response and triage skills had saved his life. If not for Doc, Joshua was convinced his life would have ended in the sand and dirt of a foreign country that didn't want him there in the first place.

After that, Joshua was emotionally and physically unable to remain in the job that he loved to do. Trained by the army to be a battlefield medic and registered nurse, his active duty time of almost nine years and three Middle East tours, had ended that hot dusty morning. He went on to endure four months of rehab at Walter Reed Veterans Hospital. The honorable medical discharge and the accompanying battlefield medals were of little solace to Joshua, whose lifelong dream of retiring from the military was taken away by the Taliban.

Now the enemy was his own government. His application to be a nurse for the Veteran's Administration had been rejected. "Too physically demanding," he was told. "Why don't you just take your disability and go on and enjoy your life?" the civilian administrator advised as he was being dismissed from the employment office at the Louis Stokes VA Center in Cleveland.

Unknown to Joshua, his military files had entries of *anger issues, emotionally unstable* and *difficulty adjusting back to civilian life* scattered throughout the thick brown folder.

Despite these damaging comments, his VA Counselor had helped him get the job at St. Luke's. "The hospital gets credit for hiring veterans," the counselor said. "They will be glad to take you on." The counselor had conveniently left out Joshua's emotional state in his report to St. Luke's and bestowed a "highly recommended for hire" status.

Joshua tried working on the medical floors at St. Luke's but the twelve-hour shifts spent mostly on his feet with few breaks proved to be too physically tiring and he was unhappy. The staff was heavily weighted to young female nurses with so many degrees that their hospital ID badges looked like random strings of the alphabet.

"Backstabbing little bitches," one male nurse described them. "All they're good for is hiding in the break room when a new admission hits the floor. They're only hired so the hospital administrator can get his rocks off bragging how his nurses have higher levels of education than the other hospitals."

Magnet Status accreditation for St. Luke's meant little to Joshua. The idea that because he did not have a bachelor's or master's degree made him less qualified pissed him off. Those so-called qualified nurses sat on their asses, got their promotions, and then when they made too much money, their positions would be eliminated so the hospital could hire a new crop of graduates at cheaper rates.

They have no passion, no empathy, Joshua told himself. Civilian nursing schools taught them nothing about "real" nursing.

Prompted by co-worker complaints at having to work with the difficult nurse, Joshua was increasingly floated off the medical floors to the Behavioral Health units, which was generally considered to be a less desirable assignment. Joshua's demeanor did not allow him to be accepted into the various hospital cliques and while people were cordial to him, the thirty-five year old vet with the chip on his shoulder was generally avoided by staff.

"He belongs on the psych ward," the Head Nurse had remarked to the hospital administrator. "He's just one pill away from being a patient himself."

Joshua found the Behavioral Health unit to be to his calling. Many of the patients were veterans themselves; homeless and addicted to drugs and alcohol. Loners, like him. He threw himself into his work with fervor, working his three twelve-hour shifts and volunteering his off time at the 1900 Hamilton homeless shelter on the near east side in downtown Cleveland. His only recreation was riding his Harley-Davidson Fat Boy motorcycle when the weather permitted. His patients and the downtrodden were his only focus. No female companionship. His only living relative, a sister, was married and lived in California. A year after she had moved from Cleveland, they stopped calling each other.

The only person Joshua considered to be trusted

enough to talk to was Doc Stafford. When Joshua felt the pressure building up and needed to vent, Doc was there. They had spent countless hours raking the hospital administrative and selected staff over the coals, mostly over beers at the Recovery Room Bar conveniently located across the street from the hospital. Maybe it was time to call Doc before he blew a gasket.

The shower felt good. He dried off, put on his street clothes, and walked out of the hospital to the black and chrome motorcycle parked in the now sun-filled corner of the employee parking lot. Although early, the July sun was heating up the morning and he chose not to wear the leather jacket or his helmet. Swinging his leg over the seat, he fired up the Harley, allowing the rumble of the exhaust pipes to massage his body. He welcomed the three-mile ride to his downtown apartment in the Metropolitan Nine, as the upscale residence was called. Between his job at St. Luke's and his military pension, he could afford it. Waiting for him were the VA-supplied Vicodin pills to ease the additional pain applied to his already damaged body from the physical demands of nursing; long hours spent on his feet and the occasional tussling with an unruly patient. The pills helped him sleep. But they couldn't always stop his brain from melding work and war into fright-night movies that played a continuous loop.

He thought about the three interns taunting that helpless girl. "Assholes!"   Twisting the throttle he turned out of the hospital's parking lot and swung north on West 25th Street, leaving tendrils of anger and bike exhaust behind.

Chapter 5

Doctor Katrina Westerly stared at the three student doctors seated at a table in the Day Area and mulled over what Joshua had told her. She didn't doubt his story but she knew he possessed an inherent dislike for authority figures, which included physicians and especially student doctors. Before she tackled that issue, she needed to talk to Nick.

Detective Nicholas Silvano had received a 3 a.m. call from Police Radio to handle the scene of a murder and she didn't get the chance to tell him to have a "safe and good day" before he slipped out of their bed. She found the yellow Post-it Note stuck to the coffee maker: "called out at 3 - call me". The note was signed with a drawing of a heart. Just thinking about it made her smile.

Kat went into the nurse's break room and using the office phone, dialed nine for an outside line followed by a phone number she knew by memory.

"Homicide Unit, Colegrove. Can I help you?"

"Hi Danny," Kat said. "Is Nick around?"

"C'mon Kat, forget about Nick. When you gonna dump that dickhead and start seeing a real man like me?" Colegrove joked.

"Aww, Danny, you know I love you best but Nicky has the money to support my lifestyle of the rich and famous," she answered brightly.

"Kat, if he's making that much dough, I want in on that action." Detectives Danny Colegrove and Nick Silvano went way back. He laughed, then his tone turned serious. "He's out at a murder scene right now with Jimmy Herron. I can put a note on his desk to call you, or if it's urgent, I can get ahold of him on the radio."

"A note is good, Danny, thanks."

"You got it, girlfriend," the detective said and hung up the phone.

Kat and Nick met at the Captain's Quarters Bar at the East 55th Street Marina where the detective docked his beloved twenty-eight foot Rinker boat that served as his summer home. She was a barmaid and he was a loyal customer. During the day she attended classes at Case Western University where she received a degree in psychiatry. After they became a couple she convinced him to move into her Gold Coast apartment overlooking Lake Erie in Lakewood, just west of Cleveland. Nick was divorced, no kids, and twelve years older than Kat, which didn't bother her in the least. He had worked in Narcotics for eleven years before asking to be transferred to Homicide. But he didn't seem happy in his new job. Living with a cop wasn't easy, she acknowledged. And any day that Kat didn't get to wish him a safe return made her feel unsettled, as if the simple phrase would serve as an invisible shield.

"It's like they go off to war every day for twenty-five years," a cop's wife had explained at a retirement party for one of Nick's old uniform partners. "I don't know how my husband did it for all those years and then came home 'normal'. Rapes, murders, abuse, and the sheer daily terror - and those cops survive it every single fucking day," the wife had told her and the other wives and girlfriends after her second bottle of wine. "I just don't know how they do it," she slurred as she went off in search of bottle number three.

Kat placed her phone into her lab coat pocket and said a silent prayer for Nick, hoping that would make up for missing her morning benediction for his safety. While she was not a practicing Christian, she'd seen too many miracles that defied explanation to discount the existence of a master creator.

Dr. Hanson came into the room, disrupting her thoughts. "Good Morning, Doctor Westerly," he said. "Have you seen any extra patient sheets lying around back here? I don't know what rooms my patients are in today. Seems like they change them on purpose just to confuse us doctors," he joked.

"Here, I'll make a copy of mine for you," Kat offered. "I haven't written on it yet." She handed him a clean copy as he made a cup of coffee from the unit's Keurig machine.

"I see you got assigned the 'baby' doctors' rotation for their psych mandatories. Any of them going to make it?" he asked.

"They are about to have a really bad day," she answered with a wry smile. Kat studied the Census sheet and saw seventeen names. "Almost a full house," she remarked to herself and after some small talk with the oncoming staff and the unit's two social workers, she approached the three student doctors seated in the Day Area.

"Good morning, gentlemen," she said without looking up from the Census sheet she carried. "I see that Doctor Cooper was your previous medical unit mentor in the ER. I'm sure he informed you that any improper language or interactions with patients at this hospital will not be tolerated." She paused, allowing her gaze to sweep over the trio, who now shifted uncomfortably in their chairs and cast uneasy glances at each other.

"Your job is to observe me. This rotation is not a vacation from your studies. Here, you will treat the war veterans, the addicts, the mentally challenged, the physically abused, and all kinds of cases that outsiders would deem impossible to fix. Just as a medical patient needs medication to keep their blood pressure in check, these patients need medication for their minds, and emotional support for their souls. Now, let's begin the daily assessments of our patients."

Kat asked an aide to bring Theresa in first. She shuffled into the room, head down, her skinny fingers clutching the front of her blue and white striped hospital gown.

"Hello, Theresa. I'm Dr. Westerly. Did you sleep well?"

No response.

"Did you eat breakfast yet?"

Nothing.

"Are you having any pain?"

Still no answer. Theresa kept her head down, avoiding looking directly at Kat or the three student doctors. Failing to receive any verbal or visual responses from the patient, Kat instructed the aide to walk Theresa back to her room.

Kat stared at the student doctors who in turn looked down at their notebooks, unable to meet her gaze. She uttered a long sigh before speaking. "That patient is an eighteen-year-old girl who was receiving excellent grades as a senior at John Adams High School. Her mother found Theresa in her bedroom after she had been beaten and raped by her stepfather. Her physical injuries will heal but, emotionally, she is scarred for life. I heard what you three did to her – taunting a patient! Now, my job to help her was compromised by your irresponsible actions in the one place she is supposed to feel safe!" The three student doctors remained silent even as Kat slapped her hand on the desk, causing the Census sheet to waft slowly onto the floor.

"If it was up to me, you'd be out on your asses today!" Kat picked up the paper then called for the aide to bring in the next patient.

Chapter 6

"Nicky, I can't move! I can't stand up!" Detective Jimmy Herron stammered through clenched teeth.

"C'mon Jimmy, stop messing around," Nick said. "We've got a murder scene to get back to." Cleveland Police Homicide Detective Nicholas Silvano, Badge #124, stood just inside the door to the Police Report room adjacent to St. Luke's Emergency Room's admissions desk. Nick leaned in the doorframe, his back to his partner, his gaze focused on the usual emergency room patient tangle in the lobby.

Nick heard a groan behind him and turned around. *What the hell?* Jimmy's arms were crossed over his chest and he was shaking almost to the point of full blown convulsions. "Get a doctor in here quick!" Nick yelled to the nurse at the intake counter, who was pounding on the keys of one of the computers on wheels.

Dr. Joseph Cooper, the hospital's Medical Director and attending ER Physician, entered the room. He had just pronounced the detectives' murder victims, a young mother and newborn son, as officially deceased. The pair had been stabbed to death with a kitchen butcher knife, the bloody weapon now encased in a plastic evidence bag and lying on the desk.

"Detective, what is it?" the doctor asked, waving his pen light into Jimmy's eyes.

"I don't know, Doc," Jimmy grimaced.

Dr. Cooper grabbed Jimmy's arm and tried to move it

away from his chest. "Get me a cart and an IV kit," he ordered one of the ER staff that had gathered in the doorway. In a matter of minutes, the skilled ER staff had an IV of Valium mixing with the 1000 cc's of normal saline flowing into Jimmy's arm.

"Let's give it a couple minutes - and get that knife out of here," ordered Dr. Cooper.

Nick picked up the evidence bag and put it inside his suit jacket and out of Jimmy's sight, but still in his possession to preserve the chain of evidence if the case made it to court. The doctor monitored Jimmy's vital signs and after a few minutes, he was able to pry Jimmy's arms away from his chest.

"Let's get up and onto the cart, Detective," Dr. Cooper instructed. "You're going to be just fine now." The doctor turned to address Nick. "Can you hold onto his gun? My people don't like guns on their patients."

Nick removed his partner's 9mm from its shoulder holster and stuffed it into his waistband.

"Put him into ER-12 for now," Dr. Cooper said.

After his partner was wheeled out of the Report Room, Nick asked, "What the hell was that all about, Doc?"

Dr. Cooper closed the door before turning to face Nick. "My best guess is that Jimmy had a psychotic episode of sorts. What happened at that house?"

"It was bad, Doc," Nick said, shaking his head. "Car 112 responded to a 911 call and found a female dead on the floor with the knife sticking out of her stomach. The husband was in the kitchen cooking something in a big pot, and gospel music was blaring from a radio. We get there pretty quick and the neighbor tells us the dead woman just came home from the hospital with a new baby boy. I was searching a bedroom when I heard Jimmy yell. I go in to the kitchen and there's Jimmy, puking into the sink."

Nick paused and took a deep breath before continuing. "Jimmy pointed at the pot; the baby's head was floating in the boiling water. The father told an officer that 'Jesus told him to do it,' because the mother and baby were possessed by the Devil."

Dr. Cooper shook his head. "The terrible things people do to each other..."

"I'm with you there, Doc. I've been a Cleveland cop for twenty-one years," Nick said. "I've seen killings, suicides, and missing kids that were later found suffocated to death inside of abandoned refrigerators. But this may top the list. Just unbelievable misery."

Both men stood quietly engrossed in their own thoughts until Nick straightened up and asked anxiously, "What about my partner, Doc? Is he going to be okay?"

Dr. Cooper took Nick by the arm and steered him out of the Report Room and into the ER's main lobby. "I've seen this before, Nick. In Afghanistan. It's a form of shell shock. Your partner witnessed an incident so horrible his physical body just shut down. He'll be fine, he just needs some time." The two men entered the curtained ER-12 room where Jimmy was now sitting up on the side of the hospital bed, the IV line still embedded in his arm.

"Hey Nick, I'm sorry," Jimmy said quietly. "I don't know what happened. I just kept thinking of my wife, Linda, at home with our two little kids and what my life would be without them. You're not gonna say anything to

Lieutenant Fratello, are you?" he asked, referring to Homicide's commanding officer.

"I won't - but it's not my call," Nick replied. "We should ask the doctor here."

Doctor Cooper regarded both men. "Detective Herron, I can't allow you to be on active duty until a complete evaluation is made. You're in the system now; reports have been generated. Too many people saw what happened and I can't jeopardize my ER Department by ignoring the incident. But, I think a couple of weeks of light duty and a follow-up with a licensed professional will get you back to full duty. Physically, you're fine. But your mental state was compromised. I suggest you take it easy for a few days."

"Alright," the patient replied, reluctantly.

"Let's make a referral for a follow-up visit with a professional and then we can get you out of here." Dr. Cooper turned to Nick and asked, "You still seeing Katrina Westerly? Any problem referring Detective Herron to see her?"

"No, that's fine," Nick said. While he really didn't like Kat knowing too much about his job for fear she'd worry, he knew that she was probably the best person to evaluate his partner.

"Alright, then," Dr. Cooper said. "Let's get you discharged."

Chapter 7

Nick pulled his silver Honda Civic into the underground parking garage of the Carlyle-On-The-Lake high-rise apartments located on the "Gold Coast" of Lakewood, just west of downtown Cleveland. It was almost 6 p.m. Kat's red Lexus occupied the assigned parking spot next to his. He parked and got out; adjusting the shoulder holster that snugly held his Cleveland Police Department's issued 9mm Smith and Wesson semi-automatic. He reached over and felt the hood of Kat's car. *Still warm.*

Nick walked to the garage elevator bank, pushed the button, and waited. He and Kat shared an apartment on the twelfth floor. Nick had lived alone for the past twelve years since he and Cheryl divorced. The parting of ways had been a mutual decision. "Maybe more her decision than mine," Nick had admitted to his friends. The job had come between them; that was the real reason for the split, but they agreed they had married too young and had grown into two separate people with different interests.

Until he met Kat, Nick had spent the summers on his boat at the East 55th Street Marina. When the cold weather came, he dry-docked the boat and lived in a studio apartment over Betty's Café at West 90th and Lorain Avenue on the west side of the city. A year ago, Kat convinced him to live with her and he had to admit, it was a much better arrangement. Betty's Café was a country bar with a jukebox that blasted until bar closing. Also, the danger of a stray bullet fired by a drunken cowboy coming through the floor and killing him in his sleep was never far from his mind.

The elevator door opened. He stepped in and punched the button for his floor. As the gold-plated door slid shut, Nick's reflection filled the polished metal door. He was an athletic-built man with dark wavy hair, some of which was just beginning to grey at the temples. The tan suit jacket he wore covered his shoulder holster and fit well on his two hundred and twenty pound body. Workouts in the police gym kept it that way. He felt younger than his forty-two years. His relationship with Kat was almost perfect, he thought. She never complained if he chose to sleep on his boat, the *Guns 'n Hoses,* as long as he let her know he was safe. While he was reluctant to take advantage of the offer, she had clinched it by pointing out, "My top floor apartment has a beautiful view of your beloved Lake Erie and you can see downtown Cleveland from the windows."

She was right. The view was spectacular – both inside and out. Sitting on the balcony with the wind carrying the water's scent was almost like being on his boat. The night view of Cleveland was augmented to a greater level when the lights at FirstEnergy Stadium where the Cleveland Browns football team played or the Indians' Progressive Field were lit up for a home game.

Nick entered the apartment and tossed his keys onto the gray granite counter separating the kitchen from the living room. The table was already set. Freshly thawed Lake Erie Perch was waiting to be rolled in the special beer batter prepared in a bowl next to a pan of hot oil already sputtering on the stove.

"There's my man," Kat said softly coming up behind him and wrapping her tanned arms gently around his waist. "I got the drop on you, Copper," she said. Nick turned and planted a kiss on her forehead before stepping back to admire her, still holding both of her hands in his.

"Dude, you look great," he said.

Already out of her hospital clothes, Kat had on gray sweatpants and one of Nick's dark blue t-shirts with a CPD badge logo over the left breast. A gold chain around her neck held a pendant of Saint Michael, the patron saint of police officers. She never removed it.

"Hey! I ain't a dude," she said in mock protest. "You hungry? I thawed out some of the fish you caught."

"That'll be great," he said and moved to the windows overlooking Lake Erie. "Looks like the Indians are getting ready to play, the lights at Progressive Field are already on."

Kat rolled the fillets in the batter and dropped the pieces into the pan. The fillets sizzled, making little popping sounds as they cooked. She removed a bottle of Jack Daniels from the cabinet over the sink and poured Nick his usual three fingers into the logo-etched rock glass, then turned to the refrigerator and poured herself a glass of wine from a box of Almaden Moscato.

"Why don't you get yourself some better wine?" Nick asked as she took a sip from the stemmed glass. "You're way past drinking wine out of a box."

"Same reason you drink Jack instead of Makers Mark. I like it." After dinner they sat on the balcony and watched the sun set over the lake. The seagulls circled a pack of fishing boats anchored over the artificial reef. The reef had been built using bricks and concrete taken from the old Cleveland Browns Stadium after it was demolished to make room for the storied hometown football team.

"How was your day?" she asked.

"Bad," he answered and reluctantly told her about the senseless killing of the baby boy and his mother. "Murder cases are different from dope cases. With dope cases, you have to carefully build them to get a conviction. Killing somebody is different. The crime has already been committed and you have to figure out who did it and why," he said, staring out over the lake. Nick had transferred from Narcotics to Homicide six months ago. He wasn't sure yet if it was the right decision.

"Oh my God," she said softly, reaching out and placing her hand on his arm. Nick was one of the strongest men she had ever met, both physically and mentally, but she could see he was deeply affected by these senseless murders, no matter how he tried to shrug it off.

Then Nick told her about Jimmy. "Dr. Cooper called it a form of shell shock. What do you think it is?"

"It sounds like Jimmy experienced what we call 'tonic immobility'. It happens when someone is exposed to an event so traumatic that it causes a physical response – like fight or flight. He had what is called an 'adaptive response' to a situation where he saw no chance of successfully being able to escape or win the fight. It can be treated and controlled by a competent licensed professional," Kat said in her doctor's voice.

"Funny you should say that," Nick said, taking another sip from his glass of bourbon. "Doctor Cooper gave Jimmy a referral to see you. Right now, he's on restricted duty –

office only - pending a doctor's slip returning him to full duty."

"Have him call my office in the morning to make the appointment. And remember, I will not discuss any aspects of his condition with you," she asserted.

"I don't want to know anything. I just want him to be okay.   C'mon," Nick said, standing up. "Let's go inside and treat my ailment."

"And just what might your condition be?" she asked.

"Lack-a-Nooky," he said.

"You're in luck. The doctor is in."

Chapter 8

S wiping his hospital ID through the time clock, Joshua saw he was three minutes early for the start of his second night of three twelve-hour shifts. "You don't get any credit for being early but if you're a few minutes late they dock your paycheck for fifteen minutes," he grumbled loud enough so the other nurses lined up behind him could hear. He turned away from the annoying machine that controlled his day and walked to the outer door of Center One.

Johanna Feighan was there, stabbing the black button that rang into the locked unit with a manicured finger. "Oh, it's you," she huffed. "Open the damn door so I can get in. I'm in a hurry."

Joshua spied the ever-present attorney sitting in a chair in the overflow visitors' room off the hallway. He was busy checking his cell phone.

"You have to wait for Security to clear your visit and give you a pass, Mrs. Feighan," Joshua calmly informed her. He inserted a key into the door's lock, purposely avoiding using the alternative keypad. Only staff knew the code and it was frequently changed. No reason to let her see the numbers, he thought.

Her protest was interrupted by the appearance of a hospital security guard who asked Johanna for ID and to sign the Visitor Log. Johanna rolled her eyes and loudly exhaled. "I'm here to visit my husband, David Feighan," she snapped.

The guard looked down at his clipboard. "He's in Room 252. What's in the bag?" the guard asked, pointing to the plastic grocery bag Johanna held.

"I brought my husband a bottle of FIJI Water. This is all he drinks and I'm *sure* you don't have this in-house," she said sarcastically.

"I'm sorry Mrs. Feighan, but outside food or drink is not allowed to be brought onto the unit. I'm sure you understand. We'll hold it for you in our office until your visit is over and you can have it back then," the guard explained politely while reaching for the bag.

"No you will not!" she cried, pulling the bag to her body and embracing it with both arms as if it contained the Ten Commandments. "My husband's doctor, Toby Abernathy, gave me permission to bring this in for David and you're not taking it from me."

Michael stood then and walked to her side in silent support. The young guard looked to Joshua, eyebrows raised in a non-verbal cue for the nurse to invoke his authority and intervene.

"Wait here, Mrs. Feighan," Joshua said. "I'll check to see if Doctor Abernathy wrote the order. Without his written order in the computer, the guard is correct. You will not be allowed to bring it onto the floor."

"Make it quick, we have places to be," she said loudly as she grabbed her attorney's arm.

Joshua passed through the double doors and approached the Nurses Station to check for the order. It would be just like that stuffed shirt to allow this woman to bring unauthorized crap onto the floor, he fumed. Other patients and visitors will see her doing it and demand the same be allowed for them.

"C'mon Joshua, we're waiting to give Report. You're late," the Charge Nurse said when she saw him.

"I'm not late," Joshua countered. "Mrs. Feighan is at the door giving Security a hard time about bringing in some bottled water for her husband and I have to check the computer for the order."

"Save yourself the trouble, Josh," she said. "Toby was in this morning and wrote the order for the bottled water. I had to put it in for him - he didn't even know how - can you believe that? He's in charge and can't even use the computer to place an order! Go tell the guard to let her in and hurry back. I want to go home," she finished.

Joshua returned to the Unit's entry doors and held them open for Johanna. The guard shrugged his shoulders as if to say "go figure" and sprinted down the hall to answer a "Mr. Strong needed right away" for an out-of-control patient in the ER.

"Next time you better listen to me or Toby will get a call," Johanna could be heard saying as she started down the hall to her husband's room.

Joshua returned to the Nursing Station, swiped his badge through the card reader, entered the room and dropped his nurse's bag onto an empty chair. Nursing areas were the same in every hospital; tables cluttered with half-full Styrofoam cups of cold coffee, pizza boxes containing uneaten crusts, and scraps of paper scrawled with patients' vital signs, lab results, and doctor's phone numbers.

"Ready to work now?" the day shift Charge Nurse asked.

"Sorry," Joshua said. He wasn't sorry at all – he was just

doing his job. When were these people going to give him some credit! He took the last open chair and pulled a Census sheet with the current list of patients from the stack on the table. He knew the Charge Nurse didn't like him – that was apparent in the patients assigned to him. If Attila the Hun's name was on the sheet, his name would be written next to it, he thought. But Joshua really didn't give a damn. He wasn't here to make friends.

Reading through the assignment sheet confirmed his suspicions. He had Trudy Freese, Derek Stanton, and the new guy, David Feighan. Both Trudy and Derek were regulars that Joshua knew well from prior admissions. Trudy was a man undergoing a sex change to make him a woman. Derek was a doper, permanently brain-damaged from years of constant use of hallucinogens and lived in group homes. His file contained a note detailing he may have been responsible for the death of another man in one of the group homes he had been in, but the circumstances were murky and nothing was ever proved. Both were psychologically damaged and unlikely to ever function in what passed for a normal society. And what passed for 'normal' on a psych unit would terrify the average person.

The Charge Nurse interrupted his patient review. "I'll go first," she said, referring to her off-going report. "I have to get out of here on time today." What was supposed to be a five minute report always turned into a twenty minute sermon with plenty of whining about hospital procedures, her personal opinions on what she thought the patients' diagnosis' should have been, and gossip about what visitors wore - all while stuffing her face with candy that was continually replenished by the nurses and doctors.

"Joshua, you're going to have your hands full," she warned. "We had to call Security and put Trudy into the back isolation room. She acted out in the Day Area and threw her dinner across the room – someone forgot the Ranch dressing for her chicken strips." The other nurses gathered in Report murmured small noises of sympathy for Joshua; thankful they were spared that assignment. "We gave her a shot of Ativan and Haldol, but that barely touched her. She's due for another dose in two hours so do what you have to do.

"Derek is still in his own world, wherever that might be, but the doctor ordered a rape kit to be done on him. That new group home he was sent to was worse than the last one and whatever he told the doctor and social worker on the morning rounds prompted a bunch of new orders relating to sexual abuse from herpes to HIV. That poor kid is about as bad as I've ever seen him. He just stays in his room playing imaginary video games. Comes out only for meals and refuses to go to group.

"Now, David Feighan, the new guy, is another case altogether. I can't figure him out," she said, pausing to unwrap a miniature Hershey bar. "Toby Abernathy is his doctor and while his patient is obviously on some sort of drugs, he didn't write any orders for blood or urine tests. We have no medical history on him. He's allowed to take meals in his room but absolutely no visitors except his wife and attorney. He's some sort of rich guy that uses drugs; another patient told me that," she said as she tore up her report sheet and tossed it into the trash can. "I miss the good old days of pot and acid," she said, shaking the last piece of candy out of the bag and dropping it into her pocket.

Joshua doodled on his paper as the other off-going day shift nurses gave their reports. After Report was over, he went out to the front counter and took a chair in front of one of the computers. He shifted position, trying to get comfortable.

Nothing can help my back. He looked around. None of the nurses behind him or the patients in front of him were looking his way. He reached into the pocket of his scrubs, extracted two Vicodin and washed the pills down with a can of Red Bull. The caffeine would give him a jump start for the twelve-hour shift in front of him and the pills would help stem the ever-present ache caused by his war injuries. Most of that time would be spent on patient charting, recording their vital signs, general demeanor, if they attended group sessions, or exhibited unwanted behaviors. The shitty new hospital charting system took up time that could be better spent taking care of patients, he thought for the thousandth time. *What a waste!*

At 8 p.m. the kitchen staff rang the buzzer for entry with the evening snacks. Joshua made up a plate of the chicken strips and carried it back to the Isolation Room where he found Trudy lying on the floor; naked and pretending to be asleep. Although her eyes appeared to be closed, Joshua could see her eyelids fluttering.

"For crying out loud, Trudy. Get up off the floor and get dressed. Nobody wants to see you like that. Don't act out on my shift - I'm in no mood for any of your crap tonight," he grumbled as he placed the snack plate on the wide ledge of the window sill.

Trudy was in her mid-thirties. Crude tattoos covered

her neck and arms that were applied in prison when she was known as "Roger". Every time she was admitted, she was the topic of much discussion among the staff members. What were they to call this person? The sex organ reassignment surgery was only partially complete with both male and female parts sharing the same body. "It", "she", "he", were all bandied about. Common agreement was to address the patient with the name currently being used: Trudy, even though some of the staff deliberately used "Roger" just to piss her off.

Then there was the room assignment. Most of the rooms were double occupancy. Should Trudy have a male or a female roommate? In the end, it usually didn't matter as the Unit was always close to being full so they did what-ever could be done to accommodate her. The "man-woman" as Henry referred to her, was assigned to whatever single room could be made available, even if that meant relocating a patient to another room.

Trudy jumped up, without regard for her nakedness, once she saw the food. "What the fuck, Josh? Chicken strips agaaaiiin?" she wailed. "I just had that for dinner. Call the kitchen and get me a couple of cheeseburgers with Ranch dressing and double cheese on them. I ain't gonna eat this shit again!" she exclaimed and with a swipe of her hairy, tattooed arm, sent the plate flying to the floor.

"No, Trudy, I'm not calling the kitchen. Quit acting out - I'm not going to medicate you. You fooled the Day Shift with your crap but I know you too well. You can stay here in isolation all night for all I care. I have patients that are *really* sick and need me so it's your choice." Joshua step-ped over the spilled food to pick up her hospital gown from the corner where she had thrown it.

"Put your gown on, now!" he ordered, holding it out to her.

"Aww Josh," she said. "Can't you take a joke? I'll be good," Trudy giggled as she sat back on the floor, still naked, and picked up a strip of chicken and began to eat.

"Cover yourself - now!" Joshua ordered again. Trudy stood and put the blue and white striped gown over her body backwards. She grinned at Joshua. Her size twelve bare feet were dirty and stuck out from the too-small gown and her hairy legs were grossly out of place in contrast to the perfectly formed sized 36C breasts paid for by the taxpayers of Ohio.

Jesus! I let her get to me again and I lost my temper, he chastised himself. This is *so not* what nursing is supposed to be about. Joshua closed the door to the Isolation Room but left it unlocked per the hospital rules. Trudy knew the door was not locked and Joshua knew it wouldn't be too much longer before Trudy came out and exposed herself to the entire unit.

"The same shit, over and over again," he muttered as he walked down the hall and into the Day Area. Trudy and her boyfriend living together on the taxpayers' money, never holding a job or even looking for one, collecting welfare and food stamps while being issued free government-funded cell phones and medical care. It was never enough for some people, Joshua thought.

Derek Stanton was carrying a plate of food down the hall to his room. "Derek!" Henry called out. "You know the rules! No food in the rooms unless the doctor says it's okay. And sit at the table where I can see you or go hungry," ordered Henry. The aide's voice was loud and authoritative. Derek turned, walked silently to a table and sat down.

Thank God for Henry. Joshua stopped in front of the door to David Feighan's room then entered, not knowing what to expect. His patient was in bed sleeping and Joshua saw the unopened bottle of FIJI Water sitting on the dresser where Johanna had left it. Joshua was preparing to wake him up when he heard a loud commotion. He rushed out of Feighan's room just in time to see Henry and a security guard dragging a naked and screaming Trudy down the hallway and back into the Isolation room.

Joshua headed for the Nurses' Station and the Pyxis machine to draw up the B-52 medications for his noncompliant patient. *Trudy wins....again.*

Chapter 9

I 'm tired, Joshua thought, exhaling deeply. *I am so tired of this same never-ending crap!*

Trudy was one of the biggest abusers. With over forty-six admissions in four years, she had her routine down to a science. Twice she had been discharged in the morning and given a cab voucher to take her home - at taxpayers' expense - only to have her tell the cabbie to drive her right back to the Emergency Room on the other side of the hospital, walk in, and tell the staff that she was going to kill herself. Under the law, she had to be admitted for observation and ended up right back at the Center One floor that afternoon, never even leaving the hospital grounds! "And I get stuck with her again, every time," Joshua complained, but nobody listened.

Joshua sat in the Nurses Station waiting for the fire in his back to subside. Wrestling with Trudy to apply the four-point restraints to her wrists and ankles to keep her in bed until she stopped fighting took everything he had not to fall to the floor in agony. It had taken five security guards, along with Joshua and Henry, to place the restraints and now Henry had to sit in Trudy's room and chart his observations every fifteen minutes per Ohio state law. That left the floor short a caregiver for the rest of the patients. Even though Trudy was asleep from the medications Joshua had administered, Henry still had to watch her until the restraints could be removed. Often, Trudy would "play possum" and pretend to be sleeping. As soon as the restraints were removed she would attack the staff and any other patients who happened to be nearby until they could wrestle her back under control. Trudy was dangerous; deemed too mentally sick for jail and too violent for a group home or a place in society. Her many admissions to St. Luke's had placed an indefinite hold on the remaining surgeries required to physically transform her from Roger to Trudy.

Joshua closed his eyes and tried to will away the pain. It was too soon for more Vicodin; the clock on the wall showed only two hours had passed since he took the pills. He logged into a computer and read the nursing notes on David Feighan. The day shift nurse had little information to report. It read;

Doctor Abernathy came in to visit his patient. No new orders given. Patient takes meals in his room. Wife called and said that patient was not to receive any visitors and not be permitted to use the patient phones in the Day Area. This was confirmed verbally by Doctor Abernathy. Patient quiet and withdrawn, non-verbal with staff. Refused group. Voicing no complaints. Will continue to monitor.

Joshua checked on Henry, who was monitoring the Day Area, before walking to the doorway of David's room. He opened the door.

"About time you got around to checking on me, Nurse Ramsey. Close the door, will you? I don't want anyone to hear us." David stood up from the bed and extended his hand to Joshua in a greeting as if they had just met for coffee rather than in the sterile room of a highly-secured mental treatment facility.

Joshua's head tilted and his eyes narrowed as if studying a new species. "What kind of a game are you playing, Mr. Feighan?" he asked.

"I can assure you, this is no game, my young friend," David replied, his voice strong. Gone was the mumbling and drooling. "Before you say anything, I want you to watch this." He reached under the mattress and pulled out an iPad.

"Where did you get that?" Joshua exclaimed. "All you're supposed to have is your hospital clothing, no personal property, and certainly not that!" he pointed to the device in his patient's hand.

"You guys really have to be more careful at this hospital. The security here is quite lax," David said nonchalantly. "For instance, anyone can impersonate a doctor. And no one would notice another doctor coming into a patient's room. I got a guy who works for me and he's quite the chameleon. Before I enter into any deals, my guy does backgrounds on the people I deal with. He checks to see if they are alcoholics, drug users, wife cheaters or thieves. Now nobody's perfect," he chuckled. "Look at me – I've dabbled in vice."

"From what I've seen in the papers," Joshua countered, one eyebrow raised. "You've done more than just *dabble*."

"Well, yes that's true," Feighan admitted, nonplussed. "As I was saying....I check people out before I enter into business with them. Never can be too careful, you know. It doesn't mean I won't do business with them – in most cases I'll just take their *pecadillos* into account. It would be a small circle if I eliminated anyone who's ever sinned," he grinned. "And you're the only person I have confided this information to but, in this case, I *have* to trust you. I'm a very good judge of character and I believe you can be trusted."

Joshua was dumfounded.   He peered out the door; the hallway was quiet and the lights were off. He closed the door and took a chair next to the bed. David handed the tablet to Joshua. "Watch this."

Johanna and the attorney stood together in a large room next to a well-stocked bar. Each had a drink in their hands.

"That's my study at home," David said, anticipating Joshua's question and reached over and pushed the Play arrow on the screen. The scene came to life.

"Serves him right," Johanna spoke. "I told you it would work. That old bastard fell for it, hook, line, and sinker. Maybe, now you'll believe me when I told you I was serious. If you do your job right, David will *never* get out of the hospital. For Christ's sake, he was sixty-three years old when I married him two years ago and I'm his fifth wife. What does he expect from me? I'm only forty! I thought with all the drugs he takes he would be dead by now and I would inherit all his money, but the old bastard fooled me."

She took a sip of her drink and set it on the bar. "I knew I couldn't wait around any longer – I had to do something so I've been lacing his FIJI Water with Ketamine. I had planned on shoving him off the cliff behind the house - he always liked Lake Erie -but this may work out better! Instead of being suspected for murder, I can be the poor wife of a drug-crazed womanizer. Are you with me on this?" she playfully asked as she tried to execute a twirl but instead, stumbled against the bar top.

"Johanna, I never thought you would go this far," the attorney said. He set his drink on the bar and placed his hands on her shoulders, both for support and to guide her to the large couch in the center of the room. He turned her to him, gathered her in his arms and hungrily kissed her before allowing her to sink to the couch. "I've been David's lawyer for the past fourteen years and represented him in his last three divorces. Those ex-wives never got a dime of his money but they didn't have the nerve or the foresight to institute anything even close to what you're planning," he said, his voice full of admiration. "I should know - I wrote the pre-nuptials and those women walked away empty-handed." Johanna lifted her hand to caress his cheek.

"You're right, this crazy idea of yours just might work," Michael said. "All we have to do now is get a judge to declare David incompetent and get him probated into a mental facility for what remains of his privileged life. We can get you appointed as the administrator of his estate and all of his holdings. I've got the legal connections to make it go our way. As long as we play it cool and keep our relationship quiet, I see no reason why, *together*, we can't pull this off." Johanna reached for Michael and the pair started making out like teenagers after a long separation.

"Holy shit!" Joshua exclaimed looking away from the screen and locking eyes with David.

"Wait, there's more," David said and motioned with his hand for Joshua to continue watching the tablet and the video it contained.

"What about Toby Abernathy?" Johanna asked. "Will he play along?"

"Don't worry about him," the attorney said. "All Toby wants is his money. David's been stringing him along for months now about a large donation to St. Luke's, anywhere from a million to more than three million, but he never makes a commitment to him and now, Toby wants to retire and leave a legacy. He wants a new surgery wing to be built and named after him; The Toby Abernathy Center. You should have seen his face light up when he said it. Amazing what accolades these assholes have for themselves. To call Toby and David both narcissists is not a big enough description for those two," Michael continued talking as he reached for the top button of her blouse and started working his way down.

"That's enough for now," David said, taking the tablet from Joshua's hands. "I already know how this movie ends," he said disgustedly.

"How did you get this?" Joshua asked, but then raised his hand. "I know, you got 'a guy'."

"I've been suspicious of Johanna's behavior so I had hidden cameras installed. I never thought she would go so far as trying to kill me! Every time I drank one of those FIJI Waters she kept pushing on me I felt out of it. I gave one of the bottles to my guy and he had it tested. Turns out she was slipping me Special K, just like she confessed in the video you just saw."

Joshua recognized the street name for Ketamine, a drug used as an animal tranquilizer. But now, it was the LSD to a new generation of drug abusers. Also called bath salts or Flakka, it was cheap, available over the internet, and very dangerous.

"Some people call it fake pot but I know better," David

said. "Shit, she bought it right off the shelf at one of those inner-city gas stations and used my credit card so it would look like I bought it. I had my guy follow her and he caught her meeting Michael at various motels - and not for legal advice, if you know what I mean! No wonder when I asked him about starting divorce proceedings he started babbling about how I should 'work harder on this marriage.' I thought he was concerned as a friend and legal advisor, not a dick who was banging my wife. Now, I know the real reason he was against another divorce.

"I had cameras installed in his office – they were getting it on there too! At first I thought I could use her drugging my water to divorce her but I listened to my guy and waited. Then, after I overheard her telling my attorney, who I pay handsomely to protect my interests - not screw my wife, that she planned on killing me, I got scared and thought that she just might pull it off. I needed a safe place to be, away from both of them, so I pretended to be drugged out of my mind." He chuckled then. "Hell, it wasn't that hard, I've been there before. That way, she'd have no choice but to put me in the hospital. I needed to protect myself until I could come up with a plan. I thought about confiding in Toby but now I'm glad I didn't make that mistake. You are the only person that knows the whole story. Josh, I need you to help me get out of this mess."

David paused and held Joshua's eyes with his own. "Can I count on you?"

"What can I do?" Joshua asked. "I'm just a nurse. Why don't you go to the cops? Hell, you're David Feighan. *And*, you have proof!"

"Look, Josh. I've pissed off some important people in

this town and given the chance, they'd stand in line to stick it to me. Michael knows a lot of judges and I wouldn't put it past him to bribe one of them to put me away for the rest of my life. The way I see it, there's only one choice."

"What's that?" Joshua asked.

"We have to kill them first!"

Chapter 10

"What do you mean *we* have to kill them first? You really are crazy!" Joshua exclaimed before realizing he was yelling. He lowered his voice but the tone failed to disguise the confusion and frustration he felt toward his new patient. "I don't want anything to do with this plan of yours. Maybe you really do belong here! You can bet that I'll be going to Administration and maybe even the cops about this. For Christ's sake, David. That woman and your lawyer are actually discussing killing you or having you committed for the rest of your life, which is probably even worse than being dead. You can't ignore that."

"I'm not ignoring it, Josh. I'm going to face it head-on and handle it, just like I have done all my life. They have to be disposed of and I can't do it myself. My perfect alibi is that I am in here under lock and key. I'm offering you an opportunity here. Name your price!"

"I'm not a killer, David. I may have killed in wartime but that was for my survival and the survival of other soldiers in my unit. This is different. This is *murder* you're talking about!"

"But Josh, that's where you're wrong!" David solemnly said. "This is a matter of survival, just like you said. It's just a different battlefield."

"Maybe your survival, not mine," answered Joshua. "Why don't you just have *your guy* do it? He seems he's very good at watching your back."

"Too risky," David dismissed the idea. "He probably would do it but then he would have blackmail material on me. And I don't need that hanging over my head."

"What makes me any different? Wouldn't I have something to blackmail you with?"

"Different situation. There are more reasons for you to help me, my young and naïve friend. You can go to whoever you want and try to turn me in but don't forget, I'm in here because I'm not in my right mind. I'll just deny ever saying anything to you. Who do you think they'll believe?" remarked David. "Besides, there's another reason you should help. Toby Abernathy and Johanna were in to see me this afternoon. They stood right by the bed and talked about me as if I wasn't even here. I played the drugged-out mental patient, refusing to engage in conversation. After they left they met that prick Michael in Toby's office. Watch this!"

David handed the iPad back to Joshua, a new video queued and waiting to play. Joshua recognized the hospital office of Toby Abernathy. Toby sat at his desk across from Johanna and the attorney.

"You wired Toby's office in the hospital too?" Joshua asked, incredulously. "How did you do that?"

"You're damn right my guy wired his office. It's amazing how much freedom he had in this hospital. All it took was a white lab coat, a stethoscope around his neck, and a 'Doctor Smith' name badge on his chest," David explained proudly. "Security even held open the door for him when he smuggled stuff in to me. Your day shift nurses never batted an eye. I told you the security here sucked. Watch this!" David pressed Play.

Joshua watched as the attorney pulled some papers from his briefcase and placed them on the desk in front of the administrator. Johanna gazed into a hand-held compact and applied lipstick, oblivious to her surroundings.

"What am I looking at?" Toby inquired.

"These are papers that state, in your expert opinion, that David Feighan, is mentally unable to function in society and due to the prolonged use of illicit drugs and alcohol he is unable to care for himself and is both a danger to himself and others. Pretty standard stuff. You're the doctor and the expert and your patient cannot function without being held in a locked facility and will require court-ordered medication for the remainder of his life. All I need is your signature and I'll get a judge to rule it official," explained Michael.

Toby picked up the papers and without looking at them said, "If I do sign them, how long before the Feighan Foundation's three million dollar donation comes in so I can break ground on my new surgery center? As soon as I get the money, other donations will follow and I'd like to break ground before the end of the year."

"Don't worry," the lawyer said. "Once everything is in order, you'll have the money."

"Before the end of the year," Toby repeated, holding Michael's gaze. "We plan to break ground at the end of the year."

"As long as Mr. Feighan is taken care of, you'll get the money when you need it," Michael stated.

Toby nodded his head, seemingly satisfied. With a flourish, he signed his name to several pages then laid the pen down on the desk. He handed the papers over to the lawyer's outstretched hand.

"Johanna, of course, will be present for the news conference when I announce the new Toby Abernathy Surgery Center was made possible by a very generous donation from the Feighan Foundation," the administrator said, his face flushed with pride and anticipation.

"Unbelievable," Joshua whispered, his eyes locked on the tablet. "Just sitting there calmly without any feeling of what they are going to do to you, David!"

"Not only me, Josh," David said. "Keep watching."

"It might take a few days for me to find the right judge," Michael said, "but as soon as Johanna is granted control of the company assets, we can get the money to you. And, as we previously discussed, there will be a separate transfer of cash made to you for assisting us in this very tragic matter," he said with just a bit of irony.

"Just how much are we talking about?" Toby asked.

"How about half a million in cash and one other small favor," Johanna answered before Michael had a chance. "I want you to fire that annoying male nurse, John or Joe, whatever his name is. I don't like him. Sign the paperwork and fire him and we got a deal."

"I think that can be arranged," Toby said. "Let me check one thing first." He logged onto his desktop computer. "Yep, there he is," Toby commented, peering over the top of his glasses at the computer screen. "Joshua Ramsey. I'd like to get rid of him anyway. I want all of my nurses to have a college degree and he doesn't have one. He got his training in the Army, of all places. I'll change his shifts and have him sent back to the medical floors. He's got some sort of a disability from the military. I don't know why he got hired in the first place," he said. "His medical records show he has a prescription for Vicodin. His annual physical is coming up next month. Once I get the money, I'll order a drug test done on him. After the Vicodin shows up in his system, I can have his license pulled by the State Board of Nursing for misuse of narcotics. He will never work again as a nurse - in this state or anywhere else. Will that be sufficient, Johanna?"

She nodded her coifed head in answer.

"Besides," Toby continued. "Nurses like him come a dime a dozen. I'll get rid of him and a couple more nurses that don't have college degrees. That way it won't look like I am picking on him and I get my chance to clean house."

"How long do we have before we can get David sent somewhere?" Michael asked.

"We have to keep him for thirty days of treatment in order to avoid any questions," Toby explained. "That's about standard in cases like this. David's not responding to any treatment and I can make sure that he doesn't get any therapists or other doctors involved in his treatment. Even if he does come out of this, it will be too late. We can blame it on the judge. All the bases are covered."

"You know, Toby," Johanna said slyly. "If I didn't know better, I'd think you've done this before."

"Johanna!" Toby exclaimed, managing to look wounded. "I'm a healer and practitioner under the Hippocratic Oath," he said, referring to Socrates' ancient "do no harm" treatise.

"Are you sure it wasn't the 'Hypocritic Oath,'" Johanna countered.

Toby ignored the jab. "You're his wife and you," he nodded at Michael, "are his lawyer and friend. We all want what is best for David. Given his pattern of behavior, this IS the best course of action."

Michael nodded. "Feighan's company is private so there are no shareholders to intervene and his competitors hate his guts. I imagine there will be a lot of happy people in Cleveland when he is shipped off. I don't think I have to remind both of you that this meeting is never to be discussed. I could lose my law license and both of you could end up in prison, so think very carefully before you answer any questions. The media is going to have a field day with this. Remember, this is a situation brought on by David's own actions. Johanna, do not lose those credit card statements used to buy the Special K, I'll need them for the court hearing to prove how reckless David was with his life. We need to show the court and the media that David did this to himself without any regard for his loving wife!"

Johanna stood, flattening the front of her dress with her hands. She looked from Toby to Michael. "I think that's it, then," she said. The tablet screen went blank.

"I can't believe this is happening," Joshua said.

David watched the nurse carefully. Joshua's demeanor went from disbelief to defeat to defiance as he straightened his form and reflexively assumed the posture of a soldier at attention. He looked at David but it was as if he wasn't really seeing the man who had just turned his life upside down. He was seeing his future; a career ruined. And if he couldn't be a nurse, what else was left for him? There was nothing else he wanted to do. "Those fuckers are going to ruin my life and I did nothing to deserve it!" he burst out angrily. "And for what - money and a name on a building? You're right David. Something has to be done. I've got to think."

"There's nothing to think about, Josh," David said. "We don't have much time, maybe a couple weeks at best. It seems pretty simple to me. I can turn off the alarms and cameras to my house remotely from here with my phone. You go in and take care of them. You get rich and I get to keep my business. Simple."

"It's not that simple, David," Joshua said. "Killing never is." Without another word, he opened the door and walked out into the hallway.

***

Joshua couldn't sleep. Even the pills he routinely took after his shift (Vicodin for the pain and Ativan for the anxiety) did nothing to ease him; he felt like a coiled spring pressed down to its base with no chance for release. He was still trying to process what had happened that morning at the hospital: David, the video, all of it! Joshua was a careful individual. His time in the military taught him patience.   Rushing into a situation without weighing all the consequences could be fatal to a soldier. Now, he faced other enemies, only this time he had advance warning.

But could he really kill in cold blood? It wasn't war time but hadn't they, in effect, declared war on him? David was his patient, for God's sake! The authorities would certainly question him. Could David really be trusted to keep his mouth shut? The man's need for revenge against his wife and attorney was dangerous in itself. But there was no doubt in his mind that David was telling the truth. Joshua had seen the videos for himself. And *his* life was going to be ruined by forces beyond his control - if he did not act. He had to do something. But what? Could he really kill two people?

"There's got to be another way," he murmured before falling into a fitful sleep.

Chapter 11

The next day Joshua was seated in the Report Room getting ready for his shift when he was approached by the Unit Supervisor.

"Josh, the Hospital Nursing Supervisor wants you to meet her in Toby Abernathy's office. I was told to have you report there as soon as you came in."

"Now?"

"Yes, now," she stated firmly. "Do you know what it's about? Should I start looking for a replacement to take over your patients?"

"I have no idea," Joshua said. "Why don't you wait till I get back."

She shrugged and watched him get up from the table and walk stiffly across the hall to the elevator. Nurse Ramsey was a pretty good nurse, she acknowledged. And everyone knew he had served in Afghanistan. But sometimes his temper got the best of him. Maybe this was one of those times, she thought.

In the elevator, he whispered, "What did I do now?" He took advantage of the short ride between floors by taking several deep breaths: breathe in – one, two, three, and breathe out – one, two, three, four. He exited the elevator and went down the hall to the administrator's office. The door was open.

"Come in," Toby Abernathy commanded.

The Nursing Supervisor was already seated in a chair in front of Abernathy's desk. She looked at Joshua and motioned with her head for him to take the chair next to hers, facing Administrator Abernathy.

"Nurse Ramsey," he said. "Do you know why I summoned you to my office?"

"No, sir," Joshua replied.

"It has come to my attention that you spoke to Doctor Katrina Westerly and complained to her about three of our fledgling doctors abusing a patient," he recounted. "Is that true?"

"Well, yes," Joshua admitted warily. "Why? What did she say?"

"*She* didn't say anything," Abernathy replied. "That's an issue I will take up with her later. The three student doctors told the Nursing Supervisor here," he gestured to the woman sitting next to Joshua, "that you lied about them to Dr. Westerly and as a result, she threatened to revoke their positions in the psych rotations. Now, did you tell her they were abusing a patient? Before you answer, let me make myself clear that this is a very serious charge," he admonished.

Joshua took a deep breath before answering. He looked squarely at Administrator Abernathy. "Yes, it's true. Those three student doctors *were* verbally abusing my patient and I took appropriate steps to make sure it didn't happen again."

"Did anyone else witness this *alleged* abuse?" Abernathy asked. "Was Doctor Westerly there when it happened?"

"No, she wasn't," Joshua answered. "It was just me." He could see where this was going, and his gut began to boil.

He was just a nurse and those poor excuses for doctors

had it in for him now.

Abernathy continued. "They also said you were acting strangely. That you might be on drugs. You take Vicodin, right? Don't you know you have to be in a pain management program to get Vicodin? And I don't see anywhere here," he paused, flipping through some papers, "that you are in St. Luke's pain management program."

"Yes, I do take Vicodin," Joshua admitted. "I do my pain management at the VA and they prescribe the medication. I was perfectly fine that morning. Those three were out of line."

"I see," Abernathy said. "However, I want you to see our hospital's Pain Management doctors and take weekly drug tests as a condition of your continued employment here. Also, you do know that St. Luke's is having all of our nurses obtain degrees, right?"

"Yes, I know."

"Have you taken any steps to enroll in a Bachelor's program to get your degree?"

"No, I haven't," Joshua admitted. "I understood that was only for diploma RN's from nursing schools. I received my license from the United States Army. I've been here for five years and nobody said anything to me."

"Well, you understood wrong," the administrator said. "It applies to you, too. You have one year to obtain your degree if you want to continue working here."

"That's impossible!" Joshua burst out. "How can I possibly do that and work full-time too?"

"That's your problem, not mine. Other people seem to be able to accomplish this," he said, then turned to the nursing supervisor. "Take Nurse Ramsey down to the ER right away and give him a drug test."

"Yes, sir," she said to Abernathy, then turned to the nurse. "C'mon Josh, let's go."

Joshua glared at Toby Abernathy, not even bothering to hide his contempt, then followed the Nursing Supervisor out of the Administrator's office. He remained silent during the elevator ride to ER and also while his blood was being drawn for the drug test. *Those damn student doctors. It wasn't right!*

Toby stared at the space vacated by the two nurses. Ramsey was so arrogant, he thought. Well, he'd fix that! And it wouldn't be too hard, considering Nurse Ramsey had already been written up several times. They were minor infractions, to be sure, but he'd get him for using drugs on the job, he was sure of it.

"Nurse Ramsey," he muttered, "your days are numbered – I guarantee it!"

Chapter 12

F ollowing the drug test, Joshua returned to the floor, much to the relief of the Unit Supervisor who dreaded the thought of trying to replace a nurse on short notice. All he had to do was make it through the night, and then he had four days off. According to the Census sheet, his patient assignments were the same as yesterday: Derek Stanton, Trudy Freese, and David Feighan. The report said that David was the same. *Non-verbal and unable to follow commands, refusing group, reclusive in his room.*

The off-going nurse did report that Toby Abernathy repeated the orders specifying no visitors except for his wife and attorney, and no phone calls. "Like that space cadet could talk on the phone anyway," the reporting nurse said. "Whatever he took really fried his brain. All that money and he just sits in his room, drooling into his applesauce!"

They really are isolating him, Joshua thought. You gotta give it to the guy. He should earn an Oscar for the act he was pulling off. After all, who would ever fake being crazy to get *into* a psych ward?

Joshua went into the Day Area just in time to see Henry trying to quell an argument between Trudy and another patient about what they were going to watch on TV. The ward's one television was attached high on the wall and covered with a heavy layer of Plexiglas designed to keep unruly patients from smashing it with a chair.

"We're going to watch *Dancing with the Stars* you motherfucker, not a stupid baseball game!" Trudy yelled, balling up her fist and moving aggressively toward the young man.

Henry grabbed her arm and pulled her away from the other patient. He looked at Joshua with a silent request: "Get some meds into this patient quick before somebody gets hurt!" It was a look that transcended language in the world of psych nursing.

Joshua shot Henry a nod of understanding and headed to the Nurses Station. Trudy would be calm in no time, or at least that was the plan.

Every night, the same shit. Joshua drew the medication into a syringe. Returning to the Day Area he saw Security standing by as Henry tossed a coin into the air, the universal Heads or Tails method to settle disputes.   "Call it," he said to Trudy. "

"Never fucking mind, Henry," Trudy said as she saw Joshua approaching with the syringe in his blue surgical glove-clad hand.   "This is for me. C'mon Josh, hurry up." Trudy shook off Henry's grasp and skipped down the hall toward her room. Joshua motioned for Henry and the security guard to follow him into the room. Trudy was on her hands and knees on the bed, her hospital gown pulled up. "Stick it in my ass, Josh," she giggled, shaking her bottom at the trio.

"Oh my God," uttered the security guard. "I'll never get that picture out of my head!"

Joshua felt a burst of pain from his back and leg when he bent over to give the shot, reminding him that if not taken care of soon, the next twelve hours of his shift would be unbearable. After giving Trudy the shot, Joshua deposited the empty needle into the red sharps container then went into the uni-sex bathroom inside the Nurses Station and locked the door. He cringed as a spasm knifed through his back. Retrieving two pills from his pocket he popped the Vicodin into his mouth and cupped some water from the sink to chase them down his throat. After his encounter with Abernathy he could have used some Ativan but he knew that would be crossing the line; he couldn't risk impairing his judgment. He had to take care of his patients.

Joshua had been sent to the emergency room eight times in the five years he had been working at St. Luke's after being assaulted by out-of-control patients and every time he had to piss in a bottle before being treated. If anything improper was found in his urine, he would be fired and the hospital would not authorize any workers' comp to pay for his on-the-job injury. Compassion was reserved for patients with insurance, not for the nurses who took care of them.

Joshua knew it would take about twenty minutes for the Vicodin to grab the pain and temporally banish it from his body. Like a coyote stalking its prey, the pain never completely retreated but the meds kept it at bay. When he requested some additional pain meds from the Louis Stokes Veterans Hospital he was told no and the young female physician's assistant gave him a sermon on how addictive Vicodin was.

"Okay, then. I'll just drink a bottle of Jack Daniels to stop hurting if you won't help me! Being blown up fucking hurts and it doesn't go away," Joshua had told her.

"Maybe you need some group counseling for alcohol abuse," the clueless PA had told him and tried to set Joshua up for the twice-weekly group meeting at the VA.

"Fuck you!" Joshua had yelled angrily as he left the examining room.

"Way to go, dude!" a young wheelchair-bound veteran sitting in the overcrowded waiting room had shouted. "I hope I'm not her next victim!"

Another nurse approached Joshua in the Day Area and said, "Your young guy, Derek, went running into his room when Trudy went off out here. Maybe you better check on him, he seemed pretty disturbed."

"Thanks, Diane." She was one of the good ones. Joshua wheeled around and walked to the young patient's room.

Derek was jumping around like a Ninja, arms swinging and chopping unseen opponents into pieces. Joshua watched as Derek performed the macabre dance in a place where he was in total control. A place where he couldn't be hurt. At that moment, in the locked and secure ward, Joshua envied him his freedom.

Derek's face was happy and Joshua was reluctant to interrupt the young man's imaginary world. "Derek," he called out. "It's me, Josh. Can you stop for a minute to talk to me? Please?"

Derek froze in place and Joshua watched the self-confidence drain from the young man's face. "Hi Josh," he said quietly. His arms dropped to his sides and were still now, and his face had a look of resignation.

"I'm sorry to interrupt you, Derek. What were you doing just now?" Joshua asked.

"Killing the bad people," he said excitedly. With those

words, Derek's face became animated and flushed with the imagery of what he was doing, even though it was only in his mind. "I'm really good at it. I sneak up on them and then cut their throats before they even know I'm there. The bad people have been hurting me. I kill them before they can hurt me again. And no one ever catches me. Wanna watch?" he asked the nurse.

"I've been watching you, Derek," the nurse responded. "You're really good at killing bad people. But you know they can't get you in here, right?"

Derek squinted and he looked left and right, then straight into the nurse's eyes. When he spoke, it was a hoarse whisper. "Bad people are everywhere....even here."

Can't argue with that, Joshua thought, recalling his earlier encounter with the hospital's administrator. Just then, a tingling rocked through him and he could feel the hairs on his neck and arms stand up. It was the same feeling he experienced while on patrol in Afghanistan, and a usually reliable predictor of impending danger that, when heeded, was followed immediately by an uncanny inspiration on how to avoid said danger. But when he didn't pay attention to this feeling, well, let's just say he was reminded of the consequences every day.

He looked at Derek, then reached out and closed the door. Inspiration had struck.

"Derek, can you drive a car?"

"Sure," he replied. "I even got my driver's license. I used to deliver pizzas but I kept getting lost and people kept taking my money so they told me I had to stop. But, they let me stay in the place where they made the pizzas and they let me help them. I really liked that," Derek said.

Joshua chose his next words carefully. "Derek, what if I told you that you could play a game with me and get to drive a real car and kill bad people? Would you like to play that game with me?" Joshua asked.

"I'd like that a lot."

Joshua left Derek in his room to slay the imaginary bad people. From reading Derek's patient file, Joshua also knew there were vague references to Derek possibly being involved in the death of another resident at one of the group homes he had lived in. Could that resident have been one of the "bad guys" Derek referred to? While it was a suspicious death, the police couldn't positively link Derek to the incident. As the line between fantasy and reality was forever blurred in Derek's mind, convincing him to kill more "bad people" wouldn't be such a stretch, Joshua thought. Convincing himself was another matter. Proceeding down this road would violate every sworn oath he had taken as a soldier and as a nurse. But there was much at stake. I've got no choice, he rationalized, watching as Derek once again started chopping at the air. These people would ruin his life. He had to use any means possible to stop them.

He went into David's room without knocking and saw his patient staring at the iPad in his hands. Looking up, David said, "I can't believe the gall of those two. He's screwing *my* wife in *my* bed and getting paid to do it!"

"You're right," Joshua said. "We have to stop them." He carefully avoided using the words "kill" or "murder" as if it would absolve him of his decision. "I may have a plan." He went to the door and looked out; the Day Area was empty except for Henry and he appeared to be fighting a bad case of the nods. Joshua saw the other two nurses, Diane and Cassie, sitting at computers behind the glass windows at the nurses' station. No patients were visible. Joshua closed the door.

"You said it would be worth my while to help you. I wasn't going to go along with you - that is until your wife and lawyer brought me into it. After what you've shown me, I'm convinced we have to do something," he paused, "but, I need your assurance that I can trust you before---"

"Stop right there," David said. He got off the bed and stood looking out the window into the night. "What we do must be done together - without any doubts. I can and I will make it very profitable for you. I have the money. You have the ability. Together *our problems* can be solved, but it has to be done soon," he urged. "Michael has a judge lined up next week to sign the court order and have me ruled incompetent. We only have seven days left. That greedy prick can't wait to get rid of me and Johanna is worse than he is. That bitch was going to murder me, so you don't have any problems about trusting me, Josh," David said. "Now, let's hear your plan." He sat back down on the bed and assumed an expectant pose, his hands on his knees and his blue eyes clear and unwavering.

"I've got two hours before I go off shift and I won't be back for four days. I need a couple of days to put some things into place. You're sure we have seven days?" Joshua asked.

"Yeah, he's got some Judge named Connor on the hook. I heard him call the judge and set it up. He wanted it sooner but Judge Connor is on vacation somewhere and won't be back for seven days. Fucking lawyers!" he hissed.

"Okay, good," said Joshua. "Just keep playing your game like you have been. Keep that tablet and cell phone out of sight. Don't give anybody a reason to search your room, got it?"

"No problem," answered David. "So, tell me, what's the plan?"

"Not yet," Joshua stalled. "I don't have all the answers right now but hopefully soon. Very soon."

Chapter 13

After showering in the hospital locker room, Joshua pulled on a pair of faded Levis and a black sweatshirt with Southeast Harley in arcing white letters across the back.

Shielding his eyes from the bright morning sunlight, he found his bike in the employee parking lot. He straddled the black and silver Harley, placed his right thumb on the starter button and pushed it. The machine rumbled to life. He sat still for a moment, feeling the power waiting to be unleashed with the slightest turn of the throttle. He put on the black half-helmet and adjusted the leather chin strap. Next, he slipped on the black rider gloves and wrap-around reflective sunglasses to protect his eyes from the morning sun along with the bugs, dirt, and gravel kicked up by the cars and trucks maneuvering their way into downtown Cleveland during the morning rush hour.

But this morning he decided to not go home. He pointed his Harley north on West 25th Street until he reached Detroit Avenue. Turning right, he drove over the majestic Detroit Superior Bridge spanning the Cuyahoga River that divided Cleveland into the east and west sides. He continued through the downtown streets and pulled over at 1900 Hamilton Avenue. The one-story, red brick building, built a hundred years ago, used to house a machine shop. After being abandoned by the bankrupt owner, the city donated the building to a ministry that assisted homeless and transient men in need of food and shelter. This was Joshua's passion. His job at the hospital allowed him to satisfy some of his need to help a segment of the population ignored by most people, but the void left by greedy hospital administrators and a corrupt system made him angry. At the 1900 Hamilton Homeless Shelter he was able to give his time and money without interference from pious, greedy doctors and ruthless head nurses looking to improve their Press-Ganey scores. Truth be told, he probably needed these people more than they needed him. The feeling of accomplishment that filled him after helping to serve a meal or find clean clothing for someone took Joshua outside himself and satisfied a hunger in him as surely as the meals they served satisfied the homeless mens' hunger. Here, helping others, he could almost forget about his own physical and emotional pain. *Almost.*

Joshua carefully placed the kickstand onto the pavement and allowed the Harley to rest in place. After locking his gloves and glasses inside a saddlebag, he locked his helmet to the bike frame and pocketed the keys then headed to the front door. Passing by several familiar men sitting on the sidewalk waiting for their morning meal he acknowledged the ones he knew by name. Some were still wrapped in blankets passed out by volunteers the previous evening, which meant the shelter was full and unable to accommodate the number of homeless men with its limited number of available beds.

He entered the front door and was greeted warmly by the staff, a mix of paid workers and unpaid volunteers.

"You here to put some time in today?" The intake volunteer was busy checking off names on a clipboard adorned with an array of colorful butterfly stickers.

"Not today, Amanda, just going to check on something,"
Joshua said as he walked behind the wooden counter and
pulled out the large cardboard box marked Lost and
Found. "The cops brought in a homeless guy last night to
the Emergency Room, no identification. He told them that
he had been here so I thought I'd check to see if his ID was
in the box," he lied to the young girl.

"Good luck finding anything in that mess," Amanda
commented. "I wouldn't touch anything in there without
putting on gloves first though," she said as she walked
away without looking up from her clipboard.

Joshua dug through the assortment of keys, broken cell
phones, and empty pill bottles until he found a small
packet of papers bound together with a rubber band. He
removed the binder and found a Wisconsin driver's
license, miscellaneous papers, and a social security card.
Jackpot! Joshua rewrapped the packet with the rubber
band, casually glanced around, then satisfied no one was
paying any attention to him, slipped it into his pocket.
"Nope, not in there," he said loudly enough for Amanda to
hear as he walked by her and out the door onto Hamilton
Avenue. He headed toward his bike when he saw an
obviously intoxicated man trying to stagger away with his
Harley.

"Hey Dude!" Joshua yelled. "Get the hell off my bike!"

"Sorry man," slurred the would-be thief. He dropped
Joshua's Harley to the pavement and staggered away.

"Jesus!" Joshua exclaimed as he rushed to pick up his
motorcycle and examined it closely to see if there was any
damage. Just some road rash to the throttle handle, he

saw. After straightening the bike, he quickly started it to make sure the gas hadn't flooded the engine. It started right up. Joshua patted his pocket. The stolen identification was still there. He drove the short distance to his apartment at The Nine and parked in the underground garage.

After entering his apartment he put his backpack onto the kitchen counter, pulled the packet of papers out of his pocket, and laid them out on the counter. "Let's see what we have here."

A Wisconsin Driver's license with a picture of a white male in his late 20's looked back at him. It belonged to a Brian Dirks. He set it aside. Sorting through the pile, Joshua discarded several pieces of paper with phone numbers, old receipts, and a faded Greyhound Bus ticket stub. Then he came to the Social Security card. That went with the driver's license. The rest of the stash went into the sink. He turned on the water and allowed the papers to soak, then flipped the switch to the garbage disposal, effectively grinding away the remaining traces of Brian Dirks. He suddenly felt tired.

Was he actually going to do this? It was approaching 10 a.m. when the thoughts became words and the words came out of his mouth. *Yes. Yes I am.*

He left his apartment, went to the garage, and got on his motorcycle. Mid-day traffic was light as he turned onto the Lorain Carnegie Bridge. He drove west on Lorain Avenue to the intersection of West 65th Street. On the corner was a small used car lot. Approximately twenty older model cars faced the street, their prices marked on the windshields. A small trailer served as the office. A hand-painted sign said,

"Pete's Motors - Buy Here - Pay Here".

Joshua examined the trailer and surrounding area for mounted cameras covering the small, run-down lot. *Nothing.* Next he drove to a Chase Bank on West 25th Street. He'd never been to that particular branch before.

Standing in line behind a young mother with two kids in a double stroller, he was thinking about his next move when the cashier said loudly, "Next please."

"I need two thousand dollars – all in hundreds," Joshua told her. She barely glanced at him as he placed his driver's license and bank card on the counter and pushed them toward her.

After entering information on her computer, she pushed his license and card back to him. "Please sign on the line," she instructed, pointing to the electronic signature capture box. She counted out the bills until she reached nineteen hundred, and with a small flourish, she said, "two thousand."

"Thank you," Joshua said, and started walking to the door.

"Sir?" the teller called out.

He turned back to see her holding his receipt in her hand. "Oh, thanks," he said. He took the receipt, shoved it into his pocket and hurriedly left the bank.

Returning to The Nine, he went to his apartment and changed from his riding clothing into a pair of black Nike running pants and a gray hooded sweatshirt. He found a Cleveland Indians baseball cap and a pair of mirrored sunglasses then set out on foot to Public Square. Using his phone he touched the UberSELECT app and summoned a ride to take him from the Square to the used car lot on

West 65th. Touching the Apple-pay icon, he confirmed to Uber that his fare was already paid for and would be removed from his bank account using PayPal. Yellow Cab kept records on their fares. And Uber was cheaper.

The Uber driver arrived quickly in a red Jeep Cherokee. Joshua climbed into the back seat and snapped his seat belt into place.

"You wanna sit up front?" asked the driver, peering at Joshua from the rear view mirror.

"Naw, this is good," Joshua answered, never meeting the driver's eyes.

"Okay. My name is Don. You're going to 65th and Lorain, right?"

"Yes." Joshua confirmed his destination then leaned back into the seat. The radio was set to 106.5 - The Lake FM radio station. The classic Pink Floyd recording of *The Wall* was playing. Well, that fits, Joshua thought. I just keep adding bricks to my wall. Wonder if they'll hold? The driver made an attempt at conversation but quickly gave up after receiving only a couple of grunts in response.

The ride went quickly even though the beginning rush hour traffic was starting. Downtown Cleveland workers were dumping out of the city and spreading out to the surrounding suburbs. The driver pulled to the curb. "Okay mister, we're here."

Joshua exited the vehicle and stood on the corner. After the Uber cab pulled away into traffic, he crossed Lorain Avenue at the light and walked the short distance to the used car lot where he loitered among the cars, peering into several windshields. After a few minutes the trailer door opened and a Hispanic male headed over to Joshua, adjusting his tie as he approached.

"I was just getting ready to lock up for the day. Are you looking to buy a car?" He spread his arms out, pointing to the array of tired looking cars.

"Yes," Joshua replied. "I'm looking for a cheap ride. I've got cash. You take cash, don't you?" he asked.

"We sure do," the salesman grinned. "How much are you looking to spend?"

"Well, I have two grand in cash – that's all I can afford. But I need to drive it off today," Joshua explained.

"No problem, we can do that, sir. My name is Pete. What's yours?" Pete held out his hand to shake with his customer.

Joshua froze. *What was the name on that license?* Buying some time, he walked away from Pete and over to a dark blue Chevy cobalt with a price of $2199 written on the windshield in bold yellow letters.

Pete pulled back his hand and spoke loudly. "That's a beauty, just took it in on a trade today," he lied. In reality, he had removed the car from a flatbed tow truck two days ago when it arrived from the car auction at the Berea Fairgrounds. He'd only started it once - to put it on the line with his other vehicles. He had eight hundred into the car and hoped he could take the two thousand off this customer.

"Will you take two - cash for everything?" Joshua asked. "That's for everything. Tax, title, and plates. And I get it now."

"I can do that, partner," Pete answered quickly before his customer had second thoughts. "Don't you want to test drive it first?"

"No," replied Joshua. "I'm sure it's okay."

"Okay, then. Let's go to the office and do the paperwork," Pete said, leading the way. This was the easiest sale he'd made in a long time.

Joshua followed Pete into the trailer, taking care to avoid a broken bottom step. Taking a seat in an old kitchen chair across from the salesman, Joshua maintained a bored countenance as if he always bought used cars without taking them for a test drive. He didn't want to do or say anything that would stand out if the salesman was later asked about the guy who bought the car.

Pete filled out the paperwork. Joshua reached into his pocket and pulled out the wad of cash secured only by a rubber band. He retrieved the stolen identity from his other pocket and, after looking at it, thought, *Brian Dirks, that's my name.* He was betting Pete wouldn't pay too close attention to the photo to notice any differences between him and the real Brian Dirks.

When Pete picked up the driver's license and Social Security card, Joshua lowered his head and began counting out hundred dollar bills on the desk. The salesman's eyes were drawn to the money and he set the identification cards aside and started filling out the paperwork.

"I'm sure you've got insurance so we can skip that part," Pete said, unwilling to slow down the process and perhaps lose the sale. "I can give you a thirty day tag today. Do you want me to use this Wisconsin address to mail out the title and plates when they come in or do you want to stop back and pick them up?"

"I'll come back," Joshua said.

"Phone number?" Pete asked.

Joshua provided the dealer a fictitious phone number. Pete completed the paperwork, took Joshua's money, and counted out the cash. Satisfied it was all there, he folded the bills over and placed them into his pocket.

"Just let me wash the price off the windshield before you go. Be pretty hard to see the road through all the writing and we don't want you to smash up that pretty little ride before you get to enjoy it," he chuckled as he grabbed a dirty rag and spray bottle of cleaner from the floor beside his desk. He hurried out the door, stumbled and tripped over the broken stair. "Gotta fix that some day before I kill myself," he muttered.

Joshua stood by and watched the salesman scrub the windshield. Then Pete placed the cardboard thirty-day temporary tag to the rear bumper of the Cobalt.

"There you go, Brian," Pete said, handing him the key. "Sorry, we only have one set but as it was a fresh trade-in, I didn't have time to get another made."

"That's okay," Joshua answered, getting in the car and turning the key. The car started up right away. Pete unlocked the padlock holding the end of the steel cable used to prevent a potential thief from stealing cars when the lot was closed. Then he pulled the cable through the eyehook of the steel post embedded into the asphalt. With the cable end in one hand he motioned with the other for Joshua to pull off the lot.

"Thanks for the business. I'll call you when the plates and title comes in," Pete called out as Joshua stopped to wait for a Number 22 RTA bus to clear his path in front of him. He gave a little wave of acknowledgement out the window and then turned left onto Lorain Avenue.

"You'll never see me again, you fucking thief," Joshua said as he checked the gas gauge and saw it was half full. He drove east on Lorain and turned right onto West 25th Street until he reached St. Luke's hospital. He pulled into the Visitor Only lot and parked far away from the main entrance but still within eyesight of the windows of the Center One floor. He wished it was darker. Maybe he should come back later.

No, he told himself. *You're just being paranoid.* Using his phone, he placed another request for an Uber ride, giving his pickup location as the front entrance to the hospital. It was only a five minute wait. He pulled the hood of his sweatshirt over the baseball cap he was wearing then got out of the car. Leaving it unlocked, he walked quickly to the hospital entrance where a silver GMC had just pulled in and parked curbside. He kept his head down to avoid the hospital lot's security cameras and approached the driver.

A young, black male rolled down the window. "Brian?" he asked.

"Yeah, that's me," Joshua replied as he climbed into the back seat. "Take me to downtown Public Square."

After being dropped off, Joshua started walking back to his apartment, feeling surprisingly calm for having stolen identification and purchased a car under a false name. He thought he'd feel different. After all, he had agreed to kill two people. That decision made, the act itself became a mission to accomplish. In his mind, the conniving lawyer and unfaithful wife weren't only a threat to the millionaire taking refuge in St. Luke's Hospital; they were a threat to his livelihood. He was tired of people screwing with him.

Even though Joshua had come to terms with his part in Feighan's plot, he waivered over taking advantage of his young patient's illness to further their goals. What he was planning went against everything he believed in as a nurse, as a soldier, and as a member of the human race.

There was so much that could go wrong. "I just hope Derek can drive a car and follow my instructions. He trusts me enough, I think," Joshua expressed his thoughts out loud while inserting the key into his door. "Right now, he's our best option." This was war. All assets needed to be employed. And Derek was now an asset.

Joshua entered his apartment and fell onto the bed without bothering to undress. After two Vicodin and three Ativan, the dreamlike state before sleep came quickly. Far off flashes of light followed by the screams of his fellow soldiers rang in his head. "Please God, no! No more....no more!" he begged.

Chapter 14

When Nick woke up, the pelting rain against the penthouse apartment windows sounded like crinkling aluminum foil. He glanced at the red numbers on the bedside alarm clock; 4:44 a.m.

"Crap," he muttered. Too early to report for his 0700 hour shift in Homicide and too late to go back to sleep, even if he could. Yesterday's murders of the baby boy and his mother lingered in his brain. He knew it would take some time for those visions to fade.

Nick padded barefoot to the kitchen. He pushed the flashing blue button of the Keurig coffee maker and watched as the machine dispensed dark roast coffee into his white Cleveland Police coffee cup, then added a generous shot of Baily's Irish Cream to the brew. His thoughts wandered. When he was a rookie cop in Cleveland's First District his training officer had given him some advice.

"Look kid, you're going to see shit on the job that will scar you forever. For me," the veteran continued, "I was working Car 121 in the First District and we got a radio run to look for two missing little brothers. One was four and the other one was seven. The older one was nicknamed Tuba. Funny how I remember that name. We were working the day shift and the kids' mom said they were playing out back of the house but now they were gone and she couldn't find them. We looked all over the neighborhood for those kids with no results. We went back to the mom's house and called a boss. The other cars heard us and came to help. We finally found them - locked inside an old refrigerator in the neighbor's garage - dead. I still can see the steam coming off their little bodies. They were holding each other when they died. You will never get used to this stuff, Nick," his mentor stressed. "A cop's career is filled with sadness and dark days but it goes with the job."

Yesterday was one of those days, Nick thought. Cup in hand, he went to the balcony windows overlooking Lake Erie. The shallowest of the Great Lakes was pissed. Six-foot waves pounded the shoreline of the Lakewood Condo and whitecaps were visible as far as he could see. Nobody was going to fish on that angry lady today.

Looking through the rain-soaked windows toward downtown Cleveland, he saw the low dark clouds obscuring the tops of the Terminal Tower and the Key Bank buildings. Downing the last of the warm liquid, he rinsed his cup, placed it into the chrome sink, then quietly walked into the bedroom and grabbed a pair of swimming trunks, taking care to not wake Kat. He thought he'd catch an early swim then go check on his boat before heading to work.

Nick rode the elevator down to the indoor swimming pool. After his swim, he returned to the apartment, showered and dressed, strapped on his shoulder holster, retrieved his gun from the nightstand, and slipped it into the holster.

"Wake up, baby," he whispered into Kat's ear. She stirred and sat up in the bed.

"You up already?" she yawned.

"Yep, I gotta go check on the boat before work. Pretty

bad storm last night. Don't forget that Jimmy is going to call you today. Try and see if you can help him get the demons out of his head. Too many good cops have quit the job after seeing stuff like we saw yesterday. The department can't afford to lose him."

"I'll do what I can for him. What about you? Any bad dreams or lingering thoughts?" Kat asked.

"Naw," Nick lied. "Just gotta tune it out and keep on going," he said, leaning down to give her a kiss goodbye. He grabbed his phone from the charging cradle on the night stand then left the apartment.

Nick drove the Civic six miles, taking the Shoreway route over the Main Avenue Bridge through downtown Cleveland past the football stadium and exited at the East 55th Street ramp. He swiped a card through the gate and the eight-foot tall cyclone fence rolled open. The parking lot was full of standing water from the previous evening's violent summer storm. He could see other boat owners checking their boats on the five floating docks that comprised the Cleveland Metro Parks marina property.

"Hey, Eddie," Nick greeted his dock mate who was sitting on a wooden picnic table in front of the aluminum ramp leading to "D" dock, smoking a cigarette. "Your boat survived the storm?" Nick asked.

"Yeah, Nicky. I came down last night and spent the night on my boat. It was pretty bumpy with all the wind and lightening. You should have called me to check on yours. Now, I'm just waiting for the Captain's Quarters Bar to open up and get a drink. Want one? I'm buying," Eddie said.

"Maybe next time. I gotta work today," Nick answered

as he walked down the dock toward D-57. The Rinker was still secure and bobbed slightly with the always moving water. The red and white vessel was twenty years old but it still looked new thanks to Nick's obsessive care. He unsnapped the stainless steel buttons holding the red mooring cover to the boat, pulled part of the canvas aside and climbed underneath to check the bilge for water. No sense taking the cover all the way off, Nick thought as he pulled open the hatch cover to reveal the engine compartment. His weight caused the bilge pump to sputter out a small stream of water from the opening on the outside of the hull before it stopped automatically. Other than that, everything was okay.

He crawled off the boat and reattached the mooring cover. Since moving in with Kat last winter, he'd been spending a lot less time on the boat. He missed the lake in the morning and the seagulls squawking and fighting over scraps of food and territory. But, she sure was worth it! He smiled to himself as he walked down the bouncing dock back to the parking lot.

At the Justice Center, Nick found a parking spot just large enough to accommodate the Honda, right between a sparkling white Ohio State Trooper sedan and a beat up burgundy Cleveland Police detective car.

"State troopers come into our sandbox and write shitloads of tickets on our streets taking money out of our pockets and then take our parking spots," he thought, then grinned as he remembered when the Cleveland Police Patrolmen's Association and the Fraternal Order of Police Union bosses got together and had the traffic unit cops ticket and tow all the trooper cars parked in the Police

Only marked spaces. That started a shit storm that was still going on today.

He placed his CPPA ID onto the dash so the meter maids could clearly see the Honda belonged to a cop and maybe he could avoid another parking ticket. His glove box was already full. He went through the large glass doors to the Justice Center and flashed his Detective badge at the uniformed officer guarding the entrance by the metal detector and punched the button on the crowded elevator to take him to the sixth floor that housed the Homicide Unit. His partner, Jimmy Herron, was already sitting at his desk, phone pressed to his ear.

"What are you doing here?" Nick asked.

"Trying to get your doctor girlfriend on the phone," he replied. "She's not answering."

"Kat doesn't get into her office until after seeing patients in the hospital and then she has to teach a new bunch of doctors. Besides, aren't you supposed to be off duty until you get a back-to-work slip?" Nick asked.

Jimmy started to answer but was interrupted by the Homicide's Unit Commander, Lieutenant Jon Fratello, dropping an armload of brown Cold Case file folders onto Jimmy's desk.

"I told him he could come in for office duty. I want you two to try to catch up on some of these cold cases that are piling up," Fratello addressed the detectives. "I put another team on your child murder case. I don't think it would hurt either of you to do something else right now. Jimmy, I know what happened at the hospital yesterday and until you see the shrink, you are office bound. Deputy Chief Gary Payne has been on my ass to catch up on these," he pointed to the pile of folders, "and now is as good a time as any. We need to update the oldest ones first so Payne can report the results to Chief Toothman and he can pass it onto the Mayor. Besides, this job is for the low guys on the seniority totem pole and that is you two!"

"For Christ's sake's, Jon," Nick said to his boss and longtime friend. "We got pending murder cases piling up and I still got Narcotics cases I made before coming here that are going to court."

"Nick," said the Lieutenant firmly. "Your murder cases aren't going anywhere and your drug cases can be handled by your ex-narcotics partners, Frank Ambrose and Danny Higgins. Just get it done, okay?"

"Sure thing, boss," answered Detective Silvano in an emotionless voice. Nick had second thoughts about transferring from Narcotics to Homicide. At least the druggies made you laugh sometimes, he thought. Murders were never funny.

Chapter 15

The noise was unrelenting. *Ouga! Ouga!* The obnoxious ringtone was assigned to St. Luke's. Joshua stared at the phone, letting it go to voicemail.

He looked at the time. Almost noon. "Shit, I've only been off for one shift and they're calling me already. I wanted to sleep in today," he moaned.

The abrupt ouga-ouga noise began again. Joshua grabbed the phone.

"Hello," he said flatly.

"Hey, Josh. This is Bill, from work."

Bill was the Medical Secretary on Behavioral Health and Joshua considered him to be a good guy. Bill used to be an aide but that was before he was assaulted by a violent patient. The resulting shoulder injury effectively left him unable to do any of the heavy lifting. The hospital told him he'd have to quit his job but Heather, the Unit Supervisor, stepped in and had him retrained to do the complicated paperwork. She had helped Bill, and Joshua respected her for that.

"I know you've been off only one day and I'm sorry to call you but the boss told me to see if you could come in tonight at seven. We're short on staff. The new RN out of orientation was supposed to start working on her own but she got punched in the face last night by a new admission high on Flakka. After she got treated in the ER she told the supervisor 'I'm supposed to be a nurse working in a hospital, not a punching bag for these fucking crazies,' and she quit! I know Center Two isn't your regular floor but they could use you if you can make it for all or any part of the shift," Bill pleaded.

"Naw," Joshua started negotiating. "I don't like working up on Center Two."

He waited for Bill to answer and he could hear him talking to Heather. "Okay," he said. "Heather says you can work your regular floor with the same patients. Will that work for you?"

"I can do that but she's got to promise to notify the staffing office that I won't be floated off the floor to another unit," Joshua replied.

Joshua could hear Bill relaying his response to and heard Heather tell Bill, "I can do that. Tell him thanks."

Bill came back on the phone and before he could speak Joshua interrupted him and said, "I heard her, Bill, I'll be there at seven."

"Thanks, Josh," Bill said. "The inmates will be waiting for you. It's not going to be bad. We had six discharges this morning and the Census is down to six. There's nothing pending right now from the admissions office."

"Let's hope it stays that way," Joshua said. "Who is the other nurse working with me tonight?"

"Hold on, I'll go find the schedule book."

Joshua waited for Bill to come back on the phone and he could hear Trudy wailing in the background. "Somebody better get me some damn medication before I have a seizure!"

"Shut up, Trudy," Joshua heard Bill tell the intrusive patient. "Geez, give it a break will you!"

"Sorry about that, Josh," Bill said. "Freaking Trudy is doing its thing. We all wanted her to be discharged this morning but no such luck. Looks like Big John will be your other nurse tonight. They're floating Henry to the sixth floor and Diane wanted to call off so it'll be just you and John and six patients."

"Derek and David Feighan still there?" Joshua asked.

"Yep, Kung Foo Fighter and the quiet rich guy are still here," Bill confirmed. "We got three new females. Two are junkies having withdrawals and the other has post-partum depression; they are no problem. Trudy is going to be the problem but I know you can handle her."

"Okay, thanks Bill." Joshua hung up.

Chapter 16

J oshua navigated his motorcycle through the light evening traffic to St. Luke's Hospital. An internal dialogue looped through his mind as he robotically slowed and accelerated according to the flow of traffic around him. He rolled into the hospital parking lot and spied the blue Chevy Cobalt still sitting where he had parked it.

Good. Still there. He circled the building then parked his Harley in the employee parking lot. He was headed toward the building when a voice called out.

"Wait up, Josh." Big John was just getting out of his Dodge Ram 3500 silver pickup truck. John was a nurse who was well suited for work in psych. At six-foot-five inches tall and three hundred fifty pounds, he was a valuable co-worker at Center One when a violent patient needed to be brought under control.

"What are you doing here?" John asked. "Aren't you off today?"

"They called me in," Joshua answered. "It's going to be just you and me. We only have six patients so it should be a good night."

"Great. Maybe I can get some studying done," John said. "Toby only gave us another couple of months to get our bachelor's degrees and I'm real close. Got a big test coming up for my clinical and I need some quiet time to cram."

"I hear ya," Joshua said. "I was put on notice the other day that I had a year to get mine. I mean, come on! You'd think that good old Army training would be enough, but no. Not for the king of St. Lukes! Anyway, don't worry, John," Joshua told his co-worker. "Tonight will be nothing but a study hall for you. I can handle the floor."

"Bless you, my son," John said, placing his heavy hand around Joshua's shoulder as they walked from the parking lot into Building A. After swiping his ID through the time clock, Joshua held the door open for Big John. They entered the floor together just as Trudy made a mad dash for the open door.

"Not today, Trudy," John said in a bored tone as he stuck his arm out, effectively stopping Trudy in her tracks.

"What the hell, Big John!" Trudy screamed, struggling to wriggle free of the nurse's grip on her wrist. "Let go of me you big motherfucker!" Other staff members came running out of the Nurses Station to see what the commotion was all about.

"It's been disruptive all day long," Bill said, refusing to acknowledge Trudy as a female. "The nurse floated over from the fifth floor medical unit assigned to It is deathly afraid and has been avoiding It all day so It hasn't had any meds."

"Well, that's going to change right now," Big John said. "Can you draw up some meds for me, Josh? I'll take her into the back and keep her there so she doesn't do anything else stupid."

"No problem," Joshua said.

"How about taking Report first?" asked one of the day shift nurses waiting to go off duty.

"Not a chance, my dear," Big John answered over his shoulder as he placed Trudy in a wrist lock to avoid her punches. "I ain't letting go of her until she gets her meds, something you guys should have done before we got here," he admonished as he steered the flailing Trudy into the back seclusion room.

"Make sure it's a good one, Joshua," Big John instructed. In the psychiatric nursing world, a "good one" meant drawing up the maximum amount of medication needed to quell the violence of unruly patients.

"Got it," Joshua replied. He entered the Nursing Station to remove the medicine from the Pyxis machine. The meds were administered to Trudy by injection and she promised to stay in the room after John told her that he would call the kitchen and get her two cheeseburgers for the evening snack if she wasn't disruptive.

The float nurse who had been avoiding Trudy all day must have decided it was safe to reappear. "Aren't you going to lock the door?" she asked apprehensively. "What if she gets out and hurts somebody?"

John looked at Trudy. "You going to behave? No burgers tonight if you don't keep your promise."

"Sure, Big John," Trudy answered giving him a sly glance. "Just one more thing..." She stood up from the bed and turned to face the float nurse. "BOO!" she screamed, and then jumped behind Big John, effectively using him as a tree to hide behind.

"That's it!" the nurse screamed. "I'm never coming back to this floor! I don't care if I get fired. You people are ALL crazy over here!" She turned and ran out of the room.

"Sorry, Big John," Trudy said, not sounding sorry at all. "I've been waiting all day to do that. You mad at me? Am I still getting my cheeseburgers?"

"Yes, Trudy," Big John said. "Might as well get you some chips and Twinkies too. That was a good one!"

Nursing Report went quietly after that and Bill reported there were no pending admissions or doctors calling to see if there was "any room at the Inn".

Joshua signed on as the shift Charge Nurse. "I'll take Derek, David, and Trudy," he told Big John. I know them and Trudy will be going to sleep after the meds and she eats your food bribe. After everybody is in their rooms, why don't you go into the Social Worker's office, shut the door and study. I'll be fine out here. I'll call you if I need anything."

"Man, that would be great," Big John said. "Much appreciated."

Joshua worked on his charting. An hour later, he checked on Trudy. She was sound asleep. The medication would keep her quiet until morning. He next checked on Derek who was sitting on his bed, his arms waving in controlled movements in the air around him, battling an enemy only he could see.

"Derek, you okay?" Joshua asked his young patient.

"Oh, hi Josh," Derek answered, his arms slicing through the air. "Are you going to make me stop?"

"No, Derek, I'm not going to make you stop." Joshua left the room, closing the door behind him. The three female patients were all asleep. He moved on to the next patient. David Feighan was sitting on the bed, his iPad in his lap.

"Wait! What are you doing here, Josh?" David asked. "Aren't you supposed to be off tonight?"

"I got called in," Joshua replied. "Where are your wife and lawyer tonight? Are they at your place?"

"Yep, the bitch and the bastard are getting drunk on my twenty-year-old scotch. Seems they are celebrating. Michael got Judge Connor to return early from his vacation. The commitment papers will be signed tomorrow!" his expression was resigned. "Looks like it's all over for us, my friend. Look at this." David turned the iPad toward the nurse, allowing him to see the images of his wife and attorney sitting in the bedroom, each with a drink in their hands, oblivious to the fact their every move and word were being transmitted by the hidden cameras David had installed throughout the house.

"Won't be long now," Michael was saying. "Judge Connor will sign the papers tomorrow as soon as he sees the donation deposited into his political action fund. Thank God for corruptible judges! Want another drink, dear?" he asked Johanna.

"I can't watch any more, David," Joshua said. "I have to get back to the Nurses Station." He left his patient staring morosely at the screen and wondered what would happen to David now. He returned to the Nurses Station and sat down. His gaze was focused on a faraway point beyond the glass windows.

Looks like he'd have to scrap his plan. Now he was out two thousand dollars and had an illegal car on his hands. David couldn't help him if he was committed. *Looks like he lost again.* Joshua sat at the Nurses' Station for quite a while, then felt a familiar tingle run through his body. *Maybe it wasn't too late.* The patients were all quiet, Big John would be studying all night, the Chevy was in the lot, and David's wife and lawyer were at home, apparently getting drunk. They wouldn't be going anywhere tonight.

He walked back to Derek's room. "Hey Derek," Joshua called. Derek twirled around, hands still chopping. "Want to play that game I was telling you about?"

"Yeah! What game, Josh?"

"A very special game. One that only you and I can play. We'll kill the bad people, together. Would you like that?"

"Yeah, yeah Josh! I like to kill the bad people," Derek responded, excited at the prospect of playing a game with the nurse. Nobody else played games with him.

"Okay. I'll be right back. Then we'll play the game."

Joshua moved from room to room, checking on his patients. They were asleep. He returned to David's room where David was still watching the live video feed from his house.

"I used to think Johanna was a classy lady," he remarked. "I'm such a dumb shit for marrying that slut. Michael kept telling me not to do it. Now she's got her hooks into him and I'm in here," he said ruefully. "Too late now, I guess."

"Maybe not," Joshua countered. "Do you think they will stay at your house tonight?"

"She's too drunk to go anywhere and Michael will most certainly stay with her. He knows she can't handle her liquor and he's not going to let her out of his sight. Why?"

"I have a plan," Joshua said. "But before I do *anything*, you have to make sure that this is what you really want. No changing your mind now."

"Yes! I want them both gone," David growled.

"Alright, then," Joshua said, knowing he had just crossed a line from which there was no return. "Give me your phone."

David reached under the mattress and handed it to Joshua.

"Do you have Skype on your phone and iPad?" Joshua asked.

"Yes," David answered. "Lots of my business is conducted that way. I can talk to anybody in the world without leaving my house."

"Okay. Make sure it's ready to go. And did Johanna bring in that bottle of water for you today?" Joshua asked, pointing to the FIJI Water bottle on the window sill.

"Yes, she was in much earlier than normal," David said. "I pretended to be asleep and she left right away. Probably anxious to meet up with Michael and start celebrating. That's why she's all screwed up already. She's been drinking for hours," he snorted.

Joshua picked up the Ketamine-laced bottle of water and put it into the side pocket of his scrub top. It was now approaching midnight. He returned to Derek's room. Derek was still playing his imaginary game.

"Here, Derek," Joshua said, handing him the bottle of drug-laced designer water. "Drink this."

Ketamine had properties that made the human mind more malleable and subject to following commands, Joshua knew from his experience on the Behavioral Unit. It would be just the thing he needed for the events he was about to put in motion.

Derek drank half the bottle before Joshua reached out and took it from his hand. He felt slightly sordid and recognized the pang of guilt, but ignored it. He had to keep going. Joshua left Derek and went into the shower room. He took a set of blue hospital scrubs, two sets of gray nonskid socks and returned to Derek's room. "Change into these and stay in your room until I come back to get you," Joshua instructed.

"Sure, Josh," Derek replied.

Joshua then went to the Social Worker's office and knocked on the closed door. Big John opened it and asked, "What is it, everything okay?"

"All is fine, John," Joshua told him. "Just letting you know everybody is asleep and we are good until morning, so stay with the studying."

Big John checked his watch and said, "Thanks, Josh. Come get me if you need me."

Joshua pulled the door closed and went back into David's room. "Is the Skype working?" he asked.

"Yes. What are you doing? What's going on?" David asked.

Joshua then told David how he had stolen identity papers and stashed a car for Derek to use to drive to David's house and kill Johanna and Michael. "You said you can control the alarm systems and the lights in your home from your iPad, right?" Joshua asked.

"Yes. No problems with that. I must say, I'm impressed, Josh," David said, admiringly. "When are we going to do this?"

"We have to move now - while we have the chance." Joshua looked at his patient, now partner in an undertaking that violated the very "Do no harm" oath he had sworn to uphold as a nurse caring for society's most vulnerable.

"Okay," he said quietly. "Let's do this."

Chapter 17

Joshua unlocked the door to the patient interview room, ushering David in before him. "Sit there," Joshua instructed, pointing to the desk. David took a seat and positioned his iPad so the screen wasn't visible through the glass windows. "Make the Skype connection between your phone and the iPad." The connection made, Joshua took the phone and walked out of the interview room into the Day Area. Looking at the phone's screen, he could see David's face in front of the laptop. "Can you see and hear me, David?" Joshua asked.

"Loud and clear, Josh," David answered.

After Joshua turned the lights off in the three hallways and the Day Area, he went to Derek's room. Derek was now wearing the hospital scrubs and non-slip socks as instructed.

"Put these on," Joshua said, handing him a pair of blue surgical gloves. "You have to keep these gloves on for the game to work and for you to get to the next level. Do you understand? If you don't follow the game's instructions you will fail and the bad people will kill all of us," Joshua issued the grave instructions.

Derek nodded his head. Joshua studied his face to confirm his level of comprehension. Did he ingest too much of the Ketamine-laced water? Years of hallucinogenic drug use had slowed Derek's brain functions and his ability to properly utilize social skills. Joshua couldn't tell if Derek could remain focused long enough to complete his "game".

He thought of all the things that could go wrong. Derek interrupted his misgivings. "I want to play the game, Josh. Don't worry, I won't let you down, I promise," he said, sounding like a child promising to do his homework if he could stay up past his bedtime.

Joshua put his immediate worries aside and handed the phone to Derek. "Here, Derek, put the ear buds in your ears and tell me if you can see and hear the Game Master."

Derek held the phone up and nodded. "Yes, I can see him but I don't hear anything," he replied excitedly.

"Say something, Game Master," Joshua spoke into the phone.

"Welcome to the game," David said in a deep, somber tone.

Derek's face lit up as he heard the Game Master's voice.

"Alright, now be quiet and follow me," Joshua instructed. "We're going outside and find a car for you to drive to the game," Joshua said. "We have to be very quiet. Bad people are all around us. We have to do exactly what the Game Master tells us so we can win the game."

"Okay, Josh," answered Derrick. He couldn't believe that Josh had asked him to play a game with him. And a game where he could kill bad people! Something he was really good at.

Joshua led Derek out of his room and down the hallway to the locked emergency exit door leading out into the hospital's parking lot. He unlocked the door using one of the keys on the nursing supervisor's key ring and opened it slowly, surveilling the visitor's parking lot. Seeing the lot was empty of people, Joshua exhaled and motioned for Derek to follow him outside the confines of the hospital and out into the humid summer night.

Swarms of bugs danced wildly around the widely spaced parking lot lights. Joshua had chosen this area of the Visitor's Lot as it was dimly lit and not covered by security cameras. He took Derek's elbow and guided him to the parked Chevy Cobalt.

"Here is your car, Derek," he said quietly and handed him the key. He instructed the young man to use the phone and test his communications to the Game Master.

"Josh, I know how to use a phone," Derek admonished and demonstrated his knowledge. "Game Master, this is Derek. Are you there?"

"Yes, Derek. I am here," David responded. "Do what Josh tells you. The game will start when you begin to drive."

"Where do you want me to go, Josh?" Derek asked. "What am I supposed to do to win the game?"

"Wait in the car and the Game Master will instruct you," Joshua said. "I am going back inside. From now on, it's up to you. And remember - after you kill the bad people, drive right back here and park in the same place."

"Okay, Josh," Derek said confidently. "I'll win the game."

Joshua fervently hoped that Derek would never understand what was happening here tonight. He went back into the hospital, praying that he had not been missed or Security had made any rounds and found the floor unmanned. He made it back to the interview room.

"You son-of-a-bitch! This is going perfectly." David beamed at Josh in admiration.

Joshua held his finger to his lips and mouthed to David. "He can hear us!" reminding David that Derek was to only hear instructions on playing the game, nothing else.

"Derek, can you hear me?" asked Joshua.

"Yes, I can," he answered. "But, where is the Game Master? You told me to only listen to him."

Joshua then realized he had to stick to the script. Derek's mind was fragile and he could only follow simple instructions.

David held up his hand to Joshua and pointed to himself. "Derek, this is the Game Master. Put the phone onto the seat and keep the ear buds in your ears. Now, start the car. Go toward the exit. Now turn right onto West 25th Street. Do you see where I want you to go?"

"Yes, Game Master, I see it," Derek replied.

"Turn right and keep driving until you get to Detroit Avenue," commanded David.

Joshua sat quietly and listened to David as he provided the turn-by-turn directions to Derek. He could hear the car's engine and the clicking of the turn signals. David's voice was calm and with each command he gave, Derek responded, "Yes, Game Master."

Twenty minutes passed. Joshua's heart raced and his thoughts tumbled over each other. What if Derek was stopped by the police for a traffic violation? What if he got into an accident or got lost? What if he just drove off in another direction? *What if! What if!*

After what seemed like an eternity, they heard Derek's voice. "I'm in the driveway, but there is a gate. What do I do now?"

"Good job, Derek," the Game Master said. "You have passed the first level. Can you see the keypad on the post next to the gate?"

"Yes."

"I want you to enter these numbers on the keypad and the gate will open. The numbers are seven-two-three-four. Got that? If I have to repeat it you will lose points."

"Seven two three four. Seven two three four," they heard him repeat out loud. Then, "It worked!" Derek exclaimed. "The gate opened! How many points for opening the gate, Game Master?"

"Uh, 500 points," David said. "You are now at level two in the game. Drive to the back of the house, stop the car and turn off the lights."

While Derek did as instructed, something occurred to Joshua. "Do you have security cameras on your property and in your home?" he whispered to David. "And, I don't mean your secret cameras. Are there real ones connected to a security company?"

"Yes," David whispered. "But I disabled them remotely from my iPad before Derek drove into the driveway. Don't worry. The only people watching are you and me." Reassuming his Game Master persona, he asked, "Are you at the back of the house? Can you see the back door?"

"Yes, Game Master."

David minimized the Skype connection and typed a code into the iPad.

"What are you doing?" Joshua asked.

"I'm remotely unlocking the rear door and turning on the kitchen lights so the kid can get in and see where he is going," David explained in hushed tones. "Now, let's make sure our intended victims are where they should be." David checked the live video feed from the bedroom he had shared with Johanna. She and Michael were both on the bed, passed out. Johanna was naked and Michael had managed to undress down to his underwear. His suit was draped over the back of a chair next to the bed.

"Showtime," David whispered to Joshua, and then in a deep voice said, "This is the Game Master. Are you ready to play the next level of the game?"

"Yes, Master, I am," Derek replied.

"Put the phone in the pocket of your scrub top and keep the ear buds in your ears so you can hear me."

They heard a rustling noise as Derek followed the Game Master's instructions.

"Now, get out of the car. You'll see a door. Open it. Go inside and you will be in the kitchen. Good," David said as he picked Derek up on one of the home's many hidden cameras. "Now, turn to your left. Take the largest knife from the knife holder on the kitchen counter and go through the door into the living room." He paced his instructions to match Derek's on-camera progress. "See the stairs in front of you?" They both watched as Derek nodded his head.

"This is a good game, Game Master," said Derek. "You can see me but I can't see you." He stood at the bottom of a long spiral staircase, the knife visible in his right hand.

"Do not speak!" the Game Master admonished. "I can see you and will tell you what to do." Joshua reluctantly pulled his eyes away from the scene playing out in front of him on the iPad and glanced out of the interview room's windows to make sure they were still alone.

"Now, go up the stairs." They watched Derek climb the stairs. When he was at the top of the landing, David continued. "When you get to the top, turn to the left. Go into the room. There will be two people on the bed. A man and a woman - they are the bad people. Your mission is to kill them both. In order to get the maximum points, you must first kill the man, and then kill the woman. *In that order.* You must be very quiet. I will not speak again until you have completed this level. Do not leave the room until I tell you it is safe to leave. Nod if you understand." The video showed Derek's head nodding vigorously. "Now go!"

Joshua and David stared intently at the iPad screen until the hidden bedroom camera showed the door open slowly and Derek enter the room. They watched as the game player approached the bed where Johanna and Michael slept. In a burst of motion that startled David and Joshua, Derek lashed out with the knife at Michael, striking the sleeping man in the throat. Joshua could see the blood spurting out from the man's neck and thought it strange that the lawyer never moved even as he lay dying. Derek next turned to Johanna who appeared to have awakened but hadn't moved. She never uttered a sound as she put her hands over her face in a defensive posture while Derek slashed at her body with the knife. It must have been thirty seconds before he stopped. David and Joshua sat in front of the iPad without speaking, surprised by the viciousness of Derek's attack.

"Holy Mother of God," David spoke first, still whispering. "He did it!"

Joshua felt bile rising up through his throat and he swallowed hard several times. Nothing he witnessed on the battlefield had prepared him for the violence expressed by his patient as Derek stabbed and slashed his way to earn points to win the game. Maybe the kid really did kill that guy in the group home, Joshua thought. From what he just saw, he certainly seemed more than capable. Joshua almost felt sorry for Johanna and the lawyer. Almost.

"We've got to get him out of there before something goes wrong," Joshua told David.

"Right," David said. "Derek, this is the Game Master. Put the knife on the bed and leave the room."

Derek didn't respond to the Game Master's commands. Instead, he remained at the bloody bedside. He dropped the knife to the floor. But instead of leaving the room, he untied the strings to his scrub bottoms. They slid down his legs, bunching around his ankles. He stood there.

"What the hell is he doing now?" David asked Joshua.

"I don't know! Command him to leave again!"

David repeated the command and even threatened to take away points but Derek remained where he was, half-naked, staring at the two dead bodies on the blood-soaked bed. Then he began to masturbate in front of the dead Johanna.

"Derek, STOP what you are doing and follow the Game Master's commands. If you do not STOP NOW you will lose the game and the bad people will come back to life," Joshua urged in a hoarse whisper through the Skype connection. Derek ignored the voices coming from the ear buds. He placed his left hand onto one of Johanna's breasts, and continued masturbating.

"Derek, this is the Game Master," David tried again. "I command you to stop and leave right now!" He turned to Joshua. "Jesus! That's all we need is for him to leave his DNA on the body!"

Suddenly, the young killer stopped. He slowly picked up

his pants and tied the waist drawstrings. He seemed en-
tranced as he turned and left the room. They watched as
he re-emerged into the kitchen.

"Derek, leave the house and get back into the car,"
David instructed.

In a few minutes, they could hear the car door slam
shut.

"Derek, can you hear me?" David asked a hint of anxiety
in his voice.

No answer.

"Derek, drive back to the hospital and park the car
where you found it," Joshua spoke next taking the place of
the Game Master and praying Derek would listen. The
sound of the car engine came through the iPad's speakers
as Derek started the car and began the drive back to the
hospital.

Chapter 18

Derek followed David's instructions and drove back to St. Luke's after completing his "game" of killing the bad people.

"Okay," David said. "You are back at the hospital. Now, turn left into the parking lot and park the car back in the same place, understand?"

Derek's voice came through the speaker. "Yes, Game Master. I understand." Joshua could hear the clicking of the turn signal as Derek turned into the hospital parking lot.

Joshua turned and looked out the window into the visitor's lot. He could see the headlights of a slowly moving car. He began to relax as the blue Chevy containing the young killer came closer, and then passed the spot where Derek was supposed to park.

"Derek, stop!" Joshua said loudly. He saw the brake lights flash and the car lurch as Derek slammed on the brakes. "Park where I told you to," he commanded.

Derek's voice was anxious. "I don't remember, they all look the same!" Joshua saw the brake lights vanish as the car went out of view.

"Oh, shit," David said. "Where is he?"

"I don't know," Joshua replied, trying to stifle a wave of panic.

"I can see the big red lights that say Emergency Room. The sign says to park here," they heard Derek say.

"No Derek! That's not the right place! Stay in the car and keep going until I tell you to stop," Joshua commanded.

"But it says to park here," Derek whined. "I'm tired Josh. I want to lie down in my room."

Joshua heard the car door slam shut. "Derek, stay there. I'm coming to get you."

He turned to David. "Get back into your room. I have to go out and get him before he goes into the ER." Joshua checked the hallway; it was clear.

David picked up the iPad and returned to his room as Joshua sprinted down the hall and out the emergency door to the parking lot. He looked for the Chevy but it was nowhere in sight. He stayed close to the building and skirted around the corner toward the Emergency Room entrance. Loud sirens were approaching as he came into view of the ER and he turned his head away as a Cleveland fire truck drove past him toward the exit.

"Damn, where is he," he muttered, scanning the parking lot for the Chevy.

"There - there it is!" The car was parked two spaces away from the ER doors. A yellow Cleveland EMS ambulance with sirens blaring barreled into the lot. Emergency Room workers rushed out to meet the vehicle and Joshua saw Derek standing next to the Chevy, watching the scene.

"Derek, come this way," Joshua whispered loudly and motioned for Derek to follow him. "Where is the phone?" Joshua asked him after they turned the corner and out of sight of the ER.

"It's here" Derek pointed to his scrub pocket. Joshua gasped when he saw Derek illuminated by the overhead lights. He was covered in blood! The blue scrubs were drenched to a dark brown and Derek's bare arms and face were streaked in blood.

"C'mon, let's go!" Joshua hissed urgently, grabbing Derek by the arm. Using his keys, Joshua opened the locked Exit door from the outside and peered into the dark hallway before pulling Derek inside. He guided Derek directly to one of the patient shower rooms.

"Take off your clothes and shower. I'll bring you some clean clothes from your room. Don't come out until I tell you to, do you understand?" Joshua asked.

"Yeah," Derek replied.

Joshua left the shower room and leaned against the door. He took some deep breaths and waited for his racing heart to slow. Pursing his lips and mouth he took several long slow breaths in and out, until he felt the pounding in his chest subside. The sound of the water being turned on confirmed that Derek had followed his instructions.

"Jesus, keep it together," he told himself.

Standing in the dark empty Day Area he glanced at the wall clock behind the glass inside the Nurses Station. Almost 5:30 a.m. The day shift would be starting to come in.

As if on cue, he heard the buzzing of the entrance doors and went to see who was requesting entry. Before he reached the door Big John came out of the Social Worker's office and stretched his arms high over his head.

"I got it, Josh," John said and unlocked the doors by pushing the buttons using the keyless code. Joshua stood while John held the doors open for a laundry worker pushing a large four-wheeled cart with fresh towels and assorted bedding, resupplying the unit for the day.

"Man, I got a lot of studying in last night," Big John said

to Joshua. "Did it go okay on the floor? Any problems with my people?" he asked.

"Nope, all your people slept through the night. No meds or anything," answered Joshua. "I got Derek in the shower now. He had an accident in his pants. Trying too hard to win his imaginary game to stop and go to the bathroom, I guess. Here, let me just take this into the shower room for him," said Joshua as he grabbed some towels off the cart. "I got to bag his soiled clothes in a red contaminated bag. There was some discussion in Report that he might have AIDS. No sense taking any chances, right?" Joshua said loudly. Joshua would permanently dispose the blood-soaked scrubs by having the hospital burn them along with all the other red-bagged items deemed too dangerous to wash or reuse.

"Give me a minute, will you?" Joshua said to the laundry worker. "I'll get the clothes bagged right now and you can take them with you."

Putting on surgical gloves, Joshua walked quickly to the shower room saying over his shoulder, "Don't leave, I'll be right back."

The shower was still running when Joshua entered and saw the blood soaked clothing lying on the floor. Opening the door to the supply locker he grabbed the large roll of red plastic bags and pulled off two of them. With his gloved hands probing through the bloody scrubs, he found the cell phone Derek had used, made sure it was turned off, then jammed it into a surgical glove and put the glove in the red bag. He carefully placed the bloody scrubs in the bag, then removed his surgical gloves and threw them in. Next, he double bagged the items making sure that nothing showed through the translucent plastic bags before twisting the top and tying a knot.

Joshua felt secure that there would be no evidence linking him to the double murder. *Nobody would look into a bag of shitty and pissy clothing.* He tossed the bag into a wheeled container marked for contaminated items and pushed it over to the laundry worker who was leaning against the wall by the front doors. The man took the cart and pushed it through the doors and off to the furnace; never to be seen again.

Joshua gave a thumbs-up to Big John, who was now sitting inside the Nurses Station, then entered David Feighan's room.

"Give me your iPad, we have to get rid of it," Joshua said taking a white towel and wrapping it up. "I'm going to dump this. I already got rid of the phone and Derek's clothes."

"What about the car?" David asked. "What are we going to do about that?"

"Nothing," answered Joshua. "It can't be traced back to us. We'll just leave it there and eventually Security will call it abandoned and tow it away. I'm not going near it. I just hope that there were no cameras catching me bringing Derek back into the hospital. I'm going to be off for the next two days. Just keep playing dumb because I'm sure the cops are going to want to talk to you when they find the bodies."

"Don't worry about me," answered David. "My alibi is rock solid. I'm locked up in here. Bet Johanna never realized she helped me by putting me in here. Anyway, I have plans. I never do anything without a plan, a backup plan, and another backup plan. And don't worry - I'm going to repay you for this, Josh," David said. "I'll never forget what you did for me, my friend," he said touching Joshua's arm. "Just be patient and wait for my call. I don't want to say anything now."

"I don't want to know anything about your plans. The only problem will be Derek but I think he will be okay. There is no way to tie him to anything. Me either," Joshua continued. "The only person the cops are gonna want to talk to will be you, so do what you have to do. If I don't see you again, good luck," Joshua said shaking David's hand.

Joshua turned and left the room holding the iPad wrapped in the towel under his left arm. Going directly to the shower he found Derek already dressed in the clean clothing he had left for him.

"Derek, remember, if you tell anybody about our game, the bad people will come alive again and hurt us. Can you keep the secret?" Joshua asked as he took a dry towel and rubbed it over the young man's still dripping wet hair.

"Sure, Josh I can keep a secret. . . It was so real. Can I go to bed now? Please, I'm really tired," he implored.

"Sure," Joshua said, taking Derek by the elbow and leading him back to his room. He casually opened a dresser drawer and placed the towel-covered iPad inside. He'd come back and get it before he went home. He left Derek in his room and after turning off the lights he went into the Nurses Station where the day shift was assembled for Report.

Nursing report was quick. "All my people slept throughout the night and no meds had to be given," Big John said.

Joshua was next. "Derek Stanton had an accident in his pants. I got him showered and put his soiled clothing into a red bag since he might have contracted HIV. The test results didn't come back yet. No sense taking any chances," he said to the other nurses in the room.

"Good thinking, Josh," said the day shift Charge Nurse.

Big John and Joshua were gathering their nurse's bags. "Dude, I can't thank you enough for letting me study last night," Big John said.

"No problem," Joshua replied as he got ready to leave. "I'm going to check on Derek before I go home."

Big John left the floor and Joshua went into Derek's room and quietly retrieved the towel containing the iPad and placed it into his backpack, zipping it shut. As he was leaving the floor, the Day Shift nurses were placing breakfast trays onto the tables in the Day Area. Approaching the Charge Nurse, he said, "Derek had a rough night. He might sleep through breakfast. Can you save his meal for him?"

"Sure," she answered. "Good night, Josh." Joshua punched out and left the building. After starting the bike, he drove around the corner and saw the blue Chevy parked where Derek had left it. Joshua stopped, bike idling, and stared at the car. Was there anything in it that could link him or David to the murders? He quickly glanced through the driver window. Nothing. Well, nothing but the blood that had transferred from Derek's clothing to the car seats but he couldn't do anything about that.

Joshua twisted the throttle and left the parking lot, pointing his Harley down West 25th Street toward downtown. Instead of taking the Detroit Superior Bridge to The Nine, he took Washington Avenue into the Flats and stopped on one of the bridges. The Flats held a combination of industrial, entertainment, and growing residential units near the banks of the Cuyahoga River. A casual observer would think he was just stopping to admire the view. Satisfied no one was paying any attention to him, he tossed the towel containing the iPad into the Cuyahoga River. He continued on until he exited the Flats using Main Street and then continued to his apartment. He turned on the television to Fox 8 News.

"Good morning, this is Fox Eight News and Wayne Dawson with Stefani Schaefer. Kristi Capel is off today," the news anchor cheerfully reported. "We have breaking news of a five car pileup on the West Shoreway so you might want to redirect yourself before using that route to get into downtown today. We have a team on the way..."

No mention of two dead bodies. Good, he thought. If they had been discovered, it would have been all over the news. Joshua flipped to the other channels. Nothing. He put on sweat pants and a t-shirt. Walking into the bathroom, he reached into the medicine cabinet and took two Vicodin and three Ativan, popped them into his mouth and chewed the pills to get the medicine into his system faster. He looked into the mirror, searching his image for any visible signs marking the betrayal of his ethics and the oath he had sworn. But there was nothing. And he felt nothing. No remorse, no guilt.

He crawled into bed praying that the meds would act quickly. He was so very tired.

Chapter 19

Nick picked up a cold case file, paged through it, and then tossed it on a stack with the others. He was a street cop. That's where he did his best work. On the street. Not at a desk. The chair squeaked a protest as he leaned back and absentmindedly ran his hand through his hair. He couldn't concentrate. Not when Jimmy was getting his psych evaluation. He lurched forward in the chair as his cell phone rang. The caller ID showed St. Luke's Hospital.

"Kat, is Jimmy okay?"

"How did you know it was me?" Kat asked. "I'm using the hospital phone on my desk, not my cell."

"I've got powers you don't even know about yet," he joked. "For example, I can see you through the phone."

"Really? What do you see, oh Great Swami?"

"I see a gorgeous chick with short blond hair, sparklingly green eyes, and a big-big brain that's going to give me my partner back so I can get the hell out of this building and do some real police work," he exclaimed, not bothering to hide his frustration. "Pushing papers is not my thing. Cracking heads and locking up the bad guys is. So – are you going to give me back my partner?"

"The short answer is yes. I put Jimmy back to work with no restrictions but you've got to promise you'll keep an eye on him. He answered all the questions honestly but he's still troubled by what he saw. He associates the dead baby with his kids at home. I told him I want to see him back in a few days for follow-up and to bring his wife Linda." She paused. "He also told me that you were in that kitchen and saw the same thing he did. Are you sure it didn't bother you more than you're letting on? This stuff will sit in the recesses of your mind and be triggered at the most inopportune time. I can set you up with one of my associates if you need to talk about it. Be honest with me, Nicky, this is important," Kat said.

"I'm fine, Kat. Cops see this stuff all the time. Jimmy is young and has kids so of course he's going to handle it differently. Really, I'm okay."

"Alright, tough guy, I have to get back to work and do rounds in the hospital. See you tonight?"

"I'll call you later but I will be home after work. You want me to bring Chinese home for dinner?"

"That sounds wonderful. Love you. Later."

As the call ended, Jimmy came in the Homicide office and dropped into the chair at his desk across from Nick. "Christ," he said. "That was worse than taking a lie detector test, but I got this!" He waved a piece paper around for all the other detectives to see. "This piece of paper proves I'm not crazy!"

"Yeah?" one of the detectives said. "They just don't know you very well, Jimmy!" The detectives laughed.

"Screw you guys," Jimmy said, grinning. "I got to show this to Lieutenant Fratello before I take it to the Medical Unit. Now, where are we with all this?" he asked, waving his hand over the piles of cold case files on the two desks.

"You are done with that stuff," a voice bellowed from inside the Lieutenant's office. "We got a hot one out on the west side! Two dead - stabbed on Edgewater Drive.

Uniforms are on the scene waiting for us so Nick, you and Jimmy take lead on this one. CSI is on the way. The place is crawling with news media so be on your best behavior."

"You got it, boss," Jimmy said, grabbing a set of keys from the desk. "C'mon Nicky," he nodded toward the door. "Let's get out of here before he changes his mind."

I hope Kat is right about Jimmy, Nick thought. "Give me the keys, Rookie," he said. "I'm driving."

Chapter 20

The cop cars were double-parked in front of the sprawling brick mansion on Edgewater Drive, effectively blocking the news media vans from getting any closer to the crime scene. Two news choppers circled above a thick canopy of tree branches looking like buzzards waiting to swoop down and devour a carcass.

"Jesus, Nick," Jimmy exclaimed. "Looks like the Lieutenant was telling the truth - we haven't even seen a body yet and look at this mess!"

A uniformed cop stood to the side of the street, allowing the detectives to pull through the elaborately scrolled iron gate. They followed the wide stone driveway around the right side of the manicured lawn to the home's rear entrance. Nick and Jimmy entered the kitchen door and went up the stairs to the master bedroom and the murder scene. SIU Detectives were taking photos and dusting for prints while the coroner's office people stood patiently in the hallway, standing by with wheeled gurneys and body bags needed to transport the victims to the Cuyahoga County Morgue where they would be autopsied for evidence.

"What do we have, Steve?" Steve Loomis was the lead detective from the Scientific Investigation Unit.

"You got a dead Johanna Feighan and a dead Michael White that somebody obviously didn't like very much. Michael got his throat cut, probably when he was sleeping because there are no defensive wounds or signs of a struggle. Just a nice deep slash across the windpipe that severed the carotid artery - he bled out in seconds. Never knew it was coming. Now, Johanna here is a different story. She fought back. See the cuts on her hands? She tried to fend off the knife but the killer overpowered and stabbed her multiple times on her face and body." Loomis paused then added, "I did find something a little strange though. Notice the bloody handprint on her right breast. We couldn't get any prints because the hand was covered by a glove, probably a surgical one like they use in hospitals."

Nick could plainly see the outline of a bloody handprint on the woman's breast and a trail of blood lines, most likely caused by the killer running his, or her, fingers on the body. Visible stab wounds to the face and hands revealed the viciousness of the attack. A twelve-inch, blood-stained butcher knife was lying on the floor next to the bed.

"This the murder weapon?" Nick asked Detective Loomis, pointing to the knife.

"Probably, but we haven't finished our work here yet. But between you, me, and the bedpost, I'd say it is. It comes from a set on the kitchen counter so we know the killer didn't bring it with him. That leads me to think this is a crime of opportunity - a burglary gone wrong. But nothing's missing from the home that we can see. No drawers were rifled through. Michael's wallet is undisturbed - still in his pants pocket draped over the chair. Johanna still has on a diamond necklace and probably a five carat ring on her finger, so the killer wasn't a robber. No signs of forced entry anywhere in the house but look at this," Loomis said, drawing the detectives' attention back to Johanna Feighan's body. "There are some other fluids on Johanna's body," he paused. "Looks like semen. We got to get her to the morgue and check it out further. In my opinion, I think this killer was a guy who wacked himself off after he killed her. I've seen this shit before. Give us a few days and maybe we can have a DNA sample that just might help you guys identify the animal that did this."

"That would be great, Steve," Nick replied. "Me and Jimmy will be downstairs checking with the neighbors while you finish up here."

Nick and Jimmy ignored the shouts from various members of the news media as they checked with the neighbors on both sides of the house and across the street. Twenty minutes later, they met a block away from the Feighan mansion to compare notes. The general consensus was no one heard or saw a thing. As they returned to the murder scene through the throng of reporters Nick heard a familiar voice.

"Hey, Nicky! You got a minute for me?"

Nick recognized Dawn Kendrick from Channel 3 News. "Hey, Dawn. How have you been?" he answered the blond reporter. Dawn was a good reporter and a friend to the cops. When other news channels were hammering the cops, she made sure her reporting was objective and fair.

"You got anything for me?" she asked again.

"Not yet. We are in the preliminary stages of the investigation. The bodies are still in the house," Nick relayed.

"Is it true that Johanna Feighan and another man were

killed? Her husband, David Feighan is still in St. Luke's Hospital, right Nick?" Dawn yelled over the voices of the other reporters clamoring for his attention.

"How does she know Feighan's in St. Luke's? We don't even have that information!" Nick quietly asked his partner. Without waiting for Jimmy's answer Nick yelled back at the reporter.

"When I find out, you'll be the first to know, Dawn." Nick and Jimmy went back into the mansion and waited for SIU to finish.

"This is a weird one," Jimmy commented. "Nothing was stolen and it looks like the killer masturbated onto the woman after she was stabbed. If he wanted to sexually assault her, why did he kill her first?"

"You know how this shit goes," Nick said. "Just when you think you got it figured out another twist pops its ugly head up! One thing we know for sure, whoever did this wanted them both dead. Let's secure the scene and leave a couple of uniforms here. If the husband is in the hospital, let's go and interview him. I think he found her with her lover and killed them."

"But he's in the hospital," Jimmy pointed out.

"Minor detail," Nick said.

Chapter 21

The volunteer staffing St. Luke's information desk looked through the admissions on her computer. "No," she
murmured. "He's not on any of the medical floors. Oh
wait! Here he is. He's on Center One, Behavioral Health,
Building A. You just go down the hall, through the doors,
and take the elevator to Behavioral Health."

"Thank you," Nick said.

The detectives followed the directions to Behavioral
Health and rang the bell for admittance. A hospital guard
came to the door. After looking at their badges he let them
in, adding, "Sorry, Detectives. No weapons allowed on the
Behavioral Health floors. Orders from my boss."

"Yeah?" Jimmy questioned. "You better go get your
boss and change his mind before I book you for impeding
a murder investigation."

"He ain't here right now," the young guard said, stuffing
his hands into the pants pockets of his blue uniform and
shifting back and forth on his feet. "I can get the nursing
supervisor for you but my boss isn't available."

"I don't care who you get," Jimmy growled, "just make it
quick."

The guard used the phone in the security office and
within a few minutes a nurse appeared from behind the
locked door of Center One.

"Identifications please," the nurse asked, holding out
her hand. After examining the IDs she held them back out
to the two men, satisfied they were actually police officers

and not reporters trying to sniff out a story on the locked ward. "What is it, officers?" she asked.

"We need to inform one of your patients that his wife has been murdered. There's also some questions we need to ask him," Nick explained.

"I don't know," she replied. "We've never had this happen before. The HIPAA Laws prevent me from even telling you if the person you want to talk to is here as a patient. And besides," she said after seeing Jimmy's gun hanging from the shoulder holster underneath his jacket, "absolutely no weapons are permitted on the floor. I'll call the administrator to get some answers. But he's in meetings; you'll have to give me a minute."

"We'll wait," Jimmy said.

She went into the adjacent security office to use the phone, leaving the door open behind her.

"Hello, Toby?" she asked. "I've got a couple of detectives here wanting to talk to one of our patients. Can you come down here and speak to them? I don't want to violate HIPAA but I think this may be more important than breaking some rules."

She returned to Nick and Jimmy. "He will be right down, Detectives. Can I ask who you want to speak to?" she asked.

"David Feighan," answered Jimmy.

"Good luck with that one," she said. "He hasn't spoken in days." Then realizing she had just confirmed that Feighan was indeed a patient at St. Luke's she said, "You didn't hear that."

"What was that?" Nick asked, grinning.

The elevator bell chimed and Toby Abernathy exited

and introduced himself while shaking the two detectives' hands.

"How can we be of assistance?" he asked.

"We need to speak to one of your patients, Mr. David Feighan, on a personal matter," Nick started. "We know he is a patient here."

"What is so important to violate HIPAA Laws and possibly even interfere with his treatment?" Abernathy asked, in a "why are you bothering me" tone of voice.

Nick spoke. "His wife Johanna was murdered last night and she was with another male who was killed also and..."

Toby Abernathy's face blanched white and he reached for a handrail on the wall to steady himself before Nick could finish the sentence. Nick shot a quick glance at his partner. By the expression on Jimmy's face, it was clear he noticed the Administrator's reaction.   The security guard and the Charge Nurse both grabbed their boss's arms to keep him from collapsing onto the hallway floor.

"You okay, sir?" the guard asked several times as Abernathy gathered himself.

Taking a deep breath before speaking, Toby responded, "Yes. Just give me a second."

Turning to the detectives, he said, "You'll have to excuse me. Johanna is....was a personal friend of mine. I just spoke to her yesterday with her attorney about David's treatment and goals and..." his voice trailed off. "Oh my God, was Michael White the man who was with her?"

"Yes, he was," Jimmy answered.

Toby Abernathy's face remained pale and pinched.

Strange, observed Nick. Not the sort of response he expected.

"Look," Jimmy said. "Either we talk to him now or we can get a court order to allow us access to him. It's up to you but time is of the essence. The longer you delay granting us access to him, the greater the chance the killer has of getting away. I don't think you want that, do you?"

"No-no of course not," Toby answered. He turned to the Charge Nurse. "Let's go onto the unit and bring Mr. Feighan into the interview room." he said still trying to compose himself.

"You understand that we need to supervise the interview, don't you?" he addressed the detectives.

Jimmy started to object but was interrupted by his partner. "No problem," Nick answered. He wanted Abernathy there. *This guy knows more than he's letting on.*

"Detectives, I'll need to lock up your guns first," the security guard said.

"Yes, yes that's right," the administrator confirmed. "Go ahead, Bonner."

The guard ushered them into the Security office, then bent down and opened a safe. He accepted the detectives' weapons, put them in the safe, closed the door and spun the combination dial to lock it.

"We can take it from here, Bonner," Abernathy said, dismissing the guard.

Jimmy gave Bonner a business card and asked him to call if he thought of anything that could help the case.

The Charge Nurse opened the door and Nick and Jimmy followed Toby and the nurse onto Center One and to the glass-walled interview room. The Charge Nurse instructed an aide to bring David into the room. Toby Abernathy took one of the chairs, tugging at his shirt collar as he sat down.

Both Nick and Jimmy noted the man was sweating profusely. As the aide arrived with David Feighan, Nick stepped aside to allow them entry.

"We will permit Mr. Abernathy to stay but the rest of you will have to leave," Nick told the nurse and other staff that had gathered in the doorway.

Closing the door, Nick took a good look at David Feighan. Dressed in a hospital gown and yellow hospital socks, he seemed oblivious to his surroundings.

"Sit down, please," said Nick.

David stood motionless, head down, staring at the floor.

"Mr. Feighan, I have some terrible news to tell you," Nick started gently. "Your wife has been murdered, along with your attorney."

Seeing no response from the patient, he repeated the news of the murders. Still nothing.

Nick allowed Jimmy to question David while he observed Abernathy, who also appeared to be anxiously watching the questioning. Finally after fifteen minutes of unanswered questions, Jimmy said, "Looks like we got nothing here, Nicky. What say we go back to the office and call the Medical Examiner?"

"Sure," Nick said.

Purposely not looking at Abernathy, Nick opened the door to the interview room. Seeing the Charge Nurse Nick asked, "Can we verify that Mr. Feighan was here for all of last night?"

"Yes, he was," she answered. "We have patient logs verifying the patients' location on the floor every fifteen minutes. I can assure you that Mr. Feighan was here the entire time for the past ten days. He never left – not even for tests of any kind. His Doctor is Mr. Abernathy here, and he would have ordered any tests but there were none," she said, a hint of uncertainty in her voice.

Turning to the director, Nick asked, "Is that true Mr. Abernathy? You are his physician?"

"Yes, I am. It's Doctor Abernathy," he responded nervously. "Before I answer any more questions, I'll have to consult our legal department."

"If you feel you have to, go ahead. But you understand, that's not going to impact our investigation," Nick replied.

Chapter 22

"I'm telling you Nicky, that guy is hiding something," Jimmy said after they retrieved their weapons and left St. Luke's Hospital. "I thought he was going to have a friggin' heart attack! The only reason he didn't hit the floor was that guard and nurse grabbed him before he hit the deck. Why would he take the news so hard?" Jimmy asked while turning and walking backwards as he spoke.

"Watch out!" Nick yelled as Jimmy almost stumbled over the bushes lining the walkway to the parking lot.

"And then," Jimmy continued, his voice rising with each word, "He says he has to *consult* with the hospital lawyers before he says anything else."

"Slow your roll, Jimmy," Nick admonished. "I agree that the esteemed Doctor Abernathy had a very peculiar response to the information that Johanna and White were killed but, we have to tread very lightly with this one. It's a high profile case. Let's go back to the office and regroup with the information we have. Forensics is our next move. Let Steve Loomis do his thing. That guy is sharp and if he says he thinks that Johanna's body had semen on it, I got to believe whatever he says. We might catch a break on a DNA match and put this one in the win column."

The two detectives got into the brown Ford Taurus detective car. Nick started the car but left it in Park and turned to Jimmy. "Look. I know you've put your time in on the street as a uniform cop, but upstairs in the detective bureau, things are different. Remember what they taught you in the Academy? Every crime - no matter how big or small - has the same parameters. Who, What, Where, Why and How. Our job is to piece those parameters together, come up with an arrest, and get a conviction for the crime.

"The Who always has two parts. First, we have a victim. Second, we have a killer. Those two are always connected either by revenge, passion, greed, or fear. Nothing was stolen so greed appears to be off the table. I don't think fear had any part in this crime either. That leaves us with passion and revenge. I'm inclined to go with passion in this case," Nick said.

"The murder weapon was a knife from the victim's own kitchen so that would leave out any sort of a contract killing. Anybody that may have been hired to kill these two would have brought in their own weapon, most likely a gun. The killer was vicious and liked to kill in this fashion. He allowed it to turn sexual, and was careful enough to wear gloves.

"We know Who the victims are but we don't know who killed them. We know What happened and Where it happened. But we don't know Why it happened. As far as the How, it appears they were stabbed to death, but I've seen many surprises come out of autopsies although this one seems to be pretty obvious. Just forget the fact that the victims were high profile people. A murder is a murder." Nick put the car in gear and turned right onto West 25th Street with the downtown Justice Center as their destination.

"The husband, David Feighan, appears to be a vegetable and has a watertight alibi," Nick continued.

His voice trailed off as the car's police radio squawked,

"Any cars in the area of Lincoln-West High School, respond to a large gang fight."

Jimmy reached for the mike affixed to the dash but Nick's hand shot out, intercepted the mike from Jimmy's hand and returned it to the holder. "We're Homicide detectives, let the uniforms handle this," Nick reprimanded his partner. "If you allow yourself to get involved in anything but our current case the Lieutenant will put you back into uniform tomorrow. You got me?"

"Yeah, I get it," Jimmy replied. Two Black and Whites with lights and sirens on screamed past the Taurus. "Probably on their way to the gang fight," Jimmy said.

"Focus on *this* case," Nick instructed. "Toby Abernathy doesn't have the balls to kill anybody but his reaction sure wasn't what you expect to hear from a guy who was 'just a friend' to Johanna, never mind being the doctor for the victim's husband." Nick pulled into the Justice Center, maneuvering the car down to Parking Level 2 and found a spot close to the elevators.

"We know robbery wasn't the motive," Nick continued as he punched the elevator's UP button. "The sheer number of stab wounds and cuts lead me to believe it was a crime of passion. But why?" The elevator doors opened and the two detectives rode in silence to the sixth floor Homicide Office.

As they walked through the office to their desks, Nick said, "Jimmy, call the morgue and see if they've started the autopsies. I'll call Loomis in the lab to see if he got anything yet. It may still be too early for answers but we have to tell Lieutenant Fratello something."

"Yeah," Jimmy said. "I'll bet his phone is ringing off the

hook from the Mayor's Office on down." Nick and Jimmy's desks faced each other in order to "foster an open environment of creativity and collaboration" or some such bullshit spouted by an overpaid consultant. While Nick secretly admitted it did make it easier to brainstorm and exchange ideas, the best part was their desks were by the windows, giving them a view of St. Clair Avenue six floors below. Nick glanced out the window. Rush hour was in full swing and gridlock surrounded the aging Justice Center built in 1977. Horns could be heard blaring through the office windows as the afternoon summer heat aggravated the workers trying to escape to their suburban homes.

Lieutenant Jon Fratello came into the office just as Jimmy was dialing the Cuyahoga County Morgue but before Nick could call Steve Loomis in the lab.

"Chief Toothman is on my ass," the Homicide boss said. "Nick!" he barked. "Find out why that reporter, Dawn Kendrick, seems to know more about this case that I do. Jesus, almost to retirement and this shit has to happen," he complained loudly as he passed by their desks to his office. It was a common refrain.

"Christ, ain't you the lucky ones to have grabbed this case," Detective Shaun O'Meara teased. Shaun was a veteran detective and had mentored Nick on his arrival to Homicide. "I warned you! Should've stayed in Narcotics!"

"Aw, Shaun...you're just jealous you don't have this case," Nick joked. "Everyone knows how you love standing in front of the camera and saying, 'We have no new leads!'"

"Nicky," the detective countered, "I got less time to do than Fratello. This kind of case would keep me going to court for two years after I retire. Me and Kathy have plans to join the rest of the snowbirds in the Florida Keys. She would not like it if I had to keep leaving Marathon to come back here and testify on the appeals and all the other bullshit that's going to come from this investigation. You and the kid there," he pointed at Jimmy, "are going for a ride. Good luck man, you're going to need it."

"Thanks a lot, Shaun," Nick said, as he dialed the number for SIU.

"Loomis there?" Nick asked the person who answered the phone in the Cleveland Police Forensics Lab, or SIU.

"This is Loomis," the SIU Detective confirmed.

"Steve, Nick Silvano here. I know it's early but do you have anything for me yet? Fratello is already on my ass so any help would be much appreciated."

"Well, I can tell you that the fluid on Johanna's body was definitely semen. I performed a Rapid Stain Identification Series test on the sample and the RSID confirmed it so we've narrowed your killer to being a male. We're going to have the DNA tests done but even in the best of circumstances it would take at least five days and then we would have to match it up in the FBI's Combined DNA Index System, which takes more time. We're going through the blood samples collected at the scene to see if the killer may have left his blood in the room or on the bodies. I know it's not much but it's only been a couple of hours. Chief Toothman's office called here and gave me the 'hurry up' order but this is science and it can't be rushed," SIU Detective Loomis explained.

"Okay. Let me know if you find anything in CODIS." Nick hung up the phone and turned to face his partner. "Anything from the morgue people yet?"

"Nope. Look Nick, I'm tired. Linda is texting me. She wants to know when I'm coming home. You think we can wrap this up for today and get a fresh start tomorrow?"

"Sure, Jimmy," Nick replied. "Let me go and tell the boss before we head out."

Nick knocked once and entered Lieutenant Fratello's office without waiting for approval. "Hey boss, we pretty much did all we can for now. The SIU lab and the morgue are doing their thing and we have to wait for some news. Loomis confirmed it was semen on the female's body so we know the killer was probably a male."

Lieutenant Fratello stood up from his desk, opened a drawer and retrieved a brown holster housing his off duty .38 caliber Colt Python snub-nose revolver and stuck it into his belt.

"Well, at least it's something," he said. "C'mon, let's go to The Roach. I'll buy you a beer. Did you get hold of that reporter like I told you to?"

"Shit! I forgot Jon. I'll call her from the car on the way to the bar. I got her cell phone number somewhere in my desk."

"Okay. I have to stop for cigarettes first anyway," the Lieutenant said.

"When are you going to kick that habit, Jon?" Nick asked what now seemed to be a familiar rhetorical question. Not expecting an answer, he moved to his desk, extracted a stack of business cards from the top drawer, and fumbled through them until he found Dawn Kendrick's card.

"I know, I know," Fratello answered, waving his hand at Nick. "I tried those Blue E-Cig electronic things but I keep losing them. I buy another one and then I find the old one.

Gets expensive. Never ending story for me," he lamented. "The nicotine gum tastes like crap and those pills they advertise can cause you to kill yourself, so I'll just stay with the Marlboros, thank you very much!"

Nick's first call was to Kat.

"Hey babe, where you at?" she answered on the second ring.

"On my way to grab a beer with Fratello at the Roach," Nick answered "I won't be long though. We caught that double homicide on the west side this morning and it's been a long day already."

"Yeah, I heard about that. The news is saying that the dead woman's husband is David Feighan. One of my nurse friends from the hospital already called to inform me that my 'extremely good looking boyfriend' was there asking him questions."

"Wow, doesn't take very long for the gossip to start," Nick said. "Do you know that patient very well? We got nothing from him and your boss, Toby Abernathy, was acting really weird when he got the news. We thought he was going to drop onto the floor and then he said he had to consult an attorney before saying anything else."

"No, he's not my patient. And even if he was, I couldn't tell you – that pesky little thing called HIPAA!" she admonished. "I haven't had any contact with him at all but word is that he's a special friend to Toby and everybody is being kept in the dark. It's not the first time that high profile patients have been admitted. They've got head problems just like everybody else – probably more! But this is the only time anybody can remember that Toby took over a case. The Charge Nurse was complaining that she had to put in the orders for Toby because he didn't know how to use the new computer system that he bought for the hospital. Shows how out of touch the administration can be to the inner workings of the healthcare system," Kat explained.

"Well, I don't think he's as out of touch in this situation as he wants people to believe."

"That's your thing, not mine," Kat responded. "I fix 'em and you lock 'em up. You need dinner when you get home? I can whip something up if you want."

"Naw, I'll grab a burger at the bar. I won't be long. See you in a little bit."

Next, Nick dialed the reporter's number.

"This is Dawn Kendrick," the Channel 3 News reporter answered.

"Hi Dawn, Nick Silvano. You got a minute?"

"That depends – do you have a scoop for me on the murders?"

"Not quite yet but I've got a question for you. How did you know David Feighan was in the psych ward at St. Luke's before I did? My boss put me on the spot about that one."

"I get along good with the uniformed cops and they told me," Dawn explained. "Said that the night shift cops took him to St. Luke's recently. Supposedly high on dope and naked in his own front yard. I wish I would have been there for that! I'm not going to tell you which cop told me though, you understand?"

"I got no problem with that, Dawn," Nick allowed. "That's what I figured but just wanted to make sure before I told the boss."

"Tell Jon to keep from getting his panties in a bunch," she laughed. "He knows I don't mess with the cops. My dad was a judge in St. Louis and his best friends were cops. I know the rules, Nick."

"Thanks, Dawn." Nick ended the call as he pulled into the parking lot.

Fratello was smoking a cigarette in front of the bar, waiting for him. "Just one or two beers," he said to Nick. "Then I gotta go."

"Yeah, I've heard that before!"

Chapter 23

J oshua got in line behind the other nurses waiting to clock in, just like any other day. He glanced around looking for cops or anyone who seemed to be looking his way, but there was no one. He exhaled deeply then froze as a large hand clamped down on his shoulder from behind.

"Josh!" Big John exclaimed. "What do you think about all the excitement around here?"

"Oh – hey John," Joshua said, relieved it was his friend and not the cops. "What are you talking about?"

"Didn't you hear?"

Joshua shook his head. "Hear what?"

"David Feighan's wife and lawyer were killed last night! I heard the cops were all over the unit today and even had Toby on the carpet. Guess he almost passed out in front of the cops. The nursing supervisor had to help him stand!" Big John reported.

"Do they know who did it?" Joshua asked as he stepped up to the Kronos machine and swiped his ID.

"Nope but they were here questioning Feighan. The social worker can read lips and was watching through the glass windows. She said they kept telling Feighan about his wife but he didn't have any response so they just took him back to his room. After the cops left, Security came on the floor and double-checked all of the rounding checks we all made last night. Good thing you marked all the boxes! Bill called me at home today with the news. He said he tried to call you too but you didn't answer. Like Feighan could get off the floor and go kill his wife and come back! He'd be lucky if he could find the door," John said as he and Joshua walked through the doors to the Center One Behavioral Health Unit.

"That's terrible," Joshua said. "If Bill tried to call me, I never heard the phone." John headed down the hall and Joshua went to the Nurses Station.

Nursing report was a blur. He was assigned Derek, David Feighan and Trudy - again. "You don't mind do you, Josh?" the Day Shift Charge Nurse asked, not really caring if Joshua minded or not. She made the assignments. "I know you get them every day but you do so well with them," she said in a patronizing tone. But this time, Joshua was glad to have the same patients. The closer he stayed to Derek and David, the better prepared he could be to handle any problems.

Center One was quiet tonight. Big John was good to work with and the other two nurses, Cassie and Diane, were both new mothers. They would spend the night exchanging baby pictures and swapping stories about how their husbands were handling their status as new fathers. Henry was on duty in the Day Area. All of the Unit's eighteen beds were full. Toby would be happy with that, Joshua thought. More patients, more money, and better justification to put his name on the new wing.

Joshua thought about what Big John had said about the cops talking to Toby and his reaction. Man, he wished he would have been there to see that! Joshua logged into the computer to check for orders. He would let Henry handle the floor. No reason to have Derek see him right away and perhaps let something slip.

He found an old order for a chest X-ray for Trudy that had not been completed on her admission from the ER, and tensed for a moment. Another example of incompetence, he fumed. Even though he knew it was probably unnecessary considering Trudy used the clinic as if it were her vacation getaway. The X-ray had been ordered and should have been done. What if something really was wrong with her and they missed it? While this was unlikely given her history and their experience with her, it was no excuse. He expected everyone to do their job and behave professionally. If they couldn't take the pressure then they shouldn't be here! He printed the order and called Radiology to see if someone could come to Center One and transport her down for the procedure.

"We don't have anybody to transport her now," the X-ray tech told him. "You guys will have to bring her down yourself if you want to get it done."

"I'll bring her down," Joshua said. He had expected this. The techs avoided the Behavior Health floors whenever they could.

"Okay, thanks," the tech answered, relief evident in his voice. "Anytime is good for us. And please bring the order with the chart."

Joshua searched for a wheelchair and found one outside the doors in the parking lot. Despite his earlier concern, his temper flared. "I have to push Trudy all the way across the hospital to the X-ray department, and she can walk better than me!" he muttered. He forced his emotions back in check and didn't even think to question that one minute he was disgusted at the missed X-ray order on his patient's behalf and the next minute his anger was directed at the same patient. He collected Trudy with no incidents – she loved being pushed in the wheelchair – and waited for Security to meet and escort them to Radiology.

While Trudy sat in the chair like it was a throne, Joshua explained to the young guard, "This patient isn't a physical threat but she has a history of accusing male staff and patients of sexual abuse – so we're never supposed to leave her alone with any male staff - for their protection."

"Hey Security Guard, can I ask you a question?" Trudy asked.

"Sure, I guess so," he said.

"How big is your dick?"

The guard, a young man of twenty-two, turned red and didn't answer. Joshua gave the guard a look and stopped pushing the wheelchair.

"Trudy, I swear to God that you will be placed into locked seclusion without any medication if you keep doing stuff like this. Jesus, don't you ever quit?"

"Screw you, Josh," she answered, but rather uncharacteristically remained quiet throughout the X-ray and the trip back to Center One.

Joshua finished his charting and glanced at the clock. Almost 3:30 a.m. He couldn't avoid it any longer; it was time to check on his patients. Might as well get it over with, he thought and went to Derek's room. Derek was fast asleep with the covers pulled up around his head. Joshua exhaled a breath of relief. Next he went to Feighan's room. David was sitting on his bed and looked up as Joshua entered the room without knocking.

"You okay, David?" Joshua asked. "I heard the police were here asking questions."

"They were but I stayed in character, so to speak, and said nothing. I'm sure we haven't seen the last of them but I'm not concerned. You should have seen Toby Abernathy's face, it was epic! The older detective kept watching Toby while the younger one was trying to get me to open up. Needless to say, he didn't have any luck. How about you? Anybody talk to you about this?" he asked.

"Not yet," Joshua answered. "I don't see any reason for them to talk to me except maybe to confirm you were here all night. They already checked the rounding sheets, everything is in place. They have no reason to speak to Derek or anybody else."

Joshua left David's room. He wasn't panicked, scared, or ashamed of his part in this tableau. Really, he felt numb. Nothing! It was vital to carry on as usual and that's what he intended to do, he told himself and continued to Trudy's room.

Empty! *Where was she?* Joshua checked the bathroom then the Day Area. "Henry," Joshua called out to the aide. "Trudy's not in her room."

While Henry headed down the hall to check closets and other patient rooms, Big John turned on the floor lights, alerted Cassie and Diane, and checked the exit doors to make sure they were still secure.

"My new patient in 230 is not in his room," Cassie told Joshua.

"Anybody checked the shower rooms yet? The main shower room is locked from the inside." Henry took the unit keys from his pocket, unlocked the door and went inside. A few seconds later he called out, "I found her! Get me some help in here!"

Three security guards arriving after hearing the alert went into the shower room. Henry came out dragging a struggling Trudy by the arm. The security guards came out with the other missing patient in an arm lock, who was wildly trying to kick at Trudy.

"You fucking pervert!" he yelled. "You're a dude! I'm gonna kill you!" he screamed.

Henry lost his grip as Trudy collapsed to the floor, gagging and shaking as if she was convulsing.

"She's faking!" Big John said. As she writhed on the floor, Trudy's gown came open, exposing what she had tried to conceal from the other patient, who had quit struggling and stared at Trudy as if he was seeing a new life form.

"Oh, Gawd!" he exclaimed and leaned forward, spewing his partially digested dinner of meatloaf and potatoes on the carpeted floor and the unfortunate guard's shoes.

Henry spoke first. "Let's get into a room before the entire floor gets up and sees this." He reached down and took Trudy's right leg while Big John and the two guards took her left leg and both arms and carried Trudy into the Isolation room.

Joshua gave Trudy a shot of Ativan mixed with Haldol as Henry described the scene in the shower room.

"Trudy was giving the new guy a head job when I interrupted them. I turned on the lights and when the new guy saw that Trudy had a dick he went nuts. Pretty funny, really!"

Joshua finished his charting on the incident and was

looking forward to having the next three days off. He made his last round before his shift was over. Trudy was still out from the meds. Derek was sleeping. He was glad he didn't have to deal with him tonight. David's room was his last stop. He was sitting by the window watching dawn break through the secure facility's thick unbreakable glass window. He didn't react to Joshua's presence and after a moment, Joshua backed out of the room, closed the door, and left for home.

Chapter 24

Streaming trails of tracer fire buzzed by his head, like thousands of bees attacking from all directions. As if in slow motion, Joshua dodged the bullets and searched for shelter from the onslaught. There was nowhere to go, nowhere to hide! *No no no noooooooo!* Joshua woke abruptly from his nightmare. Sitting up in bed and drenched with sweat, he pressed his hands to his head trying to stifle the dark thoughts that simmered in his brain. It was his personal, internal movie reel and it was always the same. He was back in combat against faceless enemies until it became too frightening and he woke up. He glanced at the face of his phone and saw that it was almost two in the afternoon.

"Crap," he said. "Only five hours of sleep."

He slowly swung his feet to the floor and stood up, stretching his arms above his head. His sweat soaked t-shirt felt cool against his skin. Ripping it off, he tossed it aside and grabbed another from the dresser drawer, slipped it over his body, and went into the kitchen. He popped a coffee pod that promised to taste like doughnut store coffee into the Keurig and turned it on. He listened to the machine whirr until the blue flashing light signaled it was ready and he pushed the button and watched it fill his cup. He reached for the full container of Ativan in the cabinet over the sink, popped three of the 1mg small white pills in his mouth, and swallowed them without any water.

Taking a sip of the coffee, he moved to the living room

and turned on the television, scrolling through the channels looking for news of the murders. *Nothing.* He picked up his phone.

"Hey, Siri?"

The automated voice responded, "Hey Josh, I'm listening."

"Call Doc Stafford," he said.

"Calling Doc Stafford," the phone replied and he watched the screen change to display his friend's name. Joshua Ramsey had few friends; Doc was one of them. Probably his only one, he concluded.

"Hey Josh, what's up buddy?" Doc answered in a deep even voice.

"Having the nightmares again," Joshua said. Whenever Joshua felt himself succumbing to the nightmares and feelings of losing control that so many battle-scarred veterans revisited in the dark of the night, he turned to his friend. Doc understood and listened.

"You gonna be okay?" Doc Stafford asked loudly over AC/DC's *War Machine* playing on the jukebox. "Where are you at now?"

"My body is in my apartment but my brain is taking me back to Ramadi. Took my meds but they aren't working. Can we meet up for a bit to talk until my brain can regroup? I'm off duty tonight."

"Sure," Doc said. "I'm off tonight too."

Doc was discharged from active duty as Joshua had been but remained in the National Guard. A vigorous advocate for veteran's affairs, Doc never judged Joshua or any other veteran that needed his help.

"I'm at the Recovery Room bar," Doc said. "Want to

meet me here? I'll wait."

"Be there in twenty minutes," answered Joshua.

The Recovery Room Bar catered to the hospital work-ers. All you had to do was walk across West 25th Street to drink away the troubles that came with working in the fast-paced environment of a big city hospital. Cops and Firemen were the groupies here, trying to hook up with a nurse to share war stories or discuss the condition of a patient they brought to the hospital or maybe just to get "lucky".

The sun was bright and the wind was warm in his face as Joshua rode his Harley south on West 25th Street to meet Doc. Usually, riding the Harley allowed the dark thoughts to slowly wane away - but not today. They rode with him. They crowded out his good sense and preyed upon his anxieties, herding them together, ever tighter, until he felt he might explode. He didn't know how much longer he could maintain control and didn't know what would happen if he blew.

He pulled into the hospital parking lot and set his bike on the kickstand. Never mind the PTSD nightmares that stretched the limits of his personal control, now he had the added danger of being linked to two murders. Sticking the keys into the pocket of his jeans, he felt like he was standing on the edge of a cliff and walked as fast as he could, crossing against the light, causing a blue van to blow his horn at the offending jaywalker. "Asshole!" yelled the Hispanic man out of his driver's side window.

Joshua pulled open the heavy wooden door and was met by the smell of stale beer and cigarette smoke. Smoking was illegal but the off duty healthcare workers would stand by the door holding it open to expel the cigarette smoke from the room.

"Hey Josh! Back here!"

Joshua spotted Doc sitting at the bar next to the pool table and made his way to an empty bar stool next to his friend. He laid his cell phone and sunglasses onto the scarred bar top and turned to face Doc.

"Hey, sounds like you got it bad this time, buddy. What's going on?" Doc asked quietly as he motioned for the attractive, red-headed barmaid to come and take their drink orders.

"Erin, I'll take another double of Cleveland Bourbon with a Bud Light." Doc said. "What do you want, Josh?"

"I'll take the same but just a single shot of whiskey. I brought my bike," Joshua replied.

"You having the dreams again?" Doc asked.

"Yeah." Joshua took a sip of the whiskey from the rock glass. "It's funny how I can be a trained psych nurse and counsel others on how their fears are imaginary, but I can't counsel myself! The VA is no help. They got some young girl Physician's Assistant just out of school in the pain clinic. She has the attitude that everybody is there just to get drugs and wanted to put me in a study group and alcohol counseling."

"Hell, you don't drink enough to need counseling," Doc said.

"I know I don't! They make us go see them and then they treat us like lab rats." Doc nodded his head in agreement.

Joshua continued. "All she did was make it worse. You go there and line up to sign in and get a number, then you piss in a bottle and get in another line. Then they stick your arm for blood and you get in another line. Then they take your blood pressure. You'll be lucky if the doctor speaks English. Never mind my panic attacks and the constant pain. All the counseling in the world won't bring back my kidney and my ribs!"

"You know those problems at the VA will never end," Doc said. "Just yesterday, I had a seventy-year-old Viet Nam veteran in the ER. He had complaints of pain in his side and his family told me that they had been sitting in the waiting room at the VA Center for over eight hours and was never seen by any of the staff. His family saw the nurses take lunch breaks and they had shift change while he was there but they never even took him back to be looked at! Finally, they got tired of waiting and brought him to St. Luke's. I examined him and sent him for x-rays and guess what. The guy had three broken ribs! It turns out he was having flash backs that he was back in a Viet Nam jungle with the 1st Marine division. His wife said he kept yelling, "Gooks in the wire! Gooks in the wire!""

"Geez," Joshua said.

"She said she tried to hold him down but wasn't able to keep him under control and he fell down the stairs. I treated him and after I told him I was in combat in Iraq, he opened up to me and said how the Viet Cong came at them every night. The Marines circled their firebases with razor wire but the Viet Cong would try to cut through it and get caught! That's why he was yelling even though he didn't remember much of what happened before he took the fall down the stairs at his house. He was there again, back in combat, fifty years later! He said the older he gets, the dreams get worse, so much so that he is afraid to go to sleep and he needs to drink heavily to knock himself out so he can sleep. The VA is so fucked up. Beyond help," Doc said angrily.

Joshua nodded his head in agreement. "I know I have problems, and I don't like it that I take all this medication, but I get overwhelmed with horrible, dark thoughts. Just talking to you makes me feel better. Especially since you were there with me. You saved my life," Joshua said, his voice cracking.

Joshua had a sudden image of Derek slashing at Johanna with the knife. He drained his glass in one quick gulp.

"Whoa, slow down there, pal," Doc cautioned, placing his hand on his friend's shoulder. He slid the empty glass to the bar rail. "There's plenty more where that came from. And you don't have to explain anything to me," Doc continued. "Let's change the subject. Hey Erin," he called out, "Give me and my buddy here another round."

Joshua thought about telling his only friend about David Feighan, what was being done to him, and how he'd gotten mixed up in the millionaire's plot for revenge, but stopped himself. It wouldn't be fair to get Doc immersed in his problems; they were just too big.

"Just another day of paradise living in the looney bin!" Joshua said as he reached for his wallet to pay for the round of drinks. He managed a small smile as he handed a twenty dollar bill to Erin and said, "I got this one."

An awkward silence followed while Erin poured the drinks and Doc allowed Joshua to regain his composure. The next couple of hours were spent on small talk. No war, no mention of work, and certainly no talk of the recent murders that everyone else was talking about.

When Joshua got up to leave, he felt better than he had in days.

Chapter 25

"It's been three days," Jimmy said, spinning his office chair around to face his partner. "Any word from Loomis on the DNA from the semen sample he got off Johanna's body?"

"Not yet," Nick replied. "He said it would take about a week for the results. Not like on television, that's for sure. Solving murders is a lengthy and time-consuming process. It's very common for investigations to be halted while waiting for forensics to be plugged into place."

"Well, I don't like sitting on my ass knowing that a killer is somewhere out there." Jimmy abruptly rose from his chair and moved to the windows. He thrust his hands in his pockets and stared out at the city. "The whole city is looking to us to give them something, anything! Makes us look like we don't know what we are doing. Even my wife is asking me why we don't have anything!"

Nick sighed deeply. "Get used to it," he advised. "Lots of hurry up and wait ahead of you."

"Herron, some guy on the phone for you," the unit's office man Chris Cheetham called over the general office hum. Chris, a veteran homicide detective, was also the department's descriptive artist. His ability to reconstruct a suspect's description from a witness was uncanny, and suburban police departments often requested his expertise to draw wanted posters. "Says he's a guard from St. Luke's. He's on hold - line three."

"Thanks, Chris." Jimmy sat down at his desk, picked up

the worn, tan plastic phone and punched the button with the blinking light.

"This is Detective Herron, how can I help you?"

"Sir? This is security guard Robert Bonner from the hospital. Remember me? You gave me your card and told me to call you if I thought of anything else."

"Sure, I remember you," Jimmy said as he motioned with his hand for Nick to pick up the extension. "What do you have for me?"

"Well, I don't know if this has anything to do with Mr. Feighan's wife getting killed but there's a car parked by the Emergency Room and it looks like there's blood smeared on the steering wheel. The keys are still in it. It has a temp tag on it for license plates and my boss wants me to call a tow truck and haul it out of here for being abandoned. I went and checked the video camera to see when it was parked there. You know, to see if maybe the owner is here in the hospital to save...."

"Get to the point," Jimmy interrupted.

"Well, it was dropped off the same night that Mrs. Feighan and that lawyer were killed. The video is time stamped 3:34 a.m. and you can see somebody getting out of it but they don't go into the Emergency Room. They walk around the corner out of sight of the cameras. Probably nothing but I just thought you guys should know," the guard finished.

Nick spoke before his partner could answer. "Leave that car right where it is. We'll be right there."

"Yes sir," the guard said.

"Grab a set of keys, Jimmy. We might have just caught a huge break."

The two detectives spoke little during the twenty minute ride to St. Luke's. "There he is," Jimmy pointed at a security guard standing by a blue car. "Right over there next to the Emergency Room."

Jimmy pulled the police car behind a blue Chevy Cobalt, put it in Park but left the engine running. The detectives headed toward security guard Robert Bonner, who was standing by the car.

Shielding his eyes from the bright mid-day sun, Nick peered through the driver's side window. Keys were hanging in the ignition. Reddish-brown smears could be seen on the steering wheel and on the tan vinyl seats.

"Take a look, Jimmy," Nick said. He stood back, allowing his partner to take his place. "Tell me what you see."

"Looks like blood to me," Jimmy reported. "But, look where it's parked. Not really out of place for being in a hospital parking lot."

"I agree," Answered Nick, "but Bonner here says the driver got out and went around the corner of the building, not into the ER. Don't you find that a little strange?" Nick asked as he circled the car looking for anything else that may be of importance.

"Yeah," Jimmy said. "I can see if a guy had an accident, then jumped in the car to drive himself to the hospital, there'd be some blood in the car. But then we should have seen him go into the Emergency Room."

"You say that you have the occupant getting out of this car on video the same night that the murders happened?" Nick asked the guard. "Can we see the tape?"

"Yes, sir. I got it keyed up in the office if you want to see it," he said.

"Okay, first we have to secure the vehicle," Nick said. "Jimmy, get on Police radio and call for a tow truck while I call Loomis in SIU to come out and process the scene. We can't leave it unsupervised – have to keep the chain of evidence intact. The keys are still in it, by some miracle. We can't have somebody driving off in it now while we're inside looking at the tape."

Twenty minutes passed before SIU Detective Steve Loomis and another forensics cop arrived at the same time as the tow truck, both drawing a few spectators.

A well-dressed, middle-aged black man came out of the emergency room entrance accompanied by the hospital administrator, Toby Abernathy. "What's going on here," the man in the suit said to no one in particular. Spotting the guard he turned his attention to him. "What are you doing out here, Bonner? Aren't you supposed to be inside watching the doors to the Behavioral Health Unit?"

"Yes, what is going on here?" Toby repeated.

"Who are you?" Jimmy asked the man in the suit.

"I'm in charge of security for the hospital - former FBI," he added. "What are you guys doing here? What's going on?" he pointed to the tow truck and two men from SIU.

Nick spoke to the man in the suit. "My partner didn't ask what you are; he wants to know who you are, like, for instance, your name?"

"Dean Winston, if you need to know," the suit answered sarcastically.

"Well, Mr. Former FBI guy, we are Homicide investigators and those other detectives are forensic investigators. This vehicle may be involved in the murders of Johanna Feighan and Michael White. Your guard here,"

Nick pointed to Robert Bonner, "was very observant and alerted us to this car. It looks like dried blood inside and we need to process it for evidence. I'm sure you don't have a problem with that, do you?" Nick directed his question to the suit but looked directly at Toby Abernathy.

"Wait, don't you need a warrant?" Toby blurted out, turning his head quickly to look at the detectives and his head of security. "This is private property and is embarrassing for St. Luke's to have the police traipsing all over the place. I must insist that you don't do anything until I contact the hospital's legal counsel for advice."

"We don't need any warrants to tow this car as we believe it might be involved in a crime," Jimmy informed the administrator. "Don't interfere with us trying to do our job."

"He's right, Toby," answered the suit, then reluctantly to Jimmy, "We'll cooperate with your investigation."

"I'm still calling the lawyer. You were hired to take care of things like this," Abernathy said as a parting shot to his head of security as he turned and walked toward the Emergency Room doors.

"Now that we've got that settled let's go inside and take a look at that tape Bonner has keyed up for us to watch. You got this, Steve?" Nick asked the forensics detective.

"Yep, we'll take care of all this," Loomis answered.

The suit glared at his security guard, angry that Bonner hadn't consulted him before calling the detectives. The walk from the parking lot was tense. Detective Nicholas Silvano had no love for the FBI, former or present.

The new breed of FBI Agents had no regard for local cops and this guy, Winston, was already looking down his nose at them, Nick thought. This Winston, if he really is former FBI, is too young to have retired normally so he was either fired or drummed out for some wrongdoing. Best to tread lightly with this one, he cautioned himself.

The security office was small and cramped with the four men crouched around a TV monitor, trying to make sense of the grainy black and white footage. Several times the video had to be rewound and started again.

"See, the person gets out and doesn't go inside our hospital," Winston said. "It's apparent to me that none of our employees or a patient is connected to that car."

"You very well could be right, Winston," Nick allowed. "But, it's too coincidental that that car was dropped off - probably within an hour of the murders and the victim's husband is a patient here. I know we were told that the floor housing Mr. Feighan is always locked and that nobody but your guards came in or out of Center One, but we want to revisit that again. Show us how you know that. Walk us through how you came to that conclusion."

Winston turned to his guard. "Bonner, explain to these officers that neither Mr. Feighan nor anybody else came onto or left Center One on the night of the murders."

"Yes, sir," the young man replied. "It's like this." He queued up the video. "Here's the night in question from the camera installed to watch the doors to Center One. The last employee to leave is a nurse going off-duty. Up until 0500, the only person that came onto and left the floor was the guard on duty and he did it two times. Once at ten minutes after midnight and again at 0445 a.m. You can see here," he pointed to a figure on the screen pushing a large wheeled cart, "the next person besides a guard was the laundry guy at a couple minutes to five in the morning bringing fresh linen. And you can see him removing a cart, probably with dirty linens."

"You guards are supposed to make rounds every hour," Dean Winston scolded his guard.

"Yes, sir, we know, but we didn't have enough help that night. The Emergency Room kept calling us away to help them with violent patients," Bonner explained.

"I don't care what your excuse is, Bonner," barked Dean Winston," I'm telling you and the other guards working here..."

Nick cut the former FBI man short. "Now is not the time or place to discuss workplace policies, Winston. Walk us through what kind of checks the guards and nurses do on night shift. How would they know if a patient left and came back? This is a hospital, not a prison," Nick exclaimed.

"Bonner, you handle this," ordered Winston. "I have to find Toby Abernathy and update him on what is going on." Bonner watched him leave then turned to the detectives, a smirk on his face.

"He left because he doesn't know the procedures and has no clue what goes on here at night," Bonner stated. "Asshole comes in and hangs with Toby and the doctors eating free food from the pharmacy reps who bring in loads of it every day."

"Okay, then," said Jimmy. "You show us what safeguards are taken to keep patients like Feighan from going off the floor, kill his wife and then sneak back unnoticed."

"These are the only doors to Center One that are used and they are on camera twenty-four hours a day," the guard explained. "You just saw all the activity from the cameras on the night in question. The only other door is an emergency fire door at the end of the hallway, but that door is kept locked all the time and nobody ever uses it."

"Another door?" questioned Nick. "Show us."

The guard bent down and opened the safe. "Sorry, but I have to lock up your service weapons – just like last time you were here. Winston already doesn't like you but he can fire me," said Bonner.

Knowing they had backup weapons in ankle holsters, both detectives complied and watched Bonner spin the dial on the small safe to lock the numbers. They followed the guard out onto the floor. Bonner used a key to open the first of the double entrance doors and Nick and Jimmy followed the guard onto the Behavioral Health floor. In a large room off the hall, a group meeting was in process. Nick observed eight or more people, all dressed in hospital gowns, sitting in a circle. A social worker stood in the middle, talking to them.

"We turn the televisions and phones off during group meetings so there are no distractions," Bonner said.

The trio walked the length of the hallway until they came to a red door marked No Exit-Emergency Only.

"What about this door?" Jimmy asked. "Could Feighan have gone out this door?"

"No," answered the guard. "This is a delayed egress fire door. You have to push on the handle for thirty seconds with constant pressure until it releases and then an alarm sounds and keeps sounding until it is reset by security or a staff member. It can be deactivated by using an employee swipe card but per hospital rules, it's for emergency purposes only."

"What about cameras?" Nick asked. "Are there cameras monitoring this door?"

"No. None." replied Bonner.

"So, it is possible to use this door without being seen?" Jimmy said.

"I guess so but from what I know about the patient Feighan, he can't even find the bathroom door much less leave, go kill his wife, and get back here without being noticed," said Bonner.

"Is it possible to talk to Feighan now?" Nick asked. "Just to put our minds at ease."

"I'll get his nurse for you. I can't authorize that," Bonner said. "You guys stay here – I'll be right back."

Nick and Jimmy watched as Bonner turned a corner, leaving them alone in the hallway. "What do you think?" Nick asked his partner.

"I don't know. Seems pretty secure," Jimmy said. "What with cameras and alarms everywhere."

"Yeah, that's how it seems," Nick said just as Bonner reappeared accompanied by a nurse.

"Hi, I'm Antonella, Mr. Feighan's nurse today. How can I help you?" she asked pleasantly.

"Can we see Mr. Feighan? Maybe this time in his room?" Nick asked the nurse. "It might be less of a distraction for him and the other patients if we had a few minutes to revisit him and verify his state of mind - if he is still unresponsive and incapable of competent thinking."

"Sort of irregular, but you're Doctor Westerly's boyfriend, right? Antonella asked Nick. "We all know about you," she said, smiling broadly. "And we really like her - so I don't think that will be a problem." Turning to the guard she asked, "Is it okay with you, Bob?"

"Fine with me, just don't let Winston know," Bonner replied.

They walked to Room 252, ignoring the stares from the patients filing out of the group meeting room.

"Mr. Feighan doesn't attend group and doesn't take his meals in the Day Area," Antonella explained as she stood aside and held out her arm for the detectives to enter the room.

David Feighan sat on the edge of his bed, head down, eyes on the floor. "Mr. Feighan?" the nurse prodded gently. "These gentlemen are from the police department and want to talk to you. Is that okay with you?" she asked.

Feighan was unresponsive. It didn't seem as if he even knew anyone else had entered the room.

The nurse looked from the patient to the detectives. "He has been this way ever since he came to us," she said. "Non-verbal and unable to follow even the slightest commands. He can eat independently and use the bathroom but that's about it. Nothing else seems to make sense to him. He doesn't take any medication. Tony Abernathy is his doctor and he hasn't ordered any meds for him, not even Tylenol."

"Isn't that unusual?" Nick asked the nurse. "No blood or urine tests for drug use either?"

"No, nothing," she answered. "To be truthful, I've been a nurse for twenty years and I've never heard of a patient not being tested. He came to us via a Direct Admit so he wasn't even seen by the emergency room but, I'm just a nurse and my boss is his doctor so you can take it from there," she hinted.

"Can I try?" Nick asked.

"Be my guest," the nurse said.

"Mr. Feighan," Nick addressed the man. "I'm Detective Nick Silvano of the Cleveland Police." Nothing. "We spoke to you the other night. We're investigating the death of your wife and lawyer." He paused, waiting for a response. Still nothing. Feighan's gaze remained on his slippered feet but Nick thought the man seemed tense, as if he was listening.

"Hey, Nick," Jimmy said, pointing to Nick's feet. "Watch out."

Nick looked down and saw a fat drop of drool pooling on top of his shoe. He stepped back from the bed. Feighan's head never moved. No one's home, Nick thought. *Poor bastard.*

Getting no response again from Feighan, the two detectives thanked the nurse and were escorted off the unit by the security guard. After the doors locked shut Nick asked, "Can you get us a copy of that tape, Bonner? We don't care if your boss or Toby knows and they won't hear anything from us. I gotta thank you for being so observant. There has got to be a connection between that car you found in the parking lot and our murders. We just have to begin connecting the dots."

"I'll make the copy for you. Okay if I drop it off at the Justice Center? I don't want Winston seeing me give it to you. He's already pissed enough at me."

"Sure," Jimmy said. "Just call me so I can meet you at the door. I'll bring you up to our office, show you around. Sound good?"

"Great," Bonner answered. "I'll have it for you tomorrow."

"Not tomorrow," Nick said. "We are both off duty the next two days. Jimmy, you call him and make the arrangements to get the video when we get back to work."

"No problem," Bonner said. "I'll have it whenever you guys want it."

Back out on the sidewalk, Nick looked at the empty space in front of the detective car. "Looks like Loomis got the car towed out of here. Jeez, Jimmy, you left our car running with the keys in it! What if somebody stole it," he admonished his young partner as he climbed into the passenger seat of the brown Taurus.

"Sorry, Nick. Just got caught up in the moment. Rookie mistake!"

Jimmy parked the Taurus in one of the homicide unit's assigned spaces on P-2 of the downtown Justice Center.

"Do you mind if I just go home from here?" Jimmy asked Nick. "Linda has her travel agent class tonight and I've got to watch the kids. I can make it just in time if I leave right now."

"Sure, go ahead on home, Jimmy," Nick said. "I'll take the keys up to the office and finish the paperwork. I want to talk to Loomis and see how long before he can process the car towed from St. Luke's today."

"Okay, Nick. Thanks," Jimmy said.

Nick Silvano needed a stress buster. He planned on heading over to The Roach for a couple beers when he finished here, then a little fishing on Lake Erie on his days off. With each passing day he regretted his request for transfer from the Narcotics Unit where he had been assigned for eleven of the twenty-one years he'd been a cop. "I never thought about retiring when I was a narc," he mused. "Now, less than six months in Homicide and it's creeping into my mind." His old Narcotics Unit Detective partners Frank Ambrose and Danny Higgins still texted Nick every day with updates on his old cases they were following since his transfer. He missed his partners. He even missed the junkies and snitches! Nick shook his head. *What a world!*

Chapter 26

J oshua spent his days off volunteering at the 1900 Hamilton Homeless Center and taking long rides along Lake
Erie on his Harley. Each person, each mile helped him
relegate the Feighan Incident, as he thought of it, to a
corner of his mind containing other things he didn't want
to think about, like his war experiences or the amount of
pills he consumed on a daily basis. That piece of his brain
was getting crowded.

Calling it an "incident" rather than "murder" down-
played the emotional impact by several degrees, dimin-
ishing the psychological impact of the actual act. While
Joshua wasn't the physical perpetrator, he certainly was
responsible for instigating the sequence of events that led
to the actual "incident". Conversely, he didn't really see it
that way. Joshua had, without conscious thought, evolved
from being a competent nurse who blindly followed
doctors' orders and worked within the system to the role
of a "protector" nurse who used his license to advocate,
some would say fiercely, for those people who he decided
needed him.

Never mind that many of the homeless he administered
to were unappreciative of his efforts, not unlike the
hospital patients. Of course it wasn't all their fault; the
people Joshua was charged with caring for exhibited a
myriad of mental illnesses that would send most "normal"
people running for the hills if they had even a fraction of
his responsibilities. Some of the homeless held a silent,

stoic anger toward a society they blamed for placing them in a position that forced them to take charity from him and others. Others were subdued by chronic drug and alcohol abuse; a common affliction in the shelter. The sidewalks outside the old building were crowded with people who were refused entry because of their use of drugs or alcohol. When that anger boiled into action they ended up in jail or in one of the few psychiatric facilities available for treatment. Like St. Luke's.

As for himself, he knew he probably needed a psychiatrist to work through his post traumatic stress disorder. While he recognized the symptoms, he was confident he was able to conceal them from others. He was wrong. There were several notes in his hospital file referring to various PTSD symptoms documented by various supervisors: *Exhibits angry outbursts toward administrative staff. Appears preoccupied with negative feelings.* Joshua was extremely self-aware, and why not? He was, after all, a licensed psych nurse. He pushed these nagging concerns for his own mental health into the corner of his mind reserved for such things. *If I went to a shrink, they would just place me on mind-numbing drugs,* he often rationalized. *I'm already numbing my body with Ativan and Vicodin. Anything more would give Abernathy the excuse he'd need to fire me!* He pounded a fist into his open palm. A fleeting thought of suicide, the patron gremlin of the ex-military, came and went. Joshua wasn't afraid to die. He was more afraid to live! But a stronger emotion always prevailed; need. *I have patients at St. Lukes and people in the shelter that need me.*

All too soon, it was time to go back to work. The evening air was still as Joshua rode his Harley to St. Luke's. He hurried to join the night shift nurses standing in line to swipe their employee ID cards through the Kronos time machine. You could tell where the nurses worked by the various colors of uniforms. Blue was the respiratory therapists, white belonged to the med-surg nurses, green was for the nurses' aides, and maroon was Joshua's group, the psych nurses. If they were even one minute late they would endure a write-up that would put them afoul of the hospital's policies.

The nurse in front of the line was known for having difficulty using the fingerprint identifier on the time clock and her repeated tries to coax the machine to chirp and acknowledge "it's me and I am at work!" caused the other employees behind her to grumble. "C'mon, you're going to make me late again," yelled a nurse at the back of the line.

After several tries the machine finally acknowledged her existence. "I don't know why it's always me this happens to," she said woefully to the line behind her. "Something must be wrong with my fingerprints."

Joshua and the others watched her heft an oversized nursing bag onto her shoulder and shift several plastic bags of carryout food onto her other arm, all while clutching a large Starbucks coffee as she scurried to the open elevator doors for the bumpy ride to her assigned floor.

"Toby would have a shit-fit if he knew what we brought in from the outside to eat," someone else said.

"Yeah," Henry agreed. "It's a wonder he doesn't have Security search our bags and toss everything he doesn't approve of." Most of the nurses brought in Chipotle, Burger King or some other fast food to survive the night.

"Administrators and doctors get to eat, but not us!" was a common complaint from night shift workers. The cafeteria closed at night and the overpriced vending machines were the only source of food. And those, Joshua thought, only contained what Toby, the hospital emperor, decided his servants should eat: diet soda and good-for-you but totally inedible munchies. "God forbid we should have a real Coke and a bag of chips," Joshua had complained on more than one occasion.

Clocking in just under the wire Joshua, along with Henry and two nurses assigned to work with him the next twelve hours, passed through the double locked doors to the Behavioral Health Unit. The hallway was empty of patients and the lights were already dimmed. Three female patients were engrossed in *The Voice* singing competition on the big screen television hanging on the wall in the Day Area.

"I'd pick Blake Shelton," one of the women said rocking back and forth on the edge of the chair. "He's soooooo cute! I'm glad he and Miranda got divorced because now he's gonna be with me!"

"What are you talking about, dumbass," the other woman jeered. "There's no way he'd ever look twice at your ugly face! Blake's going to pick me!"

Their voices faded as Joshua, Henry and Michele entered the Nurses Station. "Sorry guys," the Charge Nurse greeted them. "The Census is down to only six patients so Michele, you're going to the sixth floor and Henry, you're being floated to the emergency room."

"Great," Michele uttered under her breath in a tone indicating her displeasure at the reassignment as she turned and walked out the door. Henry went to the coffee machine, poured a generous amount of the black liquid into a big gulp 7-11 cup then followed Michele.

Nursing Report went quickly. The Charge Nurse read from a hospital directive describing ways to improve the hospital's Press Ganey Scores and Gallop Surveys. "Look for clients with a positive attitude that will...." She stopped reading in mid-sentence, crumpled the offending piece of paper and tossed it into the trash can.

"Positive attitude – my ass!" she said loudly. "The jerks in administration send out the surveys with the bills. The patients trying to read the bill wonder who the doctor was that never talked to them, much less saw them, but charged $850 dollars that their insurance company is never going to pay. We can't even call them patients anymore, they are *customers*! What are we, Walgreens? Then, the administrators blame the nurses for the low scores. It's the forty-two dollars we charge to take a blood sugar from a non-diabetic patient and the one hundred five dollar facility fee that pisses them off, not us!" she complained. "And they have the balls to ask the patients – excuse me – customers – how do you like us now? Christ!" She picked up her purse. "Have a nice night," she finished as she walked off the unit.

"Wow," said Cassie, the nurse Joshua would be working with that evening.

"She's right," he said.

"I know, Josh, I know. Don't you get started too!" Cassie held her hands in front of her face to ward off the expected rant that, surprisingly, didn't come. Instead, they got down to work. They split the patients between them; Joshua took the three male patients and Cassie the three females.

"Trudy is really a male, right Josh?" Cassie asked pleadingly, trying to duck being assigned care for the man who was not yet a woman.

"No problem, Cassie, I'll take Trudy. But you take care of the rounding sheets, deal?"

"Gladly," Cassie responded.

Joshua checked his patients. Trudy was sound asleep in her assigned room. Her meds must have kicked in, he thought. Trudy's stay usually lasted around fourteen days until the doctor discharged her. But once home to her boyfriend, another cycle of drug and alcohol abuse would ensue and it wouldn't be long before Trudy was back on the floor. It was a game and she was a high scorer.

Derek was in his room playing imaginary games and looked up when Joshua entered.

"Hi Josh," he said cheerfully.

"Hello, Derek," Joshua answered carefully. This was his first encounter with Derek since the night of the murders a week ago. "Are you doing okay?" he asked, looking for any clues in Derek's voice or behavior that may give away what had happened.

"Yep, I'm fine," he said, then lowered his voice to a whisper. "I'm really good at keeping secrets. It's like you told me, if I say anything the bad people will come and hurt us and I don't want that to happen."

"Good," Joshua whispered back, more relieved than concerned that Derek mentioned their secret. "It's our special game. Nobody else can know about it."

"I got it Josh; you don't have to worry about me." Derek continued to play his imaginary game, zoning out as if

Joshua wasn't even there.

Joshua left the room feeling a little better. There was nothing to associate Derek, David, or himself with the killings, he reassured himself. As long as Derek was afraid, he would keep his mouth shut. Besides, there was absolutely no reason anybody should even think to question Derek. It was obvious the kid was delusional.

Joshua checked his remaining patients. The new admit was snoring lightly in his room and he moved on to David Feighan's room. He deliberately left him for last. He paused before the door, steadied himself with a deep breath, knocked lightly then entered the dark room. David appeared to be asleep in his bed. Joshua used the light on his phone to search the room in case David's "guy" had smuggled additional computers or phones into the hospital. The phone they used while playing "Simon Says" with Derek had been burned in the contaminated clothing bag. The iPad was soggy junk lying at the bottom of the Cuyahoga River. Seeing that the room was clean, Joshua quietly closed the door then looked at the nurse's notes, checking for any indication that either Derek or David had aroused anyone's concern during the day.

"Good, nothing out of the ordinary," Joshua whispered. "For the psych floor anyway."

The rest of the shift passed quietly. Joshua gave his report then left the hospital. Fumbling through his backpack he retrieved his sunglasses for the ride to his apartment. He enjoyed the early morning ride home as everyone else was headed to work. Heading out of the parking lot he thought he might even be able to get some sleep.

Chapter 27

N ick hummed a few bars of a television theme song about "bad boys" and pulled the Roach's screen door open.

The infamous Cockroach Inn on Lakeside Avenue in Cleveland's lower east side industrial district was a favorite cop hangout. The surrounding factories had expelled their occupants for the day and all that remained was a ghost town; except for the Roach, as it was affectionately called by the cops who patronized the bar; an oasis from the job. Nick was looking forward to a couple of drinks and a temporary reprieve from the current murder investigation.

Willy-the-Couch stood behind the old bar, its wood top scarred from decades of cigarette burns and gouges of unknown origin, watching an episode of *Jerry Springer*. The big screen television hanging on the wall was previously occupied by a giant, stuffed moose head, until the weight of all the lead bullets from the cops shooting at it finally caused it to fall off the wall. The cops even held a funeral for their beloved "Bullwinkle" which lasted for over a week before they laid the giant head to rest in the green Dumpster behind the bar.

Willy purchased the Roach after he retired from the Cleveland Police Department. The rundown clapboard building had been built in the 1920's and operated as the Do Drop Inn for over eighty years until Willy bought it at a sheriff's sale. He renamed the working man's bar The

Cockroach Inn in an unsuccessful effort to keep civilians out. Willy only wanted cops for customers but the police groupies soon found the place and began frequenting the bar in bunches.

Groupies occupied the front of the bar and the cops gathered at the far end of the bar by the pool table. "They really don't bother anybody and they got money!" Willy told any of the cops who dared to complain.

"Keep your shop talk to a minimum," was his mantra. "These groupies all got cameras and cell phones. If you don't want your business all over Cleveland, you better keep your mouth shut! Big Brother is everywhere!"

Five minutes from the Justice Center, the bar was the closest watering hole for the thirsty cops assigned to the main police headquarters. The secluded area allowed Willy to sell alcohol past the legal 2:30 a.m. closing time when the only people on the street in this part of Cleveland were cops and delivery trucks. "No nosey neighbors to call the state on me and the cops are already here," he said.

Unlike other Cleveland bars that exhibited No Firearms Allowed placards on their doors or in the window, the only sign visible when entering the Cockroach Inn was "No FBI Allowed!"

The bar was empty except for the barmaid German Annie, Willy, and one lone customer playing on the pinball machine. His body leaned left, then right, then left again, while his hands furiously mashed the flipper buttons. The noise of the chrome metal balls hitting their target goals still weren't enough to drown out the shouts of "JEEERY!JEEERY!" emanating from the television.

"What's up, Nicky?" Willy asked without taking his eyes off the television. Two robust girls were entangled on Jerry's stage, ripping at each other, wigs askew, while the live television audience cheered wildly.

"Where's everybody at?" Nick asked, sliding onto a wooden bar stool at the cop end of the bar. "The place is empty and its happy hour."

"They'll be in later," answered Willy. "The traffic guys got an Indians baseball game at Progressive Field starting about now, SWAT is out on a big raid with the narcs, and the rest are on standby for another one of those anti-police rallies at Public Square. Fucking protestors don't understand they are protesting against the wrong people! They should be pissed at the politicians, not us cops." Willy still referred to himself as if he was on the job even though he retired several years ago.

Without even asking, Willy planted a rock glass in front of Nick and filled it with Jack Daniels. He pulled a can of Bud Light from the cooler and popped the tab, allowing the hissing foam to spill over the blue can.

"Punk ass kids just looking for reasons to break windows and steal shoes start all this shit. Then the fires start to take the attention away from the looting while the politicians hide out in their offices trying to make a politically correct statement to the news media running around sticking a microphone into every asshole's face on the street. Then the reporters start with their two cents of so-called reporting! Purple-haired little girls with training bras and pimply-faced, hot-pocket eating punks wouldn't know how to report on a real story if it came up and bit 'em in the ass. They sit in their little cubicles taking information off of Facebook, Snapchat and all the other social media websites and steal stories from real reporters," Willy ranted as he waved off the twenty dollar bill Nick held out to pay for his drinks.

Nick swirled the bourbon around in the rock glass then followed it with a swig of the cold beer while Willy continued his tirade about the misguided protestors. Nick knew enough to let Willy get his point across, even though he had heard it all before and basically agreed with everything Willy was saying.

"Back when I was in the Third District working patrol, I remember asking a Councilman why the city was pouring money into renovating the Projects, knowing full well that the people living in them would begin to destroy them the day after they were finished. Want to know what that prick told me? He told me that 'this way, we know where they are all at'!   Imagine that! Here's this elected representative of the people admitting that the politicians want to keep the blacks, Hispanics and poor white people all confined into one place. I'd be pissed too! You live in those rat-infested Projects not able to have anything nice. Can't ever have a garden or even a yard. You can't have a nice car because some low-life will steal it or bust the windows. Your kids are harassed until they have to join the neighborhood gang. The rundown public school classrooms are half-full of pregnant little girls who will never finish high school and have no place to turn but back to the compounds the politicians call housing developments. Christ, don't get me started," Willy said, furiously wiping the bar. He stopped and threw the wet rag against the back wall.

"People got to start waking up!" he sputtered. "Their enemy isn't the cops, it's the politicians who keep them locked into the Projects!   Hell, I'm ready to march with them," he huffed.

Nick nodded and took another pull of beer. He'd heard it all before.

"Wow," remarked the only other patron in the bar. Nick looked to his right. The pinball player stood next to him holding out a five dollar bill for quarters. Willy took the bill and made the change as Nick observed the new-comer. A brown pancake holster holding a black Kimber Tactical Pro II was visible under the man's loose fitting Hawaiian shirt. The gun identified him as a fellow lawman, although Nick had never seen him before. One thing was for sure, he wasn't with the FBI. Willy would have made sure of that. The guy was about six-foot tall, athletic build, and a carefully combed head of salt and peppered hair.

"Hi, Dwaine Brosemer," he said, extending his right hand out to Nick.

"Nick. Welcome," Nick said. "Don't mind him," he nodded his head at Willy. "He kind of grows on you after a while."

"Shit," Willy said, then walked to the end of the bar and sat down.

"Nick Silvano?" Dwaine continued as he firmly shook Nick's hand.

"Yeah, that's me," Nick said. "Have we met before?" he asked, eyebrows raised in inquiry.

"No. Heard about you. I'm DEA; new in town. Charley Goetz told me about you, and this place," Dwaine explained. "Didn't Charley tell you about the new, good looking agent with the perfect hair here to fight crime in your fair city?"

"No," Nick replied. "He didn't." Goetz was the Agent-In-Charge of the Federal Cleveland Drug Enforcement Administration and a good friend of Nick's. "Oh hey – wait a minute! The guy with perfect hair....Your Hairness! Is that you?"

Dwaine laughed. "Yeah, that's me. So you *have* heard of me."

"Well, I've heard about your hair anyway," Nick laughed, recalling Goetz complaining about his former partner's constant preening over his locks.

"I've heard about you, too. Charley told me about a case you worked together where you chased that drug dealer, JuJu, out of your city last year. You guys really chased him through the Florida Keys?"

"Yeah, we did," Nick confirmed. "And he wasn't just a drug dealer. He was a stone cold killer."

"What happened?"

"It was a funny thing...."

"Hey DEA!" Willy interrupted. "You gonna buy Nicky here a drink or just stand there yakking all night?"

"Yeah, get him whatever he wants," Dwaine said. The DEA Agent sat down to Nick's right. Dropping Charley Goetz's name was an instant ice-breaker.

"When did you get assigned here?" Nick asked, forgetting about Dwaine's earlier question.

"A couple of weeks ago. I was a San Diego cop before my life turned to shit. I got divorced and moved on to the DEA. How about you? How long you been on the job? You married?"

Nick held up the refilled rock glass in a silent gesture of thanks. This guy sure asks a lot of personal questions, he thought. But he worked for Charley so he must be okay. Besides, a lot of those DEA guys were wrapped tight, although he excluded himself from that description. "I've been a cop for twenty-one years now and I used to be married," Nick admitted. "But, I got to be too much of a Cowboy Cop. You know, drinking and partying too much. After seven years, she had enough of my act and we parted ways. No kids, thankfully. She got married to another cop. A good guy. We're still friends. I've got a good girlfriend now and it's working for both of us, no pressure."

Willy placed another Bud Light in front of Nick, crushed the empty can and tossed it into a large plastic recycle bin in the corner behind the bar. "Nick's wife was a looker. You screwed that up, buddy," Willy chimed in as he took Dwaine's money for the drinks.

"I know the feeling," Dwaine said. "I got married young to a Navy nurse. Only lasted two years for me. She shipped out on a hospital ship for the Middle East and I shipped out to booze and broads. She took an early leave once to surprise me but she was the one that got surprised. She caught me in our apartment with another woman. We were both too young. I got tired of playing cops and robbers and joined the DEA. Spent the last five years in Las Cruzes, New Mexico chasing the druggies there until the opening came up for Cleveland office. I thought a change in scenery would do me good. I like it here, but I'm the only single guy in the office. I got a good boss in Charley and Willy here stocks Belvedere vodka, so I'm good." He drained his glass and placed it in front of Willy for a refill.

Nick and his new drinking companion spent the next three hours buying drinks and exchanging "war stories" about their respective law enforcement careers before Nick called it quits. They exchanged business cards and Nick left the bar. Calling Kat from his car he explained that he would spend the night at the Marina on his boat. He didn't want to drive very far as he "may have" had too much to drink and the Marina was closer. She sounded disappointed but did not give him any ultimatums. "Please drive safe and call me when you get there," she said.

Reaching the Marina, he drove his Honda through a squawking flock of sea gulls occupying the parking lot. They flew a short distance away then reassumed their positions once the offending vehicles passed. Nick parked his car in a marked spot in front of D dock. The bright spotlight illuminated the large American flag towering over the gas docks; it was hanging. No wind. He could hear the music and crowd noise coming from the patio of the Captain's Quarters bar at the far end of the parking lot, but wasn't even tempted to join the crowd. He stepped onto the aluminum ramp leading to the floating wooden dock that led to his Rinker Cruiser. The effects of the alcohol caused Nick to think that the walk to his boat was longer than it really was.

"Take it easy," he kept telling himself. "Don't do what Louie did!" remembering a cop friend of his who also had a boat on D dock. One day Louie drank too much and fell into the water. He had to be rescued by other boaters before he drowned. And that was in the daytime. It was dark now. Nobody was around to fish his ass out if he fell in.

Checking to make sure the yellow shore power cord was still attached to the hull of his red and white summer home, he stepped carefully onto the swim platform, unsnapped the corner of the red Sunbrella mooring cover, and crawled underneath it. The extra weight of his presence was detected by the automatic bilge pump in the engine bay and it began to whir, generating the sound of splashing water as it spewed from the boat into the water. He entered the cabin area, turned on the light, then called Kat. She answered on the first ring.

"I'm good," he assured her. "All safe and sound on the boat."

Saying goodnight, Nick next called his friend and fellow Homicide Detective, Chris Cheetham.

"What's up, Nick?" Chris asked.

"The Lake is flat, want to try fishing tomorrow?"

"Yeah – I'm off duty tomorrow. I'll pick up the minnows at Shine's on 55th Street. I can come after I take Cindy to work at the Rocky River Library. Around nine okay?" he asked.

"Nine's good. See you then." Nick stretched out in the aft cabin bunk and allowed the gentle swaying of the boat to lull him to sleep.

Chapter 28

The next afternoon, Nick pulled into the Lakewood Gold Coast condo garage and parked next to Kat's red Lexus just in time to see her struggling to carry two large bags of groceries and a another plastic bag full of papers.

"Hey Babe, wait and let me help you carry those," Nick said. "All I got is dinner here." He held up a clear Ziplock bag with fresh fish. "Chris and I nailed the walleye today and we cleaned them at the dock."

The ride up to the top floor went quickly. "Why does this elevator always smell like metal and oil?" Nick complained.

"Apparently you haven't smelled yourself," Kat laughed as the door opened to their floor.

"Whaddya mean?"

"Catch of the day," she said nodding at the plastic bag containing their dinner.

"Hey, can you take a day off tomorrow?" Nick asked. "I've got one more day off and I thought we might go and take the boat up to the Islands. Lake is supposed to be nice."

"I can't, Nick. I have office visits tomorrow. Three patients at St. Luke's and another one at Charity Hospital. How about Sunday?"

"Can't. I'm on duty that day," he answered. "No biggie, we'll do it some other time," he said. "How about you start dinner while I take a shower? I slept in these clothes last night on the boat and besides, you said I smelled like fish,"

Nick said pinching his nose with his fingers in a comical gesture.

"No problem," Kat dropped the bags onto the kitchen island.

They exchanged small talk over a dinner of fresh walleye and corn on the cob. Kat had a glass of wine while Nick uncharacteristically passed on his Budweiser and Jack Daniels. "Still a little queasy from being out on the lake all day," he said, not wanting her to know the real reason was that he drank too much at the Roach last night with his new friend, Dwaine Brosemer.

After dinner they moved to the living room. Nick slid the balcony doors open causing the curtains to flap wildly in the strong breeze coming in off the lake.

"Whoa!" Kat chased after a bunch of papers that blew off the coffee table.

"Sorry," Nick slid the door shut. "Here, let me help you with those." He got down on his hands and knees, picked up the papers and set them on the kitchen counter.

"Where did you get this?" he gestured to the crayon drawing at the top of the pile.

"One of my patients drew it in art therapy and gave it to me," Kat answered.

"Art therapy, huh?" he commented. The drawing depicted two figures lying on a bed. Red crayon slashes cut through the figures and over the entire page.

"Are they always this gruesome?"

"It can't be all hearts and flowers when you're dealing with damaged minds," she said.

Nick sat on the couch next to Kat, the drawing in his hand.

"Why does this look so familiar," he mumbled. He set it on the coffee table in front of him, and stared. The bed, two people, lots of red. Suddenly, it clicked. It was an exact, if crude, drawing of the bedroom where Johanna Feighan and Michael White were found murdered. The bodies on the bed, the blood splashed on the walls, the knife on the floor...this drawing was made by someone who had been in that room, Nick reasoned.

"Who drew this?" he asked.

"Oh, I don't know," Kat replied. "The patients often give us the drawings they do as some sort of present. Look on the bottom and see if there is a name," she said. "Why? What's so important about that picture?"

Nick didn't answer. He smoothed out the wrinkles he made while grabbing it away from the breeze, placed it on the table, stood up, then backed away for perspective. "It can't be a coincidence!" he murmured.

"What, Nick?" Kat asked. "What are you talking about?"

He moved closer to the coffee table. Bending down he looked along the bottom of the drawing and saw a name written in small, childish lettering in black crayon. Nick took his phone and snapped a couple of pictures of the drawing.

"What's going on, Nick?" Kat repeated as Nick punched in a speed dial number on his phone.

"I'm not sure yet but this is too weird to be a coincidence," he replied. "I want to check with Jimmy before I say anything. I could be totally off-base."

"Jimmy? Nick. I'm sending a couple pictures to your phone. Take a look. Then get back to me." Nick hung up, not wanting to say anything that could influence Jimmy's perception. He paced around the sofa while he waited for his partner to call back and was rewarded after only a couple minutes.

"You trying to be a crime scene artist, Nick? My kids can draw better than that," Jimmy said.

"Seriously Jimmy, what do you see in the drawing?"

Sensing the urgency in Nick's voice, Jimmy replied, "I see a messy but very accurate depiction of our murder scene. The bodies are placed accurately, the knife is lying on the floor where we found it, and look at the clock on the bedside table. Just like in that bedroom. So again, I ask you - why are you sending me a drawing you made of our murder scene? Just how much have you had to drink?"

"Look Jimmy, I haven't had anything to drink. Kat brings home drawings that the patients give to her from their group activity. This was drawn by..." Nick paused to peer at the name, "somebody named Derek." He looked to Kat for confirmation and she nodded her head in affirmation.

"Derek?" Jimmy asked. "Is he a patient?"

"Hold on, I'm going to put you on speaker." Nick placed the phone on the table.

"Kat. Who is this Derek?" Nick queried.

"He's a patient in Behavioral Health," she replied. "And I shouldn't even be telling you that!" she snapped. "You going to tell me what's going on?"

"Sorry, I think I got a little ahead of myself. You've done nothing wrong," Nick assured her. "I needed Jimmy to confirm my suspicions."

"Again - what is going on? What suspicions?"

"That drawing is the murder scene of Johanna Feighan and her lawyer, or something pretty close to it! Her husband, David, is our prime suspect but he was admitted to St. Luke's before the killings and we can't find any evidence that he was able to leave the hospital, kill his wife and attorney, and get back into a locked ward undiscovered. The car used to transport the killer was found in St. Luke's parking lot yesterday full of blood. And now," he pointed to the drawing, "we've got this!"

"Kat," Jimmy's voice came through the speaker. "Who is Derek?"

"He's a patient. Comes into the hospital a lot from various group homes. He took a lot of drugs already in his young life and his brain is damaged," Kat explained. "Derek has paranoia and trust issues from being sexually and mentally abused but he is not dangerous. He mostly keeps to himself," she said.

"We have to question him," Jimmy said. "Hey, Nick. When do you want to get him and bring him downtown to the Justice Center?"

"Hold on you two," Kat said. "You can't legally just burst onto a hospital behavioral health unit and remove a person being treated for mental issues. It's illegal. You probably need a court order. You better check with your cop lawyers before you do anything. Derek isn't going anywhere for the time being. I'll tell you one thing," she continued, sounding like the doctor she was. "Derek is paranoid already. You two start questioning him in an aggressive manner and he will close up tighter than a clam. Never mind the hospital will block your every move to get to him by citing the HIPAA Laws and patients' rights."

"She's right, Jimmy," Nick said. "And we've already pissed off the Security Chief *and* Abernathy."

Nick turned to Kat. "Can you question this Derek for us? I'm assuming he trusts you. All you have to do is get him to talk about what he drew on that paper. He had to be there! How else could he have drawn the scene so well without being there," Nick concluded.

"You know I can't do that!" Kat exclaimed. "You're going to have to figure out another way to talk to him."

"Nick? Let's wait until SIU finishes processing the car towed from St. Luke's lot," Jimmy said. Maybe some DNA or blood tying this Derek to the murders will surface and give us a concrete reason to take him in. We know who and where he is. Another couple of days won't hurt," Jimmy reasoned. "The kid's not going anywhere."

"You're probably right," Nick relented. "Kat can't be involved." At the very least, she could lose her job. And if there was a killer roaming around in the hospital....no, he couldn't even think about that.

"I'll see you on Sunday at the Homicide office," Nick told Jimmy, and hung up.

Chapter 29

Even though it was Sunday, the traffic unit, narcotics and homicide were open; it was business as usual. "Remember all you kumquats in the suits: baseball, murder, and heroin have no holidays!" Detective Frank Ambrose yelled through the doorway on his way to the Narcotics unit down the hall.

Detective Chris Cheetham threw a wad of paper at the narc. "Get to work, Frank!" Ambrose grinned and ducked out the doorway.

"Nick, wasn't that your old partner?" Chris asked.

"Yeah," Nick sighed heavily.

"I can see why you wanted to come over to Homicide," Chris grinned.

"Silvano! Herron!" Lieutenant Fratello barked from his office. "I just got my ass chewed out on the ninth floor. Sundays are slow news days and Chief Toothman needs to feed the Press! The esteemed members of the Fourth Estate are clamoring for updates on the Feighan and White murders. You guys have anything for me?"

"I think we can help you out, boss," Nick offered. "We got the forensics back from Loomis," Nick looked at his notes. "The car towed from St. Luke's Hospital came back positive for blood belonging to both Johanna and the lawyer White. The DNA sample taken from her body tested positive for sperm but there was no match in CODIS. The car is listed to a Brian Dirks from Wisconsin and was bought last week from a used car lot over on

Lorain by West 65th Street. We ran his name but no hits - he's not local. But I've got an idea to have the name checked without going through all the proper channels - if that's okay with you?"

"Sure, do it," Fratello said. "What else?"

"Coroner's report confirms the cause of death was by knife wounds. Alcohol was present in both victims' bodies. Johanna had a 0.24 blood alcohol level. She was really drunk. White was at 0.09 so he was not as drunk as she was. But, here," Nick stood and handed Fratello the crude drawing that had been given to Kat. "Look at this."

"What am I looking at?" Fratello asked, turning the paper over in his hands.

"The Feighan murder scene," Nick said. "At least that's what it appears to be. There's Johanna, there's White," Nick pointed a finger at the figures in the drawing. "Notice where the knife is?"

"Yeah," Fratello acknowledged. "On the floor by the bed. A detail that was never reported to the public. Who did this drawing? Where did you get this?"

"Believe it or not, a patient in the Behavioral Health Unit at St. Luke's drew it in art therapy and gave it to Doctor Westerly - my Kat," he added. "We have the patient's name but the law won't allow us to bring him in or even question him. But I have an idea. I need your permission to have Chris Cheetham go undercover at St. Luke's as a guest art instructor and see what he can find out. Remember, he's got a degree in Art Therapy. I already called and got permission from Dr. Westerly. The hospital allows volunteers like those with therapy dogs and musicians to go onto the floor and assist the patients. Sort of unorthodox but it can't hurt. The kid who gave her the picture has serious brain damage from drugs, but Jesus, that drawing is spot on," Nick said, taking the drawing out of Fratello's hands and returning it to his desk.

"Okay, let me get this straight." Fratello was thoughtful as he looked out the window. "David Feighan is on the psych floor when his wife and lawyer get murdered. Then Kat's patient draws this picture, which seems to be a crude, but accurate, presentation of our murder scene." Nick nodded in confirmation. "Additionally, we have proof that neither David Feighan or this patient left the hospital on the night in question yet, this patient drew a picture of the murder scene?"

"I know how it sounds, boss," Jimmy interjected, "but seeing as how the drawing is so accurate, it needs to be checked out. Maybe Chris can get some insight to this kid. See if he knows anything or if he's really just crazy. But no one else at St. Luke's can know, not even the administrator."

"Can this case get any more screwed up?" Fratello asked. "Chris, you okay with this?"

"I got my degree in Art Therapy but I never practiced in that field. There was no money in it," he said.

"And so you switched to a more lucrative career in police work," Jimmy smirked.

"Yeah, right," Chris said. "I can do this. Might work if I can get the kid to open up. Besides, I can finally tell my mom my degree came in handy!"

"I'll run it by Chief Toothman first." Fratello said. "Now, how about the car you towed," Fratello turned his attention to Nick and Jimmy. "How are you going to handle it?"

"Well, I called the car lot where it was sold and some guy answered the phone so it's open," Nick said. "Jimmy and I will head over there and check it out."

"Alright," Fratello said. "Get to it. I want the report on my desk before you go home today."

Jimmy grabbed a set of keys from the hooks on the Homicide unit wall. "I hope the night shift left us some gas," he remarked.

The ride to Pete's Motor Sales was short and silent. No conversation was needed between the two partners and fifteen minutes later, the city-owned brown Taurus turned into the car lot's driveway.

Nick exited the detective car and glanced around, looking up at the poles and into the corners of the small, rundown car lot. "Damn, no cameras!"

"I don't see any cameras either," Jimmy said.

The door to the white metal building that served as the office swung open and a short, balding Hispanic male maneuvered the four steps down the stairs, tripping on the sagging bottom step.

"Jesus!" he exclaimed, almost falling. "I gotta get that step fixed before I kill myself." After righting himself on the asphalt, he looked anxiously at the two Cleveland Detectives standing in his car lot.

"No worries there, Hector. We ain't from auto Theft," Jimmy said as they showed the man their badges.

"My name is Pete, not Hector," the man responded. "Well, my name is Pedro but everybody calls me Pete," he offered. He made them as cops right away and decided to downplay the obvious racial slur. He ran a clean business. *Well, pretty clean.* "What can I do for you, Detectives?"

Nick held out his cell phone with the image of the abandoned Chevy Cobalt in St. Luke's parking lot that he took before Loomis had it towed away for processing. "Did you sell this car?"

Pete took the phone, squinted, and turned it away from the bright morning sun so he could make out the image. "Yeah, that's one of mine," he confirmed. "I sold that car about a week ago. It was clean. I bought it at a car auction," he said, repressing a sigh of relief that he could justify he hadn't sold a stolen car.

"We aren't asking if the car was hot. We just want to know if you have the information about the person you sold it to. You keep records, don't you?" Jimmy asked.

"I keep very good records," Pete huffed indignantly. "Just follow me." He turned and walked up the steps into the trailer, purposely not advising the detective to watch out for the broken step. Maybe the Anglo *bicho* will break his leg, he thought.

Jimmy winked at Nick as he hopped up into the trailer office with one giant leap, avoiding the broken step. Nick grinned. Jimmy just loved to piss off people he was interviewing.

"Pissed off people talk more," Jimmy had told Nick, attempting to convince his veteran partner that he was doing it all wrong when conducting interrogations.

Pete rummaged through a battered gray metal file cabinet then pulled out a manila folder and opened it on the coffee-stained desk. Spinning the open folder around so the detectives could see the contents he said, "Go ahead, and look. I got nothing to hide. That guy was supposed to come back and pick up the title and plates. He never showed. The phone number he gave isn't right either. He paid cash and had identification. What do you want me to do?" Pete asked.

Nick rifled through the papers, stopping at the copy of the driver's license.

"This guy?" he asked Pete, holding up the photo copy of the license of the car's buyer.

"Yeah, that's him," Pete confirmed, gaining more confidence now that he felt he wasn't in any trouble. "I can make a copy of the whole file if you want."

"Why don't you do that," Nick said.

"Anything else you can remember about the buyer?" Jimmy asked as the car lot owner made copies.

"Nope, I didn't see him come in. He paid me cash, I put the temp tag on, gave him the purchase agreement, and he drove off. He was wearing sunglasses," Pete said. A lot of times we got people just looking for a cheap car and I sell them with no warranty. I don't want to see them again. It ain't my fault he never came back and picked up the plates and title."

"Alright," Nick said, handing the dealer his Homicide Unit business card. "If he shows up, don't let him know we were here. Just call us right away. If you can stall him, do it. We will take it from there."

"No problem, Detective." He reached out and shook Nick's hand but purposely ignored Jimmy. Pete watched from the trailer's grimy window as the detectives avoided the broken step and walked back to their car. He recalled that Brian Dirks walked with a slight limp. Maybe that's something those detectives would want to know, he thought. But after the way he'd been treated, well – they were detectives. They could figure it out themselves. He shrugged his shoulders and returned to his desk.

"That was a dead end," Jimmy said as they walked back to their car. "No way our killer gave his real name when he bought that car. He ain't never going back for the title."

"You are absolutely right, partner," Nick agreed.

"Now – let's find Brian Dirks," Jimmy said, staring at the copy of the Wisconsin Drivers License.

Chapter 30

"Get me everything you can about this guy." Nick put copies of the car purchase agreement and Brian Dirks' Wisconsin driver's license on Chris Cheetham's desk.

"Sure thing," Chris said. "Hey Herron, some guy is downstairs by the front desk asking for you. Says he's a guard from St. Luke's. I told the cop at the front door to let him wait for you down there."

"That's got to be Bonner with our videos from St. Luke's," Jimmy told Nick. "I'll go get him."

Nick started on the report his Lieutenant requested when he was interrupted by Fratello himself. "Just tell me what happened, Nick. The Chief is waiting. What do you have?"

"Sorry Jon, I thought you were already gone," Nick said as he swiveled his chair around to face his boss.

"I'd like to be gone," Fratello said, "but this case has everyone on high alert."

Nick described the interview with the car lot owner. "I think this Pedro Vazquez who owns the lot is telling us everything he knows. He voluntarily gave us copies of the entire purchase along with a copy of the guy's driver's license. Chris is working on it now," Nick said looking over at the office man, who was on the phone.

"That's got to be our guy! He tripped up and now we got him!" the Homicide unit's commander said loudly, slapping the corner of Nick's desk. The sound attracted the glances of several other detectives in the office.

"I'm not so sure on that, boss," Nick cautioned. "It just doesn't fit. The killer was careful to wear gloves and avoid cameras. I doubt he'd be so careless as to leave a copy of his driver's license for us to discover. He had to know that we would eventually find the car and trace it back to Pete's Car Lot. He gave a phony phone number and told Pedro he would come back to pick up the plates and title but he never showed. Why would our killer reveal his real name? It doesn't fit the profile," Nick said.

"Don't rain on my parade, Nick. I gotta go down to the P-2 parking garage and have a smoke. Cheetham! Get me the 411 on the Wisconsin Driver's license Nick gave you," Fratello barked.

"Working on it, boss," Chris said.

Nick's cell phone rang. He looked at the caller ID and saw it was from St. Luke's. "Homicide Unit, Silvano," Nick answered, turning away from the other detectives in the room.

"Hey Babe, it's me," Kat said. "I'm at the hospital. They called me with two new admissions so I decided to go in and give the orders and see my patients."

"Is Derek and David Feighan still there?" Nick inquired.

"Let me check the Census sheet," she replied. "Give me a minute." After a brief interlude, Kat said, "Yes, both patients are still here but that's not why I'm calling you. You are not going to believe this," she said excitedly.

"What?" he asked.

"Toby Abernathy quit this morning!" Kat exclaimed. "The security guard told me that Toby came in early and had him help carry out boxes from his office! The whole hospital is buzzing about it."

"That *is* strange," Nick said, recalling the stricken look on Toby's face when he learned of Johanna and Michael White's murders. "Do me a favor. Find out if he gave a reason for leaving. I think it has to do with the murders."

"Sure, I'll be your snitch," Kat said seductively. "The grapevine reports he wasn't feeling well and something was physically wrong with him. But I'll see what I can find out. What's in it for me, Copper?"

"How about a couple chili dogs from the Hot Dog Inn?" Nick offered.

"Deal," she answered. "Oh, tell Chris to be here tomorrow afternoon at 2 p.m. He's cleared to be our guest instructor. I can be there and introduce him but he's got to act like he doesn't know me, okay?"

"Sure thing," Nick replied. "You really want chili dogs?'

"I love them things!" Kat said as she hung up.

Jimmy came into the office with the security guard in tow and Fratello right behind.

"This the guy with the videos?'" Fratello asked.

"Yes, that me," Bonner said, feeling very much an important piece of the murder investigation.

"Good," Fratello said. "Let's all go up to the Chief's office and watch them." It was a short elevator ride from sixth floor Homicide to the ninth floor and Chief Toothman's office.

"Hello, Nick," the Chief greeted him as the three cops and hospital security guard were ushered into his office. "You finding Homicide to your liking?   Narcotics bosses are missing you and want me to send you back," he said.

"We can talk about that another time, Chief," Nick said,

oblivious to the looks exchanged between his Lieutenant and his partner.

"Sergeant, get those videos up and running for us," the Chief ordered his administrative aide.

The occupants of the room took seats facing a monitor set up by the aide and the lights were dimmed.

"What am I looking at?" Chief Toothman asked. The grainy footage was hard to see.

"This is the night of the murders, Chief," the hospital security guard offered. "You can see from the accelerated video that nobody came onto or left the unit except for our guard until the laundry guy shows up at five in the morning."

"How about other doors? There has to be emergency exits, right?"

"Yes, there are," Bonner confirmed. "They are locked and an alarm sounds if they are pushed open. By law, if pressure is applied for thirty seconds they will open but we would have heard the alarm sounding. Both the Charge Nurse and Security have keys that would circumvent any alarms, but there was no type of emergency or fire drill that would cause the doors to be opened."

"Okay," the Chief said. "Let's see the parking lot video."

The video started with the Chevy Cobalt entering the hospital parking lot and parking. A dark figure exited the car and walked around the corner.

"That's it?" Chief Toothman asked.

"Yes, it is, Chief," Jimmy answered. "But, we have a timeline now connecting the murders to that vehicle. We just have to find out *who* got out of the car and walked away."

Nick then filled the Chief in on what he had learned from Loomis in the SIU. "The blood in the car belongs to the victims. We're waiting to see if a DNA match to the sperm on Johanna's body comes back in CODIS. And there's something else." He explained how his girlfriend, a doctor at St. Luke's, came into possession of a drawing that closely resembled the murder scene.

"We've got it lined up for Chris Cheetham to go undercover tomorrow on the psych floor as a guest art therapist. The kid that did this drawing is a patient," Nick explained. "By law, we're not allowed to interview patients. We just need to get some kind of read on the kid. If it's just a coincidence we'll cross him off the list. But maybe someone told him something which then became his art project.

"The suspect who bought the car allowed the car lot guy to make a copy of his driver's license. I'm thinking it's either a phony ID or was stolen. There's no way the killer made that big a screw up considering all the other careful actions he took to avoid detection. Our office is checking on the driver's license and Lieutenant Fratello will keep you up to date."

"What about the husband?" the Chief asked. "He'd be my first pick. What do you have on him? I've met Feighan a couple of times at City Hall functions and he is a real piece of work. If he didn't do it, maybe he messed around with somebody else's wife or girlfriend. This could be a revenge motive seeing how vicious it was."

"Doubtful, Chief," Nick countered. "He hasn't said a coherent word since he was admitted over two weeks ago. The story is that he took an obscene amount of Ketamine or Flakka and permanently fried his brain. But there is something strange that happened today." Nick told them about Toby Abernathy's sudden resignation.

"No shit!" Jimmy erupted.

Nick made a mental note to look into David Feighan's background and the circumstances that had landed him in St. Luke's hospital psych ward. All they knew was what other people were telling them.

Chapter 31

Doctor Katrina Westerly and the visiting art therapist stopped in the hallway just outside the door of the group meeting room. Kat peered in through the window, then withdrew and turned to her guest. "Derek Stanton is third from the right. He's the skinny blonde kid wearing a black t-shirt and green army pants. I want you to know - it could get rough in there," she cautioned.

"Couldn't be worse than a bunch of high school students," Chris Cheetham grinned.

"Well – maybe not," she smiled. "Just don't show any fear. You do and it's all over. You'll lose control."

"No fear," Chris repeated.

"Okay, don't say I didn't warn you," she said, opening the door.

"Group!" Doctor Westerly said to the twelve mental health patients assembled in the meeting room. "This morning we want to welcome Mr. Smith. He is going to explain how you can use art and drawing to creatively express yourselves and help work through problems in your lives,"

"Good morning," Detective Chris Cheetham, now Mr. Smith, greeted the group. Half of the patients assembled at the two tables were attired in street clothing while the others remained in hospital gowns clearly identifying them as patients, as they were deemed escape risks.

"As Dr. Westerly said, we're going to have a drawing session today. Art has been around since the dawn of time, since man created the first graffiti on a cave wall using the end of a burnt stick. Creating art lets us express our feelings in a way that words can't."

"How big is your dick, Mr. Smith?" called out a patient dressed in layers of hospital gowns with dirty bare feet resting on the blue carpet.

"Trudy! Stop it right now," Kat admonished. "Another outburst and you'll go back to your room." Kat's expression was stern but she wanted to laugh at the look on the detective's face with the jarring start to his fake art therapy session.

Undeterred by the threat, Trudy stood and lifted her gown. "Draw this!" she shouted, revealing a penis in a semi-hard condition.   The female patients in the room shrieked at the sight of Trudy's exposed genitals.

A large, black male patient stood up and advanced toward Trudy. "You are disgusting!" he shouted as three security guards rushed into the room and dragged the kicking and screaming Trudy from the room.

"Charles, please return to your seat," Kat instructed then turned to Chris. "I'm so sorry about that outburst, Mr. Smith."

Chris put a hand over his mouth, dampening his laughter with a fake cough. They'd have a good laugh about this at the Roach, he thought.

"That's quite alright, Doctor," he said. "Let's get started, shall we? First, why don't each of you introduce yourselves?"

There were eleven patients remaining after Trudy's expulsion from the group. In turn, they stated, mumbled, or sang their names.

"My name is LeBron James," the man who had yelled at Trudy boomed.

That got a rise from the group with calls of "No it ain't!" and "You're lying!"

"Prove it ain't!" the patient countered. "I can be whoever I want to be and you can't prove it," he said confidently.

"Charles," Kat addressed him in a soothing, even tone. "Let's try and behave ourselves, okay?"

"Alright Doc," he answered. "The name is Charles, but everybody calls me Chuck," he said, looking around, daring anyone to challenge him.

"That's good, Chuck," Chris said. "What about you, young man?" he addressed a young white male patient who had so far remained quiet.

"Go ahead, tell Mr. Smith your name," Kat encouraged.

Seconds passed with no response. Finally, the patient identified as Chuck blurted out, "His name is Derek but we call him Kung Foo Fighter," he said, making chopping moves with his hands.

The detective-turned-art-therapist noticed a small smile slide over Derek's face at Chuck's description.

"Okay, let's move on," said the fake Mr. Smith. "Each of you has paper and crayons in front of you. I want you to draw something that is important in your life today. Maybe it's a person, a favorite place, or pet. Or maybe it's an event that recently took place. Go ahead and get started. In a little while, I'll come by and discuss it with you."

Despite the chaotic start, the group eagerly began their individual works of art, all while looking at their neighbors' works and talking to each other. Chris and Kat retreated to a corner of the room to give the patients time to draw.

"This is probably the most interesting group I've ever addressed," Chris said.

"No doubt," Kat agreed. "I can see you know what you're talking about. Some of our patients come to us totally non-verbal. After several art therapy sessions, they start speaking again. By giving form to their internal fears and anxieties on paper, they were better able to distance themselves from the source of their problems, which allowed them eventually to vocalize them. It's especially beneficial when you compare an initial drawing to one done after several months. You can literally see the transformation of the psyche. Of course, not everyone benefits in the same way. While I've seen some beautiful images, I've also seen some pretty disturbing stuff. What are you hoping to find?"

"The disturbing stuff. I'm hoping the 'artist' who drew the picture you gave to Nick will draw it again. The person who drew that picture knew things that only the killer could know. It's not foolproof but we have to try."

After allowing twenty minutes of drawing time, Chris walked by each patient, and stopped to offer comments. "That's a beautiful dog," he told one young woman who was in her late teens or early twenties. "He must be very special to you."

"My dad killed him because I forgot to make my bed," she answered very matter-of-factly. "Then I cut myself."

Chris noticed the criss-cross of scars on her arms and knew this girl was a "cutter", someone who used the pain of cutting to experience an emotional release.

Chris moved on, spending a few minutes with each patient before coming to Derek. He sat down next to him and looked at his drawing. It was similar to the one Nick had; a childish rendering of bodies lying on a bed with bloody chest wounds.

"Derek, right?" he asked the young man. Derek nodded. "Tell me about your drawing, Derek. How is this important to you?"

Derek's head was down, his chin nearly touching his chest and his hands were clasped tightly in his lap. No answer.

"Derek? Can you tell me about your drawing?" Chris prodded.

"That's the bad people and I can't talk about them!" Derek blurted. "If I talk about them they will hurt us," he continued.

"Who is *us*?" Chris asked. "What do you mean by the bad people and who are they going to hurt?"

"They are the bad people and I can't talk about them!" he repeated. Before Chris could ask another question, Derek jumped up from his chair and sprinted out of the room.

"Well, that's enough for today," Doctor Westerly dismissed the remaining patients. She then went around the room and picked up the drawings left behind. She removed Derek's drawing and handed it to Chris.

"There you are, Mr. Smith," she grinned. "And anytime you want to come back, just say the word."

Chris rolled up the drawing. "Thanks, but I'll stick to Homicide."

Chapter 32

"So, *Mr. Smith*, how did it go?" Nick greeted Detective Cheetham upon his return to the Homicide unit. "Did you get the goods?"

Chris turned his chair to face the assembly of detectives and Lieutenant Fratello, unrolled Derek's drawing and waved it in the air before handing it to Nick.

"This kid had to have been in the room when the murders happened. The picture he drew today was almost an exact replica of the picture you got from Kat. But if he was in St. Luke's, how could he have been at the scene of the murders? I think he knows something. No doubt in my mind. But getting him to talk may be difficult. He is frightened to death! He kept saying that 'the bad people will hurt us' if he talks. He didn't say exactly who 'us' was. I couldn't get him to say anything else – he ran out of the room," Chris reported.

"What can we do?" Jimmy asked. "The law says we can't bring him in for questioning and we can't even talk to him about the murders while he's a psychiatric patient. I say we go to St. Luke's and make them give us that kid and bring him in for questioning. I can make him talk!"

"Hold on, Jimmy," Lieutenant Fratello cautioned. "While I agree we need to talk to him, we have to do it legally. Chris," he addressed Cheetham. "You and Nick get over to the County Prosecutor's office and find Tim Misny. Tell him what you saw. He might give us a legal opinion and maybe even a warrant to bring this kid in for questioning.

If there is a way to do this, Misny can get it done. He's the most cop-friendly lawyer in the prosecutor's office. Let's see what he can do."

The walk from the Police side of the Justice Center to the County Prosecutor's office on the county side of the building took five minutes as both complexes were housed in the same building and connected via a fifth floor corridor.

They found the prosecutor at his desk behind a stack of files and thick folders. Even seated, he was an imposing figure. His broad shoulders encased in a pin-striped Hugo Boss suit suggested he was every bit as tall as the six-foot-four-inches noted on his doctor's chart. With deep brown eyes and a classic bald head, women often compared him to Yul Brenner. Looking up at the detectives over the top of his glasses, Misny produced a wide grin as he saw Detective Nick Silvano.

"Coach!" he exclaimed, standing up. He maneuvered around the desk and enveloped Nick in a bear hug. "I haven't seen you since you left Narcotics and went over to Homicide. What's it been, a year or so? I don't do the murder cases anymore, I stick with the drugs and racketeering crooks."

"It's only been six months," Nick said. "Sometimes it seems like a year though. Definitely a big change.

"Tim, this is Chris Cheetham, a detective in our office," Nick said and watched the two men shake hands. "Me and Tim go way back," he told Chris. "Back before he was a prosecutor and I was a rookie cop." Nick's tone changed. "Okay, enough of that. We have a situation needing some legal interpretation."

Tim returned to his chair and a stack of files to the far side of the desk. "Have a seat," he indicated two leather chairs directly in front of the desk. "Tell me what's going on."

Nick explained the situation. "We need to interview this kid but he's a patient on the psych ward at St. Luke's. We'd prefer to do it in the Homicide interview room as it seems to inspire those 'come to Jesus' moments that produce confessions. But we don't know if we can legally remove patients from the hospital for that purpose. The question is, can we legally interrogate a patient while they are in the hospital?" Nick explained the roadblocks placed by the hospital administrator and the ex-FBI head of Security. "But now we heard that the administrator, Toby Abernathy, up and quit with no explanation. With him gone, maybe security won't be a problem anymore."

"Sounds like you got a dilemma on your hands, Nicky," the prosecutor said. "Let me do some research on the law pertaining to HIPAA and mental patients' rights. I should have an answer for you in the next twenty-four hours."

"Thanks, Tim."

"How come Misny calls you Coach?" Chris asked as they walked back to their office.

"I met Tim when he was fresh out of law school. He was a part-time prosecutor for the city of Euclid. We used to meet for beers and cigars at the Zone Car bar at the CPPA Union Hall and talk about what type of law he should practice. He started calling me Coach way back then. We've been friends ever since. If there's way for us to talk to Derek, Tim will find it."

"I hope so. Hey, let's get a twelve pack and go fishing,"

Chris said, pointing out the window of the Justice Center toward at Lake Erie. "Look at all the boats out there. The lake looks flat. Perfect day for it. "

"Sounds good to me," Nick agreed. "Let's make our duty reports and tell Fratello what we have going on with Misny. I'll call Dwaine, the new guy over at the DEA and see if he wants to go with us. Met him at the Roach. He's alright but he's got a thing about his hair."

"Sure," Chris agreed. "The more the merrier."

Chapter 33

Nick texted DEA Agent Dwaine Brosemer.

Nick: Hey, Dwaine. Want to go fishing

Dwaine: When

Nick: Now

Dwaine: Sure

Nick: Good. Meet at the Roach in 30

Dwaine: K

"Dwaine's in. Going to meet us at the Roach in half an hour," Nick said.

"Okay. I'll call Cindy and tell her to hold dinner. Maybe I'll bring some fresh Perch home," Chris said.

"You know that ain't gonna happen, buddy. While we might actually get some fish you know we'll have some cocktails after. You won't get home until late. Might as well tell Cindy you'll see her tomorrow. It's already four o'clock and we still have to get bait. And my boat needs some gas – which you and Dwaine are going to buy."

"Shit Nicky, gas is almost five bucks a gallon at the Marina," Chris complained.

"That's $2.50 for you and $2.50 for his Hairness. Lake Erie perch is twenty-one bucks a pound and you can have what we catch. I got plenty in the freezer and Dwaine has never even seen a Perch much less caught one. He's the ultimate bachelor - doesn't even own a frying pan. You're gonna make out on this trip. All we need is for the fish to cooperate!"

"Well, since you put it that way," Chris relented. "I'll buy the shiners and the gas.

Dwaine was waiting at the curb in front of the Cockroach Inn, combing his hair when Chris and Nick pulled up. "Hey man, this back seat is too small for me and it's messing up my hair," he complained, placing both hands over his head to protect his salt- and-pepper gelled wave from touching the headliner of the small Honda Civic.

They made it to the East 55th Street Marina in five minutes. "We got lucky; rush hour isn't for another hour yet," Nick observed as he swiped his gate card through the reader at the marina parking lot entrance. The gate squeaked loudly as it slowly rolled open.

"Christ, look at all the seagulls," Dwaine said from the back seat. "Hope nothing lands on my hair." Dwaine struggled to remove himself from the back seat and get a look at his hair in the side view mirror at the same time.

"Oh my God," Chris complained, extracting a cooler full of beer from the open trunk. "He never stops looking at himself!"

"You two play nice," Nick admonished. They walked the length of the floating wooden dock to Nick's Rinker. There was a slight south breeze and the lake was flat. "Nice day," Nick said.

After removing the mooring cover, Nick fired up the boat and let the engine idle for a couple of minutes. He instructed Chris to undo the two dock lines then placed the boat into reverse and carefully maneuvered away from the dock. Once clear he shifted into forward gear and slowly motored toward the marina gas dock, obeying the No Wake signs at the end of each dock. Nick stopped the pump at twenty dollars.

"I'll take it easy on your wallet today, Chris. We're only going out about a mile to where that big pack of boats is anchored. The Perch must be schooled up close in today."

"Thanks Nicky," Chris said. "Five dozen minnows enough?"

"Yeah," Nick replied. "Grab a bag of ice for the cooler too."

Chris picked up the minnow bucket, jumped off the boat and walked to the marina office to pay for the gas and minnows. When Chris returned with a full bucket of bait, Nick turned the boat and motored slowly past the buoy marking the end of the break wall protecting the marina from the onslaught of waves kicked up by frequent storms. Once past the break wall, he pushed the throttle forward and headed out onto the lake. Before reaching the pack of fishing boats, he reduced speed then dropped anchor at the outer ring of boats. Nick handed Dwaine an 'ugly stick' fishing rod.

"What am I supposed to do with this?" Dwaine asked.

"You put a minnow on each hook on the spreaders, let the line go all the way to the bottom, reel it up a couple of turns and then wait for the fish to bite. Got it?"

"How do I know when to pull it up?" Dwaine asked.

"Just wait for a good tug on the line then yank it up and begin reeling it in," Chris said.

It took only a couple of minutes before Dwaine caught the first fish. "Look at me, I'm a natural," he boasted as he allowed Nick to take the small fish off the hook and place it into the cooler.

The fishing was slow and the talk turned to work. Nick

and Chris told Dwaine about their current case. "We got a name we need to check out – a guy from Wisconsin. Chris is trying to get information. All we have is a driver's license."

"Yeah – and the official channels are slow," Chris said.

"I've got a good buddy in the Minneapolis DEA field office. Name's Brent. He may know someone in Wisconsin. Want me to give him a call?" Dwaine asked.

"That would be great," Chris said as he pulled in another Perch.

"You're going to call him now?" Nick asked as Dwaine pulled his phone out of a pocket.

"Sure, why not? What's the guy's name and where is he from?"

"His name is Brian Dirks and he's from Hudson, Wisconsin. The info is back at the office. Don't you need it?" Chris asked.

Dwaine cast an amused glance at Chris and ran his fingers through his hair. "I'm a fucking Federal Agent. I don't need anything else."

Chris rolled his eyes as Dwaine made the call.

"Hey Brent! This is your old pal Dwaine calling from Cleveland. I'm on a boat with a couple cop friends out fishing on Lake Erie – living the good life. Hold on, I'm putting you on speaker," he said. He pushed the speaker icon on the phone. "Can you hear me okay?"

"Yep. I can hear you fine. How's the hair holding up?"

"Holy shit," Chris interrupted. "Is your hair world famous?"

Laughter boomed through the phone's speaker. "It sure is! You guys tired of hearing about his hair yet?"

"Okay, okay," Dwaine conceded. "Are you done? This is serious." He introduced Nick and Chris. "These guys have a name off a Wisconsin Drivers License they need to track down. Brian Dirks – that's regular spelling of Brian and Dirks is D-I-R-K-S. City of Hudson. That's in your neck of the woods, isn't it?"

"It's about thirty miles down the road and across the St. Croix river," Brent explained. "I-94 is a straight shot from here to there so we actually cross paths with the Hudson cops quite a bit. If people knew the kind of shit that was coming down that freeway they'd hightail it to the backwoods of Wisconsin. Anyway, what do you want to know?"

"The usual," Nick said. "Does he have a rap sheet, are there any warrants out for him, and maybe they could check where he's been for the last month."

"I've got a contact over there. Give me a day and I'll get back to you."

"That would be great," said Nick. "Saves us a lot of official paperwork crap that we don't have time for..."

"Hey, I got another bite," Dwaine interrupted. "Wow, look at the size of that one," he said as he pulled in a big Sheepshead.

"Throw that one back," Chris said. "They aren't good to eat."

"Are you really fishing, Dwaine?" Brent shouted through the phone. "They pay you to go fishing? I'm going to ask for a transfer to Cleveland."

Dwaine laughed. "Ten thousand lakes in Minnesota and you don't get to go fishing? I don't believe it. Anyway, get back to me as soon as you can. Thanks, man."

Another hour passed. "That's the last minnow guys," Chris said. "We are officially out of bait but we have beer left. How about I clean the fish while you guys finish up the beer? It's still early enough for me to get home with some fresh Perch."

"Sure," answered Nick.

"Hey Nicky," Dwaine said.

"What?"

"Next time, make sure I have a fishing license so you don't break the law!'

"You're an asshole," Nick said.

Chapter 34

I t had been raining all day so Joshua opted for an Uber ride to work that evening. Joshua's Uber Driver pulled his black Jeep Grand Cherokee into the parking lot of St. Luke's, its tires splashing water from the puddles left by another of Lake Erie's late summer storms. The Jeep slowed to allow two nurses sharing one umbrella scurry across the parking lot. His ride rounded the corner of the building to the entrance of Behavioral Health. Police cars were double parked at the curb. Joshua's pulse quickened. He counted four black and whites and one Ford Taurus, probably a detective car, he thought. He fought back the impulse to tell the driver to keep going.

This can't be good. He took a deep breath, closed his eyes, and began a silent count to control his anxiety. One, two, and three... It could be nothing. It wasn't unusual to have police cars at the hospital. Four, five, six.

"Sir, are you okay?" Joshua heard the Uber Driver say.

"Yeah...I'm fine, sorry. Just haven't woke up yet," Joshua remarked as he reached over the seat and pressed a five dollar tip into the driver's hand. He opened the door and held his nursing bag over his head in a vain attempt to stay dry. He moved at a slow lope, which was as fast as his damaged body allowed, and entered the building through the door held open for him by a uniformed Cleveland cop.

Joshua stopped just inside the small lobby and shook the water from his bag. Looking around he saw several cops and hospital security standing in small groups. Employees brushed by him, racing to get out of the rain.

Big John bumped into him. "Sorry, Josh. You better get out of the way before you get run over. C'mon, let's punch in before we're both late."

"Right behind you," Joshua said. Another glance confirmed that no one was paying any attention to him. He relaxed. The line to the Kronos time clock was longer than usual. Joshua kept his eyes fixed to Big John's back, pretending disinterest in the police-filled lobby.

"What's going on, Officer? Why are all you guys here?" a nurse in front of Big John asked the nearest cop.

"Just a missing patient, don't worry. We'll find him," the officer responded as he walked away. Joshua ventured a sidelong glance at the officer's retreating back.

"Josh," Big John poked him. "Your turn."

"Oh yeah, sorry." Joshua pressed his finger to the pad and was rewarded with a chirp confirming the machine recognized him. Turning away from the time clock he felt a heavy hand on his shoulder. He stiffened. *Oh God, what now.*

"Hey, if we're lucky, maybe Trudy got away today," Big John said while removing his hand from Joshua's shoulder. Just Big John, Joshua realized. Not the police coming to throw the cuffs on and drag him away to jail.

"Josh," Big John poked him with his elbow. "What's up, no funny bone today?'

"Sorry. Just can't seem to get it going." Joshua wished he had put extra Ativan into his bag with the Vicodin. They passed through the double doors to Center One. A young nurse's aide stood in the hallway, surrounded by hospital security, Cleveland cops, and the nursing supervisor.

"I don't know where he went," the aide said loudly, throwing her hands up in the air in a futile attempt for the group to move away from her. "All I know is that I was making my final rounds and his room was empty. We looked everywhere but he was just gone!"

The nursing station was buzzing with activity. Bill, the medical secretary, stood guard at the other end of the hallway preventing the patients from leaving the Day Area. "Get your ass back behind the line," he told Trudy, "or I swear to God I'll get the drugs myself and put you to sleep until next week!"

"All I want to do is talk to that cute cop over there," Trudy waved to a young black uniformed officer, trying to catch his attention. "This is still America and I got rights!"

"Not in here. Not in my world," Bill muttered, unfortunately just loud enough to be overheard by the nursing supervisor.

"Bill, stop with that talk. Not now - please," the nursing supervisor reproached as she passed by him on her way to the group of cops standing just inside the unit's doors.

"You're gonna get it now, Bill," Trudy mocked. "You can't talk to me like that."

Ignoring Trudy, Bill turned and swiped his ID through the card reader on the door to the Nurses Station.

"Tell your guys they can't be in here with guns on," the Day Shift Supervisor said as she waved her arms in an attempt to keep them from advancing any further onto the mental health floor. "We have searched the floor several times. He is not here and that is final. Now get your weapons off of my floor!" she demanded, holding the inner door open with one hand and pointing to the exit with her other hand.

"Okay, guys, let's move this to the other side of the doors," Lieutenant Jon Fratello conceded. "C'mon Miss," he addressed a frightened young aide. "Just a couple more questions and you can go home. We're almost done here."

"Okay, now," the Nursing Supervisor addressed her staff once the last uniformed cop had left the unit. "Let's start Report before anything else happens to keep me from getting out of here. Maybe I should just friggin' move in here." She stomped her way down the hall, past Joshua and Big John, and into the nursing station. Joshua took a chair at the cluttered table in the rear of the nursing station and grabbed a Census sheet from the pile in the center of the table.

"What happened?" Cassie asked as she entered the room and dropped her nursing bag onto the floor next to the last open chair at the table. "What's with all the cops?"

"David Feighan has gone missing," the Day Shift Supervisor said. "We took his dinner into his room and found his hospital gown and pajama bottoms folded neatly on the bed. He was nowhere to be found." She looked around at her staff. "I am really beginning to hate this place."

"Beginning?" Bill teased.

She glared at him and then continued. "We had hospital security search the building and grounds but he just vanished! We had to call in the cops and now they are crawling all over. Even the Commander of the Homicide Unit is here. Probably because the guy's wife was murdered - but he couldn't have done it - he never left this unit once while he's been here."

"How did he get off the floor?" Joshua asked, feigning concern.

"We had two separate groups of student nurses coming and going off the unit all day. Couple that with visiting hours just starting and some employee or a guard buzzed the door open without checking first," she theorized. "It could have been anybody. We had students, doctors, cleaning people, respiratory therapists and who knows who else had access to the button inside the nursing station when he left. I suppose that since he wasn't in hospital clothes, whoever answered the buzzer request to unlock the door didn't have a clue that he was a patient and not some visitor. Of course, nobody is admitting to it so we may never really know how it happened. You could see on the security tape that one of the students even held the door open for him as their group left for the day. That was a little after four."

"Where did he go after that?" Cassie inquired.

"Security queued up the parking lot tape and you could see Feighan get into a waiting car in the lot and drive off - although it was raining and the camera view was blurry. You couldn't even tell what kind of car it was, that's how hard it was raining."

"Jesus," Cassie said. "That guy acted like he was a vegetable the whole time he was here. What do you think, Josh?" she asked. "You were his nurse most of the time he was here. Was he capable of doing something like this?"

"Nope. That guy never said a word around me the whole time he was here under my care," Joshua lied. "I never even saw him leave his room, much less talk. Looks like he had help if he had a car waiting for him." Joshua silently thanked David Feighan for not escaping on his shift.

"Abernathy quits, and now this," the nursing supervisor sighed. "C'mon, let's get nursing report done before something else happens."

Chapter 35

"Thank the Lord that Feighan didn't walk out on our shift," Joshua heard Cassie tell Big John as he filled her large Styrofoam cup with steaming coffee from the unit's Keurig machine. "Whoa, that's enough," she stopped him. "Have to save room for my It Works! Greens on the Go. Donna and Emily, nurses from the ER, got me started on it. Sadie from the pharmacy sells it. This stuff really works! I've lost eleven pounds," Cassie said, stirring her coffee with a plastic spoon. "Want some?" She reached into her pocket for another packet and waved it at Big John.

"Naw," he replied, "I like Jamison in my coffee but can't use it here." He laughed then. "Like anyone would notice."

Joshua checked the computer for new patient orders and was reading patient notes when he felt his pocket "buzzing" and then heard the muted ring of his phone. He looked at the Caller ID. *Unknown Caller.* Joshua pressed the green Accept button.

"Who is this?" he said roughly, hoping to discourage a potential telemarketer.

"Hi, Josh. Miss me yet?" a familiar voice said.

"What the..." It was Feighan! Joshua got up from the desk and hurriedly stepped into the nursing station's unisex bathroom, shutting the door behind him.

"Where are you?" Joshua coarsely whispered.

"Someplace safe where they can't find me," David said. "I saw my chance and I took it. Have they discovered that guy in the room across from me is missing his clothes yet? They're a little big for me but they did the job. I got lucky. A sweet little student nurse held the door open for me and let me use her cell phone to call my guy and he picked me up. All my stars lined up, that's for sure. I even got all of my money transferred into my off-shore account. You gotta love online banking," he said.

"David...."

"Hey - listen to me, Josh," David interrupted. "I heard some art therapist guy was on the floor asking Derek questions about a picture he drew. That little freak is drawing pictures of Johanna and Michael's dead bodies and showing them around! So far he hasn't said anything but it won't be long before somebody puts one and one together and comes up with two dead bodies! I'm safe but you'll be in big trouble if the kid talks. Any idea if he'll be discharged soon?"

Joshua took a deep breath before answering. "I don't know. I'll go and check the social worker's notes on the computer. Hold on." Joshua left the bathroom and returned to his computer at the Nurses Station. Balancing the phone between his shoulder and ear he logged on. Derek was being released to a group home in Akron in the morning. He began reading the note to David.

"A cab voucher has been issued to pick him up at ten..."

"Stop talking, Josh!" David commanded. "Just text the information to me at this number and be sure to clear your phone."

"Sure," Joshua replied.

"Hey - if the supervisor sees you on your phone at work, you're going to get written up again," Big John's voice boomed behind him. Startled, Joshua's phone fell from his shoulder onto the counter. "Yeah, you should be scared! The bitch wrote me up yesterday for doing the same thing. Just so you know."

"Thanks, John.   I'm just trying to get the VA on the phone to check on my scripts. They keep you on hold forever," Joshua lied as he placed the phone back to his ear.

"That-a-boy, Josh. Way to keep your cool," David said. "Text me the information on Derek. I'll contact you after he is taken care of."

"You're not going to hurt him, are you?" Joshua quietly asked.

"No. Nobody else has to get hurt if you do your part. Everything will be just fine. Keep your ears open and your mouth shut."

Joshua texted the information on Derek's discharge then erased the call records from his phone.

Chapter 36

"C 'mon, Nicky. Let's go!" Jimmy entered the Homicide office waving a piece of paper in his hand. "Misny couldn't get a warrant to bring Derek Stanton in for questioning but he got a judge to sign papers so we can question him at the hospital. Said the judge didn't want to be responsible for the kid's well-being while in our custody but as long as he was in the hospital, it's okay."

Grabbing his suit coat from the back of the chair, Nick stood up. "Wait," he said. He reached into the desk's top drawer, pulled out his snub-nose .38 Smith and Wesson revolver, and wrapped it around his left ankle with a Velcro holster. "Now, we can go."

Jimmy grinned. "Don't leave home without it."

"Hospital Security will call for that ex-FBI security director and you know he'll screw with us over carrying our guns into the hospital so bring your backup too, Jimmy. These days, I don't want to be caught unarmed. Never know when something will jump off."

"Good idea," his partner agreed.

It was still raining when they pulled into St. Luke's parking lot. "Man, it seems like it's been raining forever," Jimmy said. He got out of the passenger seat and sprinted for the doors of the Center One Behavioral Health Unit.

There was no security guard present in the office and the security office door was locked. Just as Nick lifted the hospital phone's handset to summon security, the elevator opened and a security guard came toward them.

"Can I help you gentlemen," the uniformed security guard asked.

"Yes." Jimmy handed a sheaf of papers to the young guard. "We have a court order giving us permission to speak to one of the patients on Center One."

The guard took the papers from the detective's outstretched hand and without looking at them, opened the security office door with a key and laid the papers on a desk.

"I have to call my boss," he said. "He's gonna be really happy to see you guys after everything that has been going wrong in this crazy-assed hospital." He picked up the phone, muttering as it rang. "Friggin' big boss just up and quits, a murderer walks out on my shift and now..." His tone abruptly changed. "Yes sir, Mr. Winston. There are a couple of cops here with a court order to speak to a patient. No, I did not let them on the floor," the guard said defensively. "No, I do not know what it's about. I didn't look at the court papers!" He hung up, snarling, "That's what you get the big bucks for, asshole."

The guard turned to face the two detectives. "He's on his way. Sorry, guys. My boss says he's 'retired' FBI but everyone knows he was kicked out. He still thinks he's a big deal and lets us know it every chance he gets."

"No problem – we know the type," Jimmy said. "Say, have you heard anything about why Abernathy quit? You know, was he being investigated or anything? In any trouble?"

"Naw, just the usual 'personal considerations and want-ing to spend more time with my family' bullshit," the guard reported. "Although there's been some talk that he's sick."

Dean Winston stormed into the small security office without acknowledging the detectives. "Did you lock up their weapons?" he barked at the guard.

"Not yet, I just got here," the guard answered.

"Well, do it already. You know the rules. Or do you need to go back for more training?" He picked up the papers, snapped them open and began to read.

The guard bent over and unlocked the small safe containing patient valuables. Several large brown envelopes slid out onto the floor as Nick and Jimmy waited to place their duty weapons into the safe. The guard was trying to make room for the cops' guns.

"For Christ's sakes Officer Kimble, pick that stuff up and put it back inside the safe before somebody's wallet or money gets lost."

Winston turned to Nick and flashed a conspiratorial smirk. "I keep trying to find good help but there just doesn't seem to be anybody qualified to do this job."

Before Nick could muster an answer the guard stood up and pointed to the name badge displayed prominently on his shirt, "My name is Buckley, not Kimble, and we have asked you many times for a bigger safe to hold all this crap."

Winston glared at this challenge to his authority. Jimmy quickly interjected. "Look, lock up our weapons and let's get to the interview with Derek Stanton. You guys can talk this out later after we have done our job here, okay?"

After the detectives' weapons were secured in the safe, Winston unlocked the outer door to Center One and Nick and Jimmy followed him to the nursing station.

"How can I help you?" the Charge Nurse asked.

"These officers have a court order to conduct an interview with a patient, Derek Stanton," the head of security stated. "Please have someone bring the patient to the interview room."

"I would if I could," she replied. "But he's not here. He left an hour ago for a group home in Akron. We found a place that would accept him, the social worker issued a cab voucher, and he has been discharged."

"Okay then, that's it," Winston said. "You guys can leave my hospital now."

Ignoring Winston, Nick turned to the Charge Nurse. "Can we have the address of the group home and the name of the taxi company that picked him up?"

"Absolutely," she answered. "Just a moment." She returned a few minutes later with the information. Winston held out his hand to intercept the note but she pulled it back and handed it to Nick with a look that said, "See what we have to put up with?"

Winston escorted the detectives down the hall to the exit doors.

The security door was locked and the office was empty. "Where the hell is my guard?" Winston scowled.

He fumbled with the large ring of keys before finding the one that unlocked the door. Nick and Jimmy followed him into the office and saw a large piece of paper lying on the desk. Printed in bold red letters was a message: "I quit. And my name is Buckley!" The guard's name tag and keys lay on the desk.

"Looks like somebody is not happy, Winston," Jimmy smirked. "Give us our weapons and we'll get out of your hair."

Winston looked at the locked safe then picked up one of the hand-held radios from the wall charger. He pressed the talk button. "Any guard who can come to the security office and open the safe, please respond."

A few seconds passed before the handset crackled. "Where's Buckley and who is this on the radio?"

"This is Director Winston and I need a guard to open the safe."

"Where's Buckley?" the voice repeated.

"Buckley's not here!" Winston answered tensely.

"Don't you know the combination?"

"Just come here and open the damn safe," ordered the security chief. After a couple of minutes he picked up the portable radio again. "Somebody better get here quick to open this safe!"

As soon as he tossed the radio back onto the desk a middle-aged guard sauntered into the office. "Where's Buckley? It's his turn to man the office." The sentence was no sooner out of his mouth than he saw the note. Assessing the situation, he didn't bother to wait for an answer but rather knelt over to the safe and spun the combination dial. He turned the handle, pulled the door open, and shuffled back as the Detectives' weapons and several large brown envelopes containing patient belongings spilled out onto the floor.

"Damn it!" the guard said, annoyed. "When are we going to get a bigger safe to hold all of this shit?"

"You stay here and take care of the office," Winston ordered the guard, not bothering to answer his question. He turned and stalked away. The guard gave Nick and Jimmy their weapons back.

"Thanks," Nick said.   The detectives did a cursory examination of their weapons, placed them into their shoulder holsters and walked out of St. Luke's.

"So, what's the plan?" Jimmy asked, easing the car out into traffic. "The boss is not going to be happy to hear our guy is gone. First Feighan and now Derek. We're beginning to look like the Keystone Cops."

"I know," Nick replied. "Let's try to locate the Stanton kid before we tell Fratello. I got a contact at the cab company."

Nick placed a call. "Hello, Kathy? This is Nick Silvano. Yeah, I'm fine. How are you? Listen, I need to know what cab picked up a fare from St. Luke's psychiatric ward this morning. It would have been around 8 a.m., destination Akron, one male passenger named Derek Stanton. Yes, I can hold on," Nick said, activating the speaker phone.

"You got people everywhere?" Jimmy asked.

"Yeah, you can never have enough." A few minutes passed before Kathy's voice replaced the generic elevator music.

"Nicky, this is really weird," she said. "I just spoke to the driver and he said that as soon as he left the hospital a car with a guy waving a cop badge pulled up alongside him and told him to pull over. The guy took the kid from the cab and put him into his car. Told the cabbie that the fare was wanted on a warrant and was being arrested. Our driver said he objected but the cop told him not to interfere with official police business or else he would be arrested too!"

"Jesus, Kathy," Nick responded, concerned. "We don't

have a warrant out for him. Did the cabbie get any proof of identification or a name or something?"

"Hold on, I'll ask him. He's still on the other line."

"Mel, did you ask for ID from the cop?" they heard her say.

"What the hell, Kathy!" came the driver's voice. "The guy shows a badge, looks like he's in a plain clothes cop car, who am I to question him? I ain't going to jail over some kid wanted on a warrant. The kid never said anything either. He just got out of the cab and into the back of the cop car. The cop didn't even cuff him. Just took him by the elbow, dumped him into the car and drove off. It only took a couple of minutes."

"Ask him what kind of car and which way did it go?" Jimmy said.

"I heard him," the cab driver answered. "The guy was about forty years old wearing a brown suit. Driving a blue Taurus and went south on West 25th Street. That's all I know."

"Tell the driver thanks and if he thinks of anything else to call us," Nick said. "You got my number, Kathy."

"Will do," Kathy said.

"Let's head back to the Justice Center and tell the boss," Nick said. "This is beginning to sound like one big conspiracy."

Chapter 37

Minneapolis DEA Agent Brent Anderson drove over the I-94 bridge from Minnesota to Wisconsin. Fishing boats dotted the St. Croix River below and he silently promised himself a day on the river, and soon!

He eased into the exit lane for Hudson and reduced his speed to the posted twenty-five miles per hour as he coasted past the marina and into the city's downtown. Once known primarily as a bedroom community of the Twin Cities of Minneapolis and St. Paul, Minnesota, its proximity to the Twin Cities made it convenient for many of its citizens to commute to work in the metropolitan areas. Criminals who worked at theft, forgery, drugs, and the occasional murder, also found its location convenient.

Brent passed the Dairy Queen, several bars, restaurants, and antique shops that lined the city's historic downtown. He turned left on Vine Street, then right at the entrance to the police department's parking lot. He parked his government-issued Dodge Challenger into a spot marked Police Vehicles Only and tossed a US Government Official Vehicle placard onto the dash.

The small brick building adjoined the library and housed a staff of twenty-four full-time cops and ten more who had part-time positions.

Sergeant Barb Delander, a ten-year veteran, was sipping her second cup of coffee of the morning when her desk phone rang. The Caller ID showed it was Vanessa at the front desk.

"Yes?" she inquired.

"Sergeant Delander, there's a Brent Anderson here to see you. Says he is from the Minneapolis DEA."

"Thanks Vanessa. I'll be right there," Barb replied, wondering what brought her colleague across the river. She rose from her desk, brushed a strand of brown hair across her forehead, and walked down the short hallway to the locked entrance that separated the officers and office staff from the general public. She opened the door to the entrance area.

"Hi Brent!" she greeted him. "What happened, did you get lost or something?"

"Hey Barb, good to see you," the DEA agent replied. "No, didn't get lost. A buddy in Cleveland reached out to me with questions about a guy from Hudson so rather than make a phone call, thought I'd get out of the city and drive over."

"C'mon into my office. Want a cup of coffee?"

"That'd be great." Brent settled into a chair across from Barb's desk. His casual attire of blue jeans, a blue jeans shirt, and Red Wing work boots contrasted with Barb's crisp black uniform. His brown hair touched the top of his shirt collar; he looked like any average guy on the street. Someone you wouldn't glance twice at; which was the desired goal of an undercover agent.

Brent explained what his friend needed and Sergeant Delander took notes. "Brian Dirks. D-I-R-K-S," she repeated. "Yeah, the name sounds familiar. What do the Cleveland cops want with him?"

"Right now he's a person of interest in a murder," Brent explained. "The cops have his driver's license and are trying to establish his whereabouts for the last couple of weeks."

"Okay, let's take a look," Barb said. She typed the name into the VISIONS records management system which would tell her if Brian Dirks had contact with any law enforcement agency in St. Croix County.

"Well, well," she said. Brent looked at her expectantly. "Unless he has teleporting superpowers, there's no way he could have committed a murder in Cleveland during the time frame you're asking about. He's currently a guest of St. Croix County where he's been sitting in jail for the past thirty days."

"What's the charge?" Brent asked.

"He had an outstanding warrant for possession for sale of a dangerous drug...methamphetamine."

"Well, how about that," Brent said. "I guess I should have checked into our system first before coming out here. He would have shown up there with a crosscheck. Sorry I took up your time, Barb. How did you guys get him?"

"Routine traffic stop," she said, "and you know, you never waste my time, Brent. Our department might be on the small side from what you are used to but we do get the big city problems also. It's always good to stay in touch."

"Since I'm here, think I can talk to this Dirks guy?" the agent asked.

"Sure. I'll call the jail and let them know you're on your way over."

"Okay, great. Hey, my wife and I were planning on coming over to have dinner at Sunsets. You and Mike want to join us? My treat," he added.

"Getting Mike off the tractor might be hard at this time

of the year. I'll tell him you're buying. He might come down off the combine for that," Sergeant Delander laughed.

"Uncle Sam has lots of money and the Hudson cops have always cooperated very well with the DEA so there won't be a problem. Just let me know when you guys can make it," Brent said

The Sergeant escorted her visitor to the station lobby. "Thanks again, Barb. I'll let you know how it turns out." The DEA Agent went out the door and the Sergeant noticed Vanessa also staring at the retreating agent.

"Put your eyes back in your head, Vanessa, he's married," Barb said.

"Shit, I don't care," Vanessa said, still gazing at the empty doorway. "He's one hot guy! Where do you know him from?"

"We worked together on a case, years ago," Barb explained. "A guy was selling meth in Minnesota; Woodbury and Lake Elmo. Turns out he was manufacturing it over here in Burkhardt. He stayed in the woods so the smell wouldn't alert any neighbors. Brent had an informant who led us right into the woods and the would-be chemist. Took a lot of meth off the streets that day. We stay in touch and help each other occasionally," Barb said.

Five minutes after leaving the Hudson Police Department, Brent reached the St. Croix County Jail. An officer greeted him and showed him to an interrogation room. Brent took a chair opposite the table from where Brian Dirks was already seated. Brian was twenty-eight years old and already had a long rap sheet; mostly for petty crimes like theft and drug possession. *Had he graduated to murder?*

"Hi Brian, I'm DEA, Agent Anderson from the Minneapolis office."

"Yeah?" Brian asked warily. "What do you want from me? I didn't do nuthin' in the Cities."

"I know that, Brian. I'm not here to hassle you. I just want to ask you some questions. Okay?"

"I guess," Brian answered sullenly.

"Have you ever been to Cleveland, Ohio?"

"Yeah."

"What were you there for?"

"Was living there for awhile. Got busted for drug possession and sent to a halfway house. Got kicked out of there."

"What'd you do then?"

"Nuthin' much. Hung out."

"Where'd you stay?"

"Homeless shelter."

"Which one?"

"Why do you wanna know that for?" Brian asked.

"Humor me," the agent answered.

"Think it was called Hamilton."

"Okay. How'd you get back to Wisconsin?"

"My mom sent me some money for bus fare and I came home."

"And then got stopped by the cops here," Brent prompted.

"Yeah," he said.

"Do you have your wallet here at the jail?"

"No. I lost it in Cleveland."

"At the homeless shelter maybe?"

"Yeah, maybe," Brian said. "That's the last place I remember having it. Somebody probably took it from me when I was sleeping. That happens a lot. You have to put your stuff in your crotch if you want to keep it but I forgot and it was gone."

"Well, I know for a fact that you lost it at the shelter, Brian. Want to know how I know that?"

"I guess."

"Because someone was using your ID. And the Cleveland cops are looking for you."

"Yeah, well. I've been right here. Couldn't have done nuthin'. What do they want to talk to me for anyway?"

"They think you killed two people."

"Oh man!" Brian exclaimed, animated for the first time since the DEA Agent came to talk to him. "Well hey – it wasn't me! I've been in here! You know that, right?" he asked anxiously.

"Yeah, Brian. It couldn't have been you. Turns out sitting in jail has been a lucky thing for you."

"What about my ID – can you get that back for me?"

"Don't worry, I'll let the Cleveland cops know your situation and maybe you'll get your ID back. You may need to testify to your whereabouts should the case go to court. You okay with that or do we have to make you testify?"

"I'll testify. I didn't have nothing to do with any murders," Brian answered nervously.

Brent ended the interview and a guard escorted him out of the jail building. Back in his car, Brent found Detective Silvano's number where he'd scribbled it on a piece of paper. He dialed the Cleveland cop.

"Hi Nick, its Brent Anderson from the Minneapolis DEA office. Dwaine's buddy."

"Brent – what's up, you find out anything on the Brian Dirks guy?" Nick asked.

"I don't know if this helps or not but Brian Dirks has been sitting in the St. Croix County jail over in Hudson, Wisconsin for the past thirty days. I talked to the Hudson cops and even went to the jail and talked to the kid. Looked at the arrest reports and booking sheets too. It wasn't him in Cleveland. He's been here the whole time. Locked up."

"Shit," Nick said. "I knew it couldn't be that easy. He can't be our guy then, the timeframe doesn't fit. Someone must have gotten hold of his driver's license."

"Well, he said he might have lost it at the Hamilton Homeless shelter. That was the last place he remembers having it," Brent said.

"You saved us a lot of paperwork and phone calls, Brent," Nick said. "We owe you one."

"Maybe I can get a few days off and come down to see Dwaine and you can get me out fishing," Brent said.

"You got it," Nick answered. "Anytime." He hung up the phone.

Damn it! Now they had to start looking for a new suspect.

Chapter 38

"What's wrong, Nicky?" Nick and Kat had finished dinner and were sitting on the balcony of their apartment watching the sun set over Lake Erie. "You haven't said a word since dinner," Kat asked.

"It's this friggin' murder case that's got me wound up tight. Two dead bodies, two missing suspects; what am I missing here? There's got to be a common denominator. I just haven't found it yet."

"Give it time, you'll find it," she assured him.

"Kat - who has keys for the emergency doors to the psych ward? If there was a problem on the floor and they had to use the emergency doors, how would they get out?"

"Well, I suppose hospital security has keys and I think there's a set of master keys that the Charge Nurse on each shift carries. They hang them on a hook behind the door to the supply closet inside the Nurses Station. I know because one time I watched them get the keys to unlock a shower door. A patient had locked herself in and wouldn't come out. Really anyone on staff knows where they are and anyone could get to them if they needed to."

Nick's eyebrows raised and he tapped a forefinger to his lip. "So, the Charge Nurse could unlock the emergency exit doors, go outside and then come back inside the hospital without sounding any alarms?"

"Well, sure, I guess so," she answered. "But, in reality, anybody who knew the location of the keys could use them. Since they are located inside the locked Nurses

Station and are not marked as master keys, any staff member who had access to the nursing station - from a physician to the cleaning person - could use them."

"That's it!" Nick exclaimed.

"What's it?" Kat returned.

Nick stood up from the patio chair and smacked his fist into his open palm. "It had to be somebody on staff with the keys to unlock the emergency doors, allow David Feighan or Derek Stanton or maybe even both of them, to leave, commit the murders and then return to the hospital floor without being picked up by the cameras. They screwed up when they parked the car within view of a security camera."

Turning to Kat he placed both of his hands onto her shoulders. "You may have just solved a double murder. Now, we just have to find out who was on staff the night of the murders. But that Security Chief prick, Dean Winston, won't want to give us any access to the staffing schedule..."

"You don't need him, Sweetie," Kat interrupted. "You forget, I'm also a staff member but one with access to all nursing notes and charting activities. And I can do it from right here," she said, moving into the living room and pointing at her laptop computer sitting on the coffee table. "All I have to do is log into the hospital's system and I can tell you every note on every patient that was entered and who put the information into the charts on the day in question."

"Well, okay then Inspector Clouseau," Nick said. "Let's do it!"

Kat opened up her laptop and playfully pushed Nick away from her. "Go on - pour me a glass of wine. This might take some time. And it's going to cost you," she said as she turned on the computer and started logging in.

Nick poured the wine and then filled a rock glass with a generous amount of Gentlemen Jack for himself. He walked back to the couch where Kat sat bent over the computer, set the glass down on the table, gently turned her face to his and gave her a long, slow kiss.

"There," he said. "That's your first payment. There's more where that came from."

"Thanks," Kat said. "I think I like these working conditions!" She picked up the wine glass with her right hand and took a sip while her left hand moved across the keyboard.

"Okay," she said. "Here is the night of the murders. There were only six patients that night so the staffing would have consisted of a minimum crew." She turned to Nick. "Believe me, Toby Abernathy would have had the head nurse's job if she allowed more than the minimum number of people to take care of our patients...oops, I mean customers! Before each shift the head nurse in the hospital checks the patient count for each floor and assigns the staffing," Kat explained. "Then, they will pull nurses or aides from one floor and send them to another floor to even out the staffing levels. If they don't need a nurse or aide, they'll call them at home and tell them not come in. Trust me, night shift nurses hate to be called off after they slept all day and are ready for work. They already slept. Day shift is another story. They can roll over and go back to sleep."

"Thanks for the education on the inner workings of Behavioral Health," Nick said. "Now, tell me who was there and had access to the master keys."

"Okay, there were no admission or discharges. Only two staff nurses were assigned to that twelve hour shift and they were the only ones who made any computer entries."

"Names?" Nick prompted.

"John Archibald and Joshua Ramsey. I don't see anybody else, but then again, this is not from the staffing book on the floor. This is just who made computer entries that night."

"Well, that's a good place for me to start," Nick remarked. Glass of bourbon in his hand, he walked over to the balcony windows. He stared out over Lake Erie, sipped his bourbon and watched a large iron ore boat inch across the horizon. He turned back to Kat.

"What about those two nurses? Do you think they could be somehow involved?"

"John Archibald, we call him Big John, is a good nurse. He's studying for his RN degree to conform to Toby's requirements for all of his nurses to have degrees. Now, Joshua Ramsey is a different story. He is an Army trained RN. He was wounded in Iraq and has some difficulty physically doing his job. There's some talk about him and pain meds; he may be in more pain than he lets on and some suspect he's a pill popper – but he has a Veterans Administration prescription for Vicodin, so he's safe. He is a good nurse and a strong advocate for his patients. He also does a lot of volunteer work at the homeless shelter on Hamilton Avenue."

"I know that place," Nick said.

"Well, I know Joshua spends a lot of his off time there,"

Kat repeated. "That's the only thing he ever talks about doing when he's off duty. No women, no hobbies, no anything. Just the hospital and the Hamilton shelter."

"Hamilton Shelter.....hey, wait a minute!" Nick said, snapping his fingers. "That's where Brian Dirks stayed when he was in Cleveland!"

"Who's Brian Dirks?" Kat asked.

"Someone who may just be the key to solving this thing."

Kat then relayed the story about Joshua's reaction to the student doctors taunting a patient. "He was angry. Anyone would be but his reaction was out of proportion to the situation – that's what I thought anyway. I thought about talking to somebody in administration about it but then I got busy and it left my mind. But of the two, Joshua Ramsey would be my choice to do something out of character for a nurse. But to be involved in a murder? I don't know about that."

"Well, *somebody* killed Johanna Feighan and Michael White," Nick said. "What about Abernathy? Where was he?"

"Probably at home. He only works days."

"Well, somebody at that hospital was involved. I'm going to find out who...first thing in the morning. Now," he turned to her smiling, "let's work on that second payment installment."

Chapter 39

"You ready to solve a murder, son?" Nick asked his partner.

Detective Jimmy Herron had just walked into the sixth floor Homicide office and dropped into his worn chair across from Nick Silvano's desk.

"Hell, no," Jimmy said loudly. "We haven't solved our last ones yet and you want to go chasing another one? I just had two wonderful days away from this place. I almost threw a shoe and called off this morning," Jimmy said, referring back to the days when cops patrolled on horses.

If the horse threw a shoe, you couldn't work until the blacksmith was able to put on a new horseshoe.

"Good to see you were paying attention to your academy history lessons," Nick said.

"Yeah, well if you have that much enthusiasm, you can go and find yourself another partner...where's my coffee cup?" he yelled. "Which one of you assholes stole my coffee cup again?" Jimmy stood up and looked at the other detectives in the office.

"Look in your top drawer, Herron. It's right where you left it the other day," Nick said.

Nick waited while his partner filled his cup from the worn BUNN coffee maker that occupied an unused desk in the corner of the office.

"Hey, Chris!" Jimmy called out to their office man. "We're almost out of coffee!"

"Make it yourself," Chris said without looking up from his computer screen. "I'm busy."

"Jeez, sorry dude," Jimmy said. "Just trying to be helpful!"

"Yeah, right," Chris muttered. "If you really wanted to be helpful...."

"Yes?" Jimmy asked.

"Nothing," Chris said, a wry smile on his face.

Jimmy turned his attention back to Nick. "Okay, partner, what do we got?" he asked, sinking back into his chair.

"We don't have a new murder. We're going to solve the Feighan and White murders," Nick stated.

Lieutenant Fratello was just walking out of his office and overheard Nick. "How so?" he asked.

"Glad you're here, boss" Nick said, "Now I don't have to repeat myself."

Nick explained how Kat was able to look into her hospital files and the insight she provided into how the psych floor was staffed.

"Anyone who knew the location of the master keys could have used them. There are no cameras on those two doors and both open into the hospital parking lot. Anybody with the key could have disabled the alarm, left the floor and return without being seen. The only video we have is on the night of the murders we had someone park the car, with the victims' blood inside, and walk around the corner of the hospital building where the emergency exit doors are located. So, now, we are back to David Feighan being our main suspect since he was obviously faking his condition. But, then again, we have that kid, Derek Stanton, who drew those uncannily accurate pictures of the murder scene. Then, he goes missing - just like Feighan. Vanished, like in thin air," Nick snapped his fingers.

"We know there's got to be an accomplice on the outside. The guy who picked up Feighan in the hospital parking lot is probably the same person who faked being a cop and snatched Derek out of that cab. Plus, Nurse Ramsey seems to be a common denominator in a couple areas. One," Nick held up a finger, "he volunteers at the Hamilton Shelter, and two," he held up another finger, "Brian Dirks was a one-time visitor to the homeless shelter where he lost his wallet. Also, his identification was used to buy the blue Chevy but we've confirmed that while all this was going on, Brian Dirks was a guest of the St. Croix County jail in Hudson, Wisconsin." Nick looked around at the rest of the detectives who had now gathered around his desk.

"From the video evidence, we know for sure that nobody came in or left through the main doors the entire shift," he continued. "That leaves the emergency exits. And we have two nurses, John Archibald and Joshua Ramsey, who were working that night. Both nurses had access to the master keys. That's the common denominator; either one or both of those nurses had to be involved. I think we bring them both in for questioning and see what happens. What about it, boss?" Nick asked Fratello. "You think we have enough to haul them in?"

"Go get them," the Lieutenant said. "What about Abernathy, the administrator. Didn't he quit rather suddenly? And didn't I see something in the news about a large donation from the Feighan Foundation to the hospital?"

"Yeah, I already checked that out," Jimmy reported. "It's true he was expecting a donation from the Feighan's that would have put his name on a building. But Abernathy really *did* quit for personal reasons. Seems he'd been diagnosed with stage four pancreatic cancer and wanted to spend his remaining time with his family. So that rules him out," Jimmy concluded.

"Alright, go bring the two nurses in," Fratello instructed. "I'll go up to the ninth floor and let Chief Toothman know. Good work, Nick, Jimmy." Nick retrieved the business card of St. Luke's head of security, Dean Winston, and made the call.

"Winston? This is Detective Nick Silvano."

"Yes, Detective. What can I do for you?" Winston asked, his tone cautious.

"We need to talk to a couple of your nurses. And I need their addresses."

"What for?" Winston asked, his voice raised. "Are they suspects? Why don't you just talk to them here when they are at work?"

"You know the drill, Dean," Nick answered using the security chief's first name to disarm the man's animosity. "People tend to have come to Jesus' moments when they are in a police interrogation room. You must have seen that yourself when you were on the job," Nick said, trying to ingratiate himself while thinking, "C'mon asshole, work with me here!"

"Yeah, okay, I don't see a problem," Winston relented. "I can extend you the professional courtesy. Hold on and I'll go get that information for you."

Nick gave the thumbs up sign to Jimmy and wrote down the information as Winston read it over the phone. Nick's next call was to Cleveland Police Radio.

"Yes, this is Detective Silvano in Homicide; let me talk to the Chief Dispatcher, Maggie," he said to the intake person in Radio.

Holding his hand over the receiver on the phone, Nick said to Jimmy, "We have to coordinate this right. I don't want these two nurses to have a chance to talk to each other before they bring them in here. Maybe they're both involved."

"Agreed," Jimmy said.

"Yeah, Maggie. Nick Silvano here. I need a favor." Nick explained he needed both nurses picked up but they were to be kept separated until they got to the Justice Center.

"Sure, we can do that for you, Nicky," Maggie confirmed. "I'll get a couple of Zone Cars out to pick them up right away.

"Now it's time to turn up the heat and see who starts getting rattled."

He made another phone call. "Hi Dawn," Nick said to the Channel 3 news reporter. "I promised you the exclusive on the Feighan murders. I can tell you that we have narrowed our list of possible suspects to include employees of St. Luke's hospital..."

"Sure you have" she said, cutting him off in mid-sentence. "I know that David Feighan has gone missing from the hospital. We picked that up by monitoring police radio. Tell me something I don't already know."

"David Feighan is our main suspect but we think he may have had help from somebody who works at the hospital.

You can report that the cops are questioning employees of the hospital for their possible involvement."

"Oh, I get it," Dawn said. "You need me to stir the pot for you, right?'

"I knew you'd understand," Nick said. "You okay with that?'

"Sure, Nicky. I'll get your vague message out to the world and see who goes scurrying around. Appreciate the scoop. You got any names for me?"

"Not yet, but maybe soon," Nick answered.

"I'll be live at noon on Channel 3 News. Is that timely enough for you?" she asked.

"Perfect. Thanks," Nick replied.

"Okay, the table is all set," Nick told Jimmy. "And we never even left the office. Ain't life grand!" he said, smiling widely and flashing his perfect white teeth at his partner.

"Yeah," Jimmy said. "Now the fun starts!"

Chapter 40

N urse John Archibald was seated next to Detective Silvano's desk when Joshua Ramsey entered the Homicide office accompanied by two uniformed Cleveland Police officers. John looked up at his friend and called out, "What's going on, Josh? Why are we here?"

"No talking to each other," Chris Cheetham admonished, pointing to a chair next to his desk at the opposite end of the office from where John was sitting.

Nick stood up and looked down at John Archibald. "Follow me." The two men had to walk past Chris's desk and Joshua as they moved out of the office and into the interrogation room. Nick motioned for the nurse to take a seat.

"John," Nick addressed the nurse. "My name is Detective Nicholas Silvano and before you answer any questions I have to inform you of your Miranda Rights. You have the right to remain silent. Anything you say may be used against you in a court of law. You have the right to consult an attorney and to have an attorney present during questioning. If you cannot afford an attorney, one will be appointed for you. If you decided to answer questions now without an attorney present, you will still have the right to stop answering questions at any time until you talk to an attorney. Do you understand these rights?"

"Yes."

"Are you willing to answer my questions without an attorney present?"

"Sure, go ahead, I have nothing to hide," John spoke confidently.

Nick asked John about the night of the murders. "Did you leave the floor that night or did you give anybody the master keys to the emergency exit doors?"

"No sir," the nurse replied emphatically. "I spent most of the night studying in the Social Workers office. Nurse Ramsey was out on the floor. I remember him telling me that it was a good night for me to lock myself in the office and study for my bachelors degree, so that's what I did. I can assure you that I never left the floor. Josh made the rounds and monitored the floor by himself. There was only the two of us 'cause there weren't enough patients for more staff." He paused then and looked at the detective. "Do I need a lawyer or something?"

"No, you answered my questions, John," Nick said. "I'll get a car to take you back home."

Nick escorted John back into the Homicide Office. "Chris, get a Zone Car to take Nurse Archibald back home. He's all done here." Nick pointed to Joshua. "Jimmy, take him into the room. He's next."

"Oh, look," Jimmy nodded to the television set hanging on the wall. "Dawn Kendrick is talking about us on the noon news." Someone turned up the volume.

"....the murders of Johanna Feighan and lawyer Michael White. The police are now looking at the staff of St. Luke's hospital. They have several leads they are pursuing."

Perfect timing, Nick thought. He glanced at Joshua Ramsey; the nurse was not looking at the television. Instead, his face was turned toward the window and his right foot tapped a staccato beat on the floor.

"Is that why I'm here?" John Archibald pointed at the television.

"Yep," Chris replied. "C'mon, let's go. Your ride is in the parking garage." Nick watched as John followed Chris out of the office. The nurse never even glanced back at Joshua Ramsey.

"Your turn," Nick said to Joshua. "Follow me." Nick repeated what he had told John Archibald and advised Joshua of his Miranda Rights.

"Did you have anything to do with the murders of David Feighan and Michael White?" Nick asked him pointedly.

"No, of course not," Joshua answered defiantly but Nick heard the uncertainty in his voice. Years of talking to suspects had given him the ability to discern the truth from the bullshit. He began to press the nurse.

"Tell me what happened on your shift that night. John Archibald said you told him to stay in the Social Workers office and study. Is that when you opened the doors for David Feighan and Derek Stanton to leave and kill Feighan's wife and his lawyer? I hear that you have some anger issues. You did the hospital admission for Feighan. Did his wife and lawyer piss you off? Is that why you murdered them?"

"No! That's ridiculous! I didn't murder anyone," Joshua vehemently denied.

"I think you did, Nurse Ramsey, and I'm going to prove it," Nick said.

The next thirty minutes were spent with Nick and Jimmy both trying to break the nurse into confessing until finally Joshua blurted out, "That's it! I want a lawyer! I have nothing else to say to you."

"Okay, Joshua. You can have your lawyer. But you know once they get involved we can't help you," Nick said.

"That's right," Jimmy confirmed. "And if you are innocent," he paused, letting that word hang, "having a lawyer will just make you look guilty. But that's your call."

"One last question," Nick cajoled. "Where did you go after your shift that morning?"

"Where I usually always go," Joshua answered, feeling a bit of relief. He couldn't get into trouble for this. "I went to the Hamilton Homeless Shelter. I volunteer there."

Joshua Ramsey sat silently in the back seat of the detective car as Nick and Jimmy drove him back to his apartment at The Nine in downtown Cleveland.

"You know what I'm going to say next, don't you Ramsey?" Jimmy called out to the nurse's retreating form. "Don't leave town!"

"I don't think he likes us, Nicky," Jimmy commented after they pulled away from the curb.

"He's involved in this somehow," Nick said. "I can smell it!"

"You and your schnoz," Jimmy said. "Why so?"

"C'mon kid, use your brain and remember what I taught you. You saw the video of the suspect who got out of the car in the hospital parking lot."

"Yeah, I did," Jimmy said. "What about it?"

"That nurse John Archibald is a really big man. There's no way that was him getting out of that car. I know it was raining and a poor video but there is no mistaking that the person who got out of that car was not six-foot-five-inches and three hundred and fifty pounds! And, Joshua Ramsey is on the small side so I don't think it was him either. I think it was Derek Stanton. He drew the pictures. He is a follower who has been sexually abused and male victims of abuse like to return the favor when given a chance to retaliate. He is just 'off' enough to allow somebody to convince him to do the killings and that somebody did not want him around to talk. My bet is that Feighan and Ramsey were in on it together and had Stanton snatched and maybe even killed to keep him from talking. According to what we know, the Stanton kid's life is just one big video game and the games these kids play nowadays are all so violent that they lose their sense of reality. My money is on that kid. We have to get Loomis to check Stanton's DNA against the sperm left on Johanna's body."

"Man, you've been living with Kat too long," Jimmy said. "You're thinking like a shrink. But maybe you've got something there. I'll call Loomis right now."

Jimmy called the SIU forensics detective from the car. "Hey, Steve. Detective Herron here. Can you check the sperm from Johanna Feighan's body against Derek Stanton? He had a rape kit taken on him while he was in the hospital and you should have it in the lab. Can you process it now? We need it quick." Jimmy hung up the phone and turned to his partner.

"Loomis says he can have a preliminary result in an hour. Won't be official enough for a court hearing but close enough to begin the final testing."

"That's good enough for us," Nick said. "Let's head back to the office and wait. My bones are telling me we're on the right track."

"Guys," Chris Cheetham said when they entered the

Homicide office. "I overheard Ramsey say he was at the Hamilton Homeless Shelter so I called over there. One of the volunteers was nice enough to check something for me after I told her that she could maybe solve a murder. And guess what?"

"I'll bite," Herron said. "What?"

"Brian Dirks was there, but it was quite a while ago."

"I knew it!" Nick exclaimed.

"Nick, I know that Minneapolis DEA agent checked with the Wisconsin cops and verified Brian was in their jail at the time of the murders," Chris continued. "A young lady named Amanda told me that Joshua Ramsey was at the shelter the day the car was purchased. He was going through the lost property box. Ramsey told her that he thought maybe a patient who was brought into the hospital with no ID or wallet might have left it there. But the hospital records don't have any admissions for any John Does or any males without identification that night. There were three male patients on the night of the murders and they were all already admitted into the hospital and had the proper paperwork. So Ramsey lied to her. She had marked Ramsey on her clipboard as being there to work before he said he was just looking for a lost wallet so she drew a line through his name. She still has the sheet with the date and time and is saving it for me. *And* our bad boy nurse withdrew two thousand bucks in cash on that same day from a bank on West 25th Street a couple hours before the car was bought at Pete's Car lot for the same amount of money in cash!"

"Bingo!" Nick exclaimed. "Let's update the Lieutenant."

"Good work," Lieutenant Fratello said after hearing the

details. "Gather everything together: the DNA results from Loomis, the bank video showing Ramsey taking out the money, the sheet from the Homeless shelter and get it to Misny. Tell him we want a Grand Jury indictment. I want this by the book and airtight! The Chief is demanding quick results after Dawn Kendrick's noon report." He paused then and looked at his two detectives. "I don't suppose any of you guys had a hand in that did you?" Nick and Jimmy were uncharacteristically mute. Fratello raised his eyebrows in mock disbelief. "Yeah, yeah, you're all innocent. You know, when you stir the pot it stirs on my end too. Toothman wants it done and over. As soon as we can legally lock up this weirdo nurse, let's do it!"

Chapter 41

What was he going to do now? Even though the cops had zeroed in on him, they didn't seem to really know anything or he'd be sitting in jail and not back at his apartment, Joshua concluded. They were just fishing. But they weren't stupid. While Herron struck him as a loose cannon, that Detective Silvano was a shrewd one. And if they connected him to either Feighan or Derek outside of a nurse/patient relationship, the wall would fall fast. The way he saw it, he had two choices: suicide or run. He had plenty of Vicodin and Ativan to end his life, but that would be quitting and he wasn't a quitter. After everything he'd been through he wasn't going to kill himself because he helped a man avoid being wrongly committed to a mental institution!

He could run, but where to? His passport was expired. He could always get on the bike, head west, and hide out in some dinky town. People disappeared all the time. Or, he could stick it out, act normal, go to work, and hope that everyone continued to ignore Derek and his talk about "killing bad people" and that David Feighan would quietly disappear and forget all about him. He didn't even care about David's repeated promises for a generous payback.

Joshua went into the kitchen where he kept his bottles of pills. He took four Ativan and four Vicodin to just to calm his nerves. He thought about calling Big John to find out what he told the detectives but decided against it. As the afternoon wore on he realized he was supposed to work that evening. He picked up the phone and called the Unit.

"Center One, this is Bill speaking. How may I help you?"

"Hi Bill, this is Joshua. I'm not going to make it in tonight. I guess you all have heard the news already," he said.

"Yeah. The place is full of rumors. We heard you were arrested and in jail! And hey, Dean Winston called and said he wants to be notified the minute you show up for work. Looks like they're gunning for you. I don't know what to tell you, buddy, but if I were you I wouldn't come near this place!"

"Well, the rumor mill has it wrong. I wasn't arrested and wasn't put in jail. But I guess to some people, I might as well have been. Anyway, I'm calling in sick. I'm not feeling very well."

"Okay, Josh," Bill answered.

"Thanks, Bill. Maybe see you later," Joshua said solemnly, ending the call.

He slumped into the couch and placed both hands over his forehead as if to contain the jumble of thoughts swirling through his mind. *You fight for your country and fight to stay alive after getting blown up in battle. You fight to rehab yourself, then fight to help others.* He was getting tired of the fight. But it was all he knew.

His phone rang. Unknown Caller. He pushed the button to accept the call and managed a dull, "Hello?"

"Where are you right now?" It was David.

Joshua sighed. "My place. You know, the cops had me in for questioning."

"You okay?"

"I guess so. That detective, Silvano, is suspicious but they don't have anything.....yet," he said. "But it looks like I'll lose my job anyway."

"Forget about your job. Go look in your mailbox. My guy left a gift for you. Use it. You don't have much time!"

"What are you talking about?" Joshua asked, but David had already hung up.

Joshua went down to the lobby, opened his mailbox, and removed a large, brown envelope.

"What the hell." He left the other mail that had been accumulating in the box and returned to his apartment.

"Oh my God!" he exclaimed after opening the envelope. He looked at the bundle in his hands and everything became clear. He was holding his chance for a new beginning. *Maybe the fight was finally over.*

Picking up his phone, he ordered an Uber ride to Cleveland Hopkins Airport, then went into the bedroom and hastily packed a small bag with a change of clothes, medications, and his Army dog tags. He looked around the apartment. There was nothing else he needed. He could walk away from it all.

In the back seat of the Uber ride, he rechecked the contents of the envelope. One thousand dollars cash - all in twenties - airline tickets, a driver's license and passport with his photo, and a new name.

***

"Nick, you're so quiet," Kat said over dinner that evening. "You've barely made a dent in your lasagna."

"I'm sorry, honey," he said. "Just can't stop thinking about the Feighan case. There's something funny going on at St. Luke's and Joshua Ramsey, is the key – I can *feel* it!"

"Oh Nick, are you sure? I know Josh has his own issues, but from what I've seen, he's a very good nurse," she said. "I know there's been some complaints about him but you've got to consider the source. Mostly they were from other staff he had gotten after for not doing their jobs or paying the proper attention to their patients."

"Okay, so he's Nurse of the Year. That doesn't mean he hasn't gone off the rails," Nick commented. "He wouldn't be the first nurse to flip out. Look at the Angel of Death – the nurse who killed those elderly patients. He thought he was doing the right thing too."

"I don't know," Kat put her fork down and looked at Nick. "What about David Feighan? He was catatonic! How could Joshua have gotten him out of the hospital without being seen?"

"Yeah, we still don't know how Feighan got out of the hospital or even where he is now. Of course, Feighan's a wealthy man. Who knows – maybe someone kidnapped him and there will be a ransom call tomorrow. Everyone we talked to said the man was basically a vegetable. Hard to believe he could pull something like that off by himself."

"Plus, Joshua was volunteering at the Hamilton Homeless Shelter the day David disappeared," Kat supplied. "He was nowhere near the hospital."

"Yeah, that's a problem," he agreed. "But there's a solid connection between Joshua Ramsey, Brian Dirks, and the Hamilton Homeless Shelter. I think Jimmy and I will pay Ramsey another visit tomorrow. If we apply more pressure, maybe something will shake loose."

Chapter 42

Delta Flight 2636 departed on time from the Cleveland Hopkins Airport. Joshua transferred to Delta flight 559 in Atlanta and after a short layover continued on to San Juan, Puerto Rico. He had lunch in a concourse bar before boarding the Seaborne Airlines Flight 4600 for the final hour and a half of his flight.

Only one runway serviced the small, but modern, Vance W. Armory International Airport on the independent Caribbean island of Nevis. This little island was home to an extinct volcano, tropical rain forests, beautiful beaches, and ex-patriots from all over the world.

A wall of ninety-four humid degrees started Joshua's sweat glands working as he grasped his bag and boarded the shuttle bus that would take him to the Four Seasons Private Residences.

The shuttle driver was silent during the short trip and Joshua stared out the window at the brilliant scenery flashing by. How beautiful the island was! And far away from Cleveland...far away from Detective Nicholas Silvano. This would be his second chance, he decided. He'd cut back on the pills, build a life. He'd avoided any relationships beyond a couple people at work and Doc Stafford for so long, maybe it was time to change that. Start trusting people. He was surprised to see a little smile had formed on the face in the window's reflection.

Fifteen minutes later, the shuttle stopped in front of Palm Grove Villa. Joshua admired the Villa as the driver handed him his bag, then pressed a twenty dollar bill into his outstretched hand and thanked him. The van pulled away leaving Joshua alone on the curb. He followed the snow-white walkway of crushed shells that snaked through the impeccably groomed lawn to the covered entrance of the villa and knocked lightly on the door. It swung open.

"Hello, Josh," David Feighan said, smiling broadly and embracing his nurse-savior in a bear hug.

"You look very well, David," Joshua commented after David released him.

His former patient was dressed in white cargo shorts with a brown braided belt and a light blue polo golf shirt with a dolphin embroidered over the left breast. Tan and fit, he had the look of success about him. He looked nothing like the bewildered, emaciated man Joshua had admitted to St. Luke's Hospital Center One Behavioral Health Unit just weeks ago.

"It's all thanks to you, Josh! Come in, come in. I was just getting ready to have a drink. What's your pleasure?" David grinned broadly, playing the benevolent host. Joshua followed David across the plush, light green carpet to the fully stocked wet bar. The blue shimmering water of the villa's private in-ground pool lay beyond the large windowed cabana doors.

"You have any beer?"

"Whatever you want, my friend, whatever you want." David opened the small bar refrigerator, removed a green bottle, twisted the top and handed it to Joshua while motioning for his visitor to follow him outside.

"Now, let's get to the reason you're here," David said,

swirling a glass of Macallan scotch in his hand. He sat down on one of the blue lounge chairs circling the pool and indicated Joshua should take the adjacent chair.

"As you know, Josh, I am a very rich man. It took me many years to build my construction and real estate management business. Along the way, I did some pretty stupid things. I was on the verge of losing it all to Johanna and Michael before you stepped up with your sense of righteousness and put yourself in harm's way for me. Now, it's my turn to help you."

"I saw what they were trying to do to you and I stopped it. I would have done the same for anybody," Joshua paused, "whether they had money or not. And besides – you got me out of Cleveland. That's thanks enough."

"You are a rare bird, Josh. You jeopardized your job and your own freedom – for me! And God knows I'm not worth it – I have no illusions about myself. I'm a self-centered, greedy man. But thanks to you, I escaped that life with my freedom *and* my money." He lifted his glass in a toast. "To second chances."

"Second chances," Joshua said, touching his glass to David's.

"Now," David leaned forward, his gaze intent. "What can I do for *you*?"

"I'm not sure," Joshua replied. "I doubt I can ever get another nursing job. Even if those detectives don't figure it out and I go back, the suspicion hanging over my head will follow me wherever I go. I had some savings and my army pension, but I can't get at it now that I've left the States," he said, resignation heavy in his voice. "Christ, I'm not even Joshua Ramsey anymore," he said, thinking about the forged passport with someone else's name.

"Stay here," David said. "Lord knows I could use someone like you to keep me on the straight and narrow. Sort of like a personal assistant. I plan on keeping what I worked so hard for and another screw up could be just around the corner. See," he smiled, "I know what I'm capable of. Stay here. Work for me." Joshua just stared at him.

"I sold my businesses. I'm staying here in Nevis. My investments will provide for me for the rest of my life. And a new start for you," he added.

"What else could I do here, David?" Joshua asked. "Yeah, I could work for you. But you really don't need me. There are others out there that need me more. You saw them in the hospital. People who've been dumped on by the system – they have no power, no voice. Being a nurse isn't what you do, it's who you *are*. I just can't turn it off, even in a place as beautiful as this," he finished, waving a hand in the direction of the glistening pool and gently waving palm trees.

"I've never known anyone like you, Josh," David shook his head in amazement. "Most people would jump at the chance to ditch their job for a life in paradise. Okay. Since you feel you have to do something, there's the Medical University of the Americas just a few miles from here. If you don't fancy watching over me full-time, or being a man of leisure, you could go back to school, become a full-fledged doctor. We're only two hundred miles from Puerto Rico and lord knows there are plenty of impoverished Caribbean islands that are desperate for medical attention. You have the compassion to help and I have the money to put that compassion to work."

"You'd do that for me?" Joshua questioned warily.

"Yes! Yes! What do you think I've been trying to tell you!" the millionaire exclaimed. "You opened my eyes to a whole new world of opportunity. Before you saved me, all I cared about was making money and getting high. I told you – I owe you and the best way for me to repay you is to give you the chance to do what you do best - help people in need. And I'm one of those people. What do you say? Take this offer and stay here with me," David cajoled. "At least take some time and think about it."

Joshua took a long swallow of his beer without tasting it. What did he want? Could it be that simple? Stay here and let Feighan be his patron of sorts?

"Well, I certainly don't have anything to look forward to in Cleveland," Joshua said.   "I keep thinking that detective – Silvano – will find some new evidence and haul me away to jail in handcuffs." He paused, took a pull off the cold bottle of beer and met David's stare.

But that could happen anyway if David got high or drunk and let something slip to the wrong person. It might be better for him to stay here where he could keep an eye on David, at least for now. Besides, the really weak link was Derek, but he couldn't do anything about that. Derek was thousands of miles and several jurisdictions away. He felt confident that no one would believe anything Derek might say. The poor kid was so messed up.

He put the beer down on a table between the chairs. "How would that work, David?" he asked. "I can't just stay here forever on this passport."

"That's the beauty of this place, Josh," David answered

excitedly. "You *can* stay here forever if you wanted; and legally too. I chose this island for a reason. We both know that at any minute Detective Silvano could find something to lock us up. The Nevis government has a program called Citizenship by Investment. We can buy ourselves permanent citizenship of St. Kitts and Nevis by making a 'donation' to what they call the Sugar Industry Diversification Program. It will give us full citizenship rights and protection under local law and also a permanent passport and visa to travel to more than one hundred and twenty countries with no questions asked. I already contacted one of the companies that negotiate with the government and they will handle all of the paperwork - for a fee of course. It's a win-win for us, Josh. As citizens of St. Kitts and Nevis, we will be protected from being arrested and extradited to the United States -even if the police dig something up. C'mon, how about it?"

Joshua knew David was right. Detective Silvano didn't strike him as someone who would quit – he'd keep looking and eventually link him to Derek and the murders. "I've got nothing in Cleveland," Joshua replied. "I'll stay."

Chapter 43

The next few days passed by in a pleasant blur. Joshua had his own villa and David left him alone. Joshua never even turned on the big screen television; he wanted to avoid the news. Instead, he walked all over the hotel grounds, swam in the private pool, ate fresh seafood, and slept. Oh, how he slept. Deep, healing, dreamless sleep. He hadn't felt this good since...well, he didn't really know when.

Five days after his arrival, David summoned Joshua to his villa. As before, they sat out by the pool. After some preliminary inquiries after his health and activities the last five days, of which David already knew since Joshua's villa was wired, he said, "Now, there's something I want to discuss with you."

"Is there a problem with getting our citizenship or something?"

"No, no," David said. "Nothing like that." He hesitated slightly. "I have an associate that does business in Mexico. This person is having great difficulty. He's discovered his business partner is diverting funds from their partnership and depositing the money into an off-shore account." David paused and looked away before continuing. "This associate of mine is willing to pay a great deal of money to have his business partner, shall I say, go away and never be found. He and his partner will be here in a couple weeks for a conference at the Four Seasons. You follow me?" he ended quietly.

Joshua stared at the pool, following individual ripples of water with his eyes. He felt his internal gyroscope tumble off its axis and the hairs on his neck and arms stiffened.

"I follow you, but I'm not sure I like where this is going. I was willing to help you because I couldn't live with myself if I thought a sane person would have to spend the rest of their life in an institution! And besides, I'm not a murderer," Joshua answered, struggling to maintain a neutral expression. He should have known there had to be a catch, he scolded himself. Despite his comments to the contrary, David Feighan hadn't changed. His kind never did; it was all take, never give!

"I know, Josh," David replied. "Come with me. I want to show you something." David rose out of his chair and motioned for Joshua to follow him back inside. They walked down a hallway and stopped in front of a closed bedroom door. David opened the door. "Look who I found."

"Hi Josh!" Derek Stanton greeted the nurse. He was sitting cross-legged on the bed playing a video game. "Look what David bought me, a brand new X-Box 360!" he said, returning his attention back to the game, fingers furiously maneuvering the game's buttons in a quest to achieve the next level.

"Can we play another game like the last one we played, Josh? I liked that one a lot, especially driving a car. It was so real."

Joshua's mind reeled and he took a half step backward. Beads of sweat appeared on his forehead despite the cooled air circulating through the villa. *Derek!* What was he doing here? What could David Feighan possibly want with this poor, deranged kid?

Then it hit him. Leverage! David knew Joshua, by himself, might someday leave. But not with Derek here. No, Nurse Ramsey would protect and watch over Derek.

David Feighan was truly the Game Master, Joshua silently acknowledged. And if he wanted to protect his patient and win his own game of Staying Alive, it looked like he was going to have to play by the Game Master's rules. *For now.*

Epilogue

Nick and Jimmy were at their desks going over case files when the noon news update came on. "Hey Chris, turn it up, will ya?" Nick asked.

Chris pointed the remote at the television screen and turned up the volume.

Dawn Kendrick stood in front of the Cuyahoga County Courthouse, the early September-dried leaves shed from nearby trees swirling on the steps behind her.

"...detectives say the investigation continues into the whereabouts of hospital patient David Feighan following the murders of Feighan's wife Johanna and attorney Michael White. The millionaire, who was admitted last summer to the Behavioral Health Unit of St. Luke's Hospital, is believed to be suffering from an unspecified mental disorder and is considered to be a vulnerable adult. A nurse, Joshua Ramsey, is a person of interest and the Cleveland Police are trying to locate him in the hopes he can supply them with information.

"Cleveland Police are also trying to establish the whereabouts of Derek Stanton. Stanton was discharged from St. Luke's and on his way to a halfway house in Akron but never arrived. If anyone knows the whereabouts of any of these people, call CrimeStoppers at ....."

Also From The Authors of *Angry Nurse:*
BAD JUJU IN CLEVELAND

<u>Prologue</u>

Cleveland Police Detective Nicholas Silvano, Badge #124, lounged on the rear deck of his twenty-eight foot Rinker cruiser and stared out over Lake Erie. Nick and his good buddy Jack Daniels had been hanging out since his Narcotics Unit shift ended – seven hours ago. At 3 a.m. the Great Lake's waters were calm and a slight breeze kept the humidity level manageable.

His six-foot-two-inch frame was a solid presence in the ephemeral pre-dawn hours and filled the deck chair without spilling over, thanks to regular workouts at the police gym that held his weight at 220 pounds. You didn't have to know his last name to peg him as Italian. His ancestry was reflected in the tanned complexion, distinctive cheekbones, dark eyes, and wavy, slate-colored hair he controlled with a short haircut and gel.

He watched a mosquito land on his exposed arm. Can a mosquito get drunk by sucking blood from a drunk? He decided it didn't matter and swatted it dead. The hypnotic sway of the boat and the whiskey's influence lulled him back in time. Twenty-one years ago he was a rookie fresh out of the Police Academy when he was "officially" welcomed to the job.

"There are four stages to being a cop, Kid," a grizzled veteran told him. "The first is Rookie stage. You always wear your hat when you get out of the car. You have clean underwear on in case you get shot, stabbed, or end up in a hospital emergency room. Next is Cowboy Cop. You drink to excess. If you're married, you'll probably get divorced. You get a military buzz haircut, probably a couple tattoos, work out constantly, wear black fingerless gloves, and pound the piss out of anybody who challenges your authority.

"Helpless and Hopeless mode hits around year fifteen. Much of your time is spent in Federal Court defending yourself against lawsuits filed by the people you pounded the piss out of during your Cowboy Cop years. You probably get a part-time job to keep up with child support and alimony payments. You'll be lucky if alcohol is your only vice. But you hang on because now you're vested in your pension.

"The last stage is Auto Pilot. You try to make it to retirement without being too big of a drunk. You'll put in transfer requests to any inside job that will take you off the streets and wonder if your liver will last long enough for you to get that first pension check. And even that may not amount to much after the ex-wife, or ex-wives, get their cut."

The old-timer had looked him straight in the eyes then with an expression that was half pity and half humor. "It happens to everyone; you can't escape it. Welcome to the job, Kid!"

At the time it sounded like a load of bullshit, but now it seemed prophetic. Nick thought he was entering Auto Pilot stage. He took another pull from the bottle. *Empty.*

Chapter One

One last squinting glance in the rented Dodge Caravan's rear-view mirror confirmed the two Jamaican accomplices, Dion and Tarik, were in position a few car lengths behind. JuJu's gaze returned to the windshield before his two passengers registered there might be something of interest behind them, then turned into the narrow driveway and put the van in Park. Despite the windshield wipers' valiant efforts to defend the view, the mid-day July thunderstorm made it seem like he was peering through wavy block glass.

He turned the ignition off and the wipers ceased their battle, causing the two-story house in front of them to waver like a mirage in the desert. The only sound was the muted thudding of the rain bouncing off the roof of the van. While the conditions were not ideal for driving, they were perfect for murder.

JuJu twisted slightly to the right and unbuckled his seat belt. The movement caused a corresponding nudge in his side from the knife sheath attached to his belt. The van's passengers unbuckled their seat belts and one of the men hoisted a black duffel bag onto his lap. The passengers were couriers, employees of a Mexican drug cartel who traveled 1,200 miles non-stop from Miami to Cleveland with a load of cocaine. Just twenty minutes earlier JuJu had picked them up in the parking lot of the Independence Inn Hotel and brought them to their destination on Dickens Avenue.

As the Cartel's Protector, it was JuJu's job to ensure the deal was completed without any complications. So much could go wrong. Prior successes had earned him a cautious degree of trust from his employers. A trust that would soon be betrayed. Today, JuJu was only protecting himself.

"Ogun - may your warrior spirit protect and guide me,"

JuJu mumbled the familiar mantra under his breath, instantly feeling the electric tingle of Ogun's power in his veins as he and the two passengers exited the van. Despite the noise created by the heavy downpour, one of the passengers nodded in JuJu's direction as if acknowledging a silent instruction from the large man charged with protecting the drug exchange.

The three men climbed the dilapidated steps of the tired looking house. The front door opened quickly and a diminutive black man motioned them inside. In those few seconds, JuJu both assessed and dismissed him as a threat. The man's dove grey suit was elegantly tailored in a way that suggested a wiry strength despite the slim stature, but he was no match for JuJu.

Sylvester "Pookie" Ashford stepped aside, allowing the new arrivals to enter. JuJu noticed another black man standing in the opening between the front room and the dining area about four feet in front of where he stood. Definitely the muscle. His alert eyes swept over both men looking for weapons.

"Right on time," Pookie said. "I like that."

The group stood quietly for a moment, taking measure of each other. Drug deals this large had inherent risks but yielded vast rewards.

JuJu spoke first. "My associates," he nodded toward the Mexicans, "don't speak much English. I will conduct this transaction. Do you have the money?" he asked Pookie.

"Yeah," Pookie said, turning toward the other man in room. JuJu pegged him as "Track Suit" since he was dressed in matching navy sweat pants, T-shirt and jacket. The man was tall and looked like he could block an elephant. A dark blue duffel bag hung by his side suspended from a hand that could cover a basketball. JuJu eyed the partially zipped nylon jacket and saw the familiar bulge of a weapon. *I'll have to take care of him first.*

Pookie turned back to JuJu. "Let me see the product."

JuJu nodded and one of the couriers stepped up and placed his duffle bag on the battered coffee table top and unzipped it, revealing white, tightly wrapped bricks of cocaine. Pookie removed one of the bricks and turned it over in his hand as if to gauge its weight. Then he performed a careful count of the number of white bricks in the bag, turned to Track Suit and nodded. Track Suit set his duffel full of cash next to the black bag and backed away. JuJu kept his eyes on Pookie and Track Suit while one of the Mexicans counted the bundles of hundred dollar bills. With everyone focused on the money, nobody noticed as JuJu stealthily faded back from the assembled group.

The front door flew open and the two Jamaicans rushed in, brandishing Mini-Mac 10 machine guns. "What the hell!" Pookie yelled, looking to JuJu for reassurance. JuJu held his gaze for a moment, then calmly looked away.

"What the fuck!" one of the couriers shouted, frantically reaching for his gun only to remember it was back in Mexico. They traveled without weapons in case they became the subject of a traffic stop.

"On your knees," JuJu calmly instructed the group. "All of you," he said, including the couriers in his command. He was in charge now.

The four men did as ordered. Pookie's mouth tried to

form words but there was no sound to support them. In that instant, Track Suit reached for his weapon. Before he could remove it, JuJu sprung with a rattlesnake's deadly accuracy, jumping over the coffee table at his prey. With one slashing strike, Track Suit's neck split open and his body jerked violently.

JuJu held Track Suit's eyes with his own, forcing the dying man to his knees, his hands clawing desperately as if to close the hole at his throat. "I knew you were the one to watch," he hissed, "but my power is stronger!" The man's blood pooled warmly over JuJu's forearms, then wrists, then hands, before finally breaking off onto the tributaries of his fingers.

"Ogun shoro shoro, eyebale kawo!" JuJu roared, abandoning his usual formal style of speaking in the frenzy of the moment. The Jamaicans kept their weapons trained on the Mexicans, but the men didn't move. Even if escape were possible, their days would be numbered. Returning to Mexico without the cartel's money was the same as a death sentence; they would be burned alive. Better to die here with some measure of honor.

JuJu approached the couriers. Even in the face of death, their eyes met his as if acknowledging they had been a part of his plan all along. "For Ogun!" he screamed. The bloody knife easily passed through skin, cartilage, and sinew of the first courier's neck. He turned to the courier's partner.

"For Ogun! Again, the knife performed the task for which it was created.

The drug couriers' bodies slumped and folded over themselves onto the bare wooden floor, their blood and breath mixing to create red bubbles still laboring to escape through the smiling holes in their throats.

"Don't do this man!" Pookie pleaded, finally finding his voice. He scrambled toward the front door, his feet trying to propel his body out of the room like a long jumper. "I can get more money!" He didn't make it. Tion hit him in the head with the gun and he crumpled to the floor. JuJu picked Pookie up by the back of his suit coat and enfolded him in a violent embrace. The Obeah Man would make sure his warrior god Ogun would not be denied his sacrifices. Almost unconsciously, his arm moved against Pookie's neck and it was over. He watched, fascinated, as the soft grey material of Pookie's lapels darkened to a hellish maroon. Using the back of Pookie's suit coat as a rag, he wiped the knife clean. It is done.

The Jamaicans stared, mesmerized at the carnage brought by the Obeah Man. If only they could have played too! But the big man's orders were clear - this time, it was hands off.

"Give me the bag!" JuJu demanded. Darik removed the brown leather messenger bag that had been slung over his shoulder and handed it to the man who had just killed four people in a matter of minutes. JuJu removed a small iron cauldron containing an eleke necklace of green and black beads with white shells and placed it in the middle of the obscene square created by the four bodies.

"This is my offering to you, Ogun," he spoke loudly, wearing a wild look of exhilaration mixed with pride. One-by-one, he positioned each body on its back and using the knife, cut each of the men's blood-soaked shirts open, exposing their chests. He extracted a glass jar containing black paint from the bag and dipped his index finger into the mix, then like an artist wielding a paintbrush, drew a black cross onto each man's chest. When he was done, he wiped his finger clean on one of the courier's legs. "We must leave now," he said, standing quickly. He caught Tion frisking Track Suit's body. "Leave them!" JuJu roared, just as Tion removed a 9mm Smith and Wesson. "You two don't need a gun! Anything that exposes you will expose me as well." He pointed to the duffel bags. "Take a bag!" he commanded. Regretfully, the Jamaicans left the bodies as they were, picked up the bags, and headed for the door. The pair weren't accustomed to merely being spectators where violence was concerned. JuJu looked at the dead bodies one more time, and then followed the Jamaicans out the door.

"What did you say to them?" Darik asked as he and Tion dropped the duffel bags in the backseat of the van. "I've never heard that language before."

"It is the language of my ancestors, the Lucumi," JuJu answered, then translated, "Ogun speaks loudly, blood sacrifice - observe what the Gods have decreed!"

Get It Now!
www.bort-madsen.com
Facebook: Bort-Madsen Books
Amazon.com

ABOUT THE AUTHORS

KARL BORT was a United States Air Force jet mechanic in Texas and Georgia before joining the Cleveland, Ohio Police Department. During his 27-year police career, he worked Patrol, Auto Theft, and spent 11 years as a Narcotics Detective. He worked closely with the DEA, including a two-year assignment on national cases, often in an undercover role. As the elected president of the Cleveland Police Patrolmen's Association, Karl was responsible for negotiating contracts and protecting the rights of all Cleveland Police Officers. Following retirement, he returned to school, became a Licensed Practical Nurse, and worked 15 years as a medical surgical nurse and psychiatric nurse for the Cleveland Clinic. Karl now spends his second "retirement" in Ohio with his wife, children and grandchildren, indulging in his new career – writing crime thrillers.

THEKLA MADSEN was a corporate business analyst, technical writer, and marketing consultant. She has worked for cooperative and corporate businesses in the agriculture, medical, and banking and financial services industries, was executive editor, writer and photographer for a regional women's magazine, and has published articles in national trade magazines. Thekla and her husband live in Wisconsin on the family's century farm.

THE AUTHORS are working on the third book in the Detective Nicholas Silvano Crime Thriller series.

FIND US
www.bort-madsen.com
Facebook: Bort-Madsen Books

ABOUT OUR PARTNERS

CHRIS CHEETHAM is an award-winning graphic designer and illustrator based in Cleveland, Ohio. His work focuses on branding, logo development, conceptual design and illustration. Chris enjoys working with clients and creating visuals that bring their ideas to life. His works have been recognized locally and nationally by: The Society of Illustrators, NY, Graphic Design Magazine, BPAA, PRO-COMM Awards, Cleveland Addy Awards, International Gold Quill Awards, Automotive Aftermarket Global Design Awards, and Graphic Design USA-American Design Awards. Find Chris at: Chrischeethamdesign.com

ROB BIGNELL (Inventing Reality Editing) provides a variety of editing services including proofreading, copy editing, substantive editing, and developmental editing. In a marketplace where your manuscript faces heavy competition, it needs a second eye to ensure success. His professional services are among the most writer-friendly you'll find – and he'll polish your manuscript until it shines bright! Rob is the author of the "7 Minutes A Day" writing series and the "Hittin' the Trail" series. Find Rob at: inventingrealityediting.wordpress.com/home.

Made in the USA
Monee, IL
02 June 2022

97370906R00174